THE REFORMER'S APPRENTICE

THE
REFORMER'S
APPRENTICE

A novel of old San Francisco

Harriet Rochlin

FITHIAN PRESS, SANTA BARBARA
1996

Published by Fithian Press
A division of Daniel and Daniel, Publishers, Inc.
Post Office Box 1525
Santa Barbara, CA 93102

Book design by Eric Larson
Endsheet photograph courtesy The Bancroft Library

LIBRARY OF CONGRESS CATALOGING-IN-PUBLICATION DATA
Rochlin, Harriet, date
    The reformer's apprentice : a novel of old San Francisco / Harriet
Rochlin
        p.   cm.
    ISBN 1-56474-167-2 (cloth : alk. paper)
    I. Title.
PS 3568.O3247R44 1996
813'.54—dc20   95-52134
                                               CIP

In memory of my teacher,
Miss Finley,
who saw the writer in me
when I was eleven.

My parents were steadfast Jews, but they had no interest in maintaining ties to their Eastern European homeland. Occasionally they turned nostalgic about St. Louis, where my mother grew up and where Father came as an immigrant youth. But they reserved their love for their new home in the forward-looking West. From early childhood on, I, a native of Los Angeles, fed on their newcomer *delights* (the spaciousness, mild climate, scenic diversity, verdancy, relaxed manners) and their *terrors* (the exotic social mix, con artists, anti-Semites, fires, floods, earthquakes). Every *first* spawned a story: starting a business, learning their customers' language (Spanish), building a house, and discarding unsuitable clothing, foods, and religious rites. Business setbacks, illnesses, ruptured relationships, social slights, they bore in silence. Life was supposed to be easier, fuller, more egalitarian out west. If it wasn't, it had to be made so.

But neither nativity nor devotion made me a *real* Westerner. That distinction belonged to descendants of pioneers who wagoned or sailed west in the first two thirds of the nineteenth century, to my knowledge no Jews among them. Nor could I link myself via gender to the western past. Women were almost as absent from the record as Jews and other ethnic minorities.

At twenty, self-supporting, I left for Berkeley and—my mother feared—*radicalism*. Hardly. At forty I was a wife, mother, Reform temple teacher, and part-time writer. Then came the mid-1960s and the *who-am-I's*.

My rabbi denounced hippies as the "scum of the earth." To my ears *doin' your own thing* had a clarion ring. The Democratic congressman I backed supported the Vietnam War, the same war I despised first on principle, then in memory of a nineteen-year-old friend. Even the temple class I taught on home observances had me out on a limb. I could write the manual, memorize the prayers, test the recipes, organize family training sessions, but I couldn't get my husband and children to attend.

Just before Passover in 1966 I came down with a wracking cough and a monumental headache. Two days later, I was in the hospital shivering under a mound of blankets, my chest and back aching as if I'd been machine-gunned. The diagnosis was viral pneumonia. My temperature soared, 103, 104, 105. I heard the voices of absent relatives, saw green gnomes in the corner, and newspaper banners on the wall. One read THINGS ARE NOT WHAT THEY SEEM. The doctor said "toxic psychosis." Crazy or not, those words had a definitive ring.

During my convalescence, my thoughts drifted back to my abandoned birth community. I had feelings about Boyle Heights—attachment, pride, shame, guilt—but no facts. Information about that transitory Jewish neighborhood was scant. But I did find books and articles about Jewish life elsewhere in Los Angeles, San Francisco, and other early far-western centers. Jews had rushed onto the western frontier in the hundreds, then thousands, exuding a pioneering zeal that reminded me of my parents. I began to research and write, soon full time.

Of the diverse materials I gathered, the most compelling were the diaries, letters, and memoirs—especially the women's. "She asked me if I was proud of being a Jewess, and just as frankly I told her I was emerging from a soul struggle involving my religion" (Rebekah Bettleheim Kohut). "…The [San Francisco] Jewess developed not alone physically, but mentally and spiritually—in fact she keeps pace with the world's advancement equally with her sisters of other creeds" (Rebecca Gradwohl). "Drop all the dissension about whether you should take off your hats during a service and other unimportant ceremonials and join hands.…" (Ray Frank). "Why [Jewish] Poles lacked the virtue of [Jewish] Bavarians I did not understand, though I observed that to others the inferiority was obvious...." (Harriet Lane Levy). "...She [an unwed twenty-one-year-old] would have to go to the interior...the market for all marriageable material that could not be advantageously disposed of in the city" (ibid.). A novel took shape and grew into a trilogy.

Readers who know me well will detect traces of family lore in this, the opening novel. Those who know San Francisco history will recognize the hard times that gripped that boom–bust city between 1875 and 1880, the years this novel spans. And those who know that city's Jewish history will nod knowingly when I say my fictional central character, Frieda Levie, and her female associates were inspired by real-life counterparts.

Much of this novel appeared as the first half of *So Far Away,* a paperback original published by Jove Publishing Company in 1981. Presented as a mass-market historical romance, the novel reached few libraries. Fortunately, a number of authorities on Jewish, women's, or western fiction saw past the trappings. They praised the work as an authentic recreation of the pluralistic Far West peopled by both sexes, and lauded its author as a superb interpreter of Jewish types in the West.

They, and the believers who shepherded the novel to this more enduring edition, have my profound gratitude. As do those optimistic pioneers who help me see myself as a Jewish Westerner with roots in the region's past and a stake in its future.

As a Women's Rightist, I sought to teach our girls to use the powers of their feminine nature to improve themselves and their world.... Some parents vehemently condemned me and my views.... Remembering their opposition and my subsequent doubts, I take pleasure in noting that some of our city's most exemplary women were my pupils at Lincoln Grammar School and members of the Sisters of Service.

MARY ELLEN O'HARA
The Sisters of Service Scrapbook: 1872–1885

THE REFORMER'S APPRENTICE

A NOVEL OF OLD SAN FRANCISCO

CHAPTER ONE

Miss O'Hara's Parlor

IT WAS THE LAST MEETING before eighth-grade graduation and Frieda was memorizing the room as if it were a
homeland she might never see again. The palms in the blue
Chinese ceramic tubs that teach Miss O'Hara that nature can
be trimmed and trained to grace the human habitat. The
potted cymbidiums and begonias that keep Miss O'Hara in
touch with the eternal cycle of birth, flowering, withering,
death, and rebirth. The Japanese woodcuts, Polynesian tapa
cloth, Navajo baskets, that assure Miss O'Hara the creative
urge is universal. The view of the Golden Gate that reminds
Miss O'Hara to open her heart to newcomers, as she had to
Frieda, and so many others. Miss O'Hara, herself, erect,
white-haired, strong-minded, inspiring.

She was signaling for the opening song, "Sisters of Service Work and Sing." Frieda rose on watery knees and sang
with the others, her voice swelling and receding. The final
notes still lingering in the room, Miss O'Hara tilted her long,
luminous face toward the ceiling, and called for Silent Dedication. They were supposed to visualize themselves climbing
a mountain slope to a gathering of Elevated Feminine Spirits
at the summit. Miss O'Hara and some members of long
standing regularly reported vivid ascensions. Frieda never
mustered more than blobs of light. Eyes closed, she worked at
joining her heaving breath to the beat of her palpitating
heart. When a full-blown image of herself flashed on the
backs of her eyelids, she straightened, startled.

She was wearing a white dress with a scoop neck, long
sleeves, and a bustle she'd seen in a shop on Kearny Street

and wanted for eighth-grade graduation. The dress fit her full-breasted, narrow-waisted body perfectly. With her long, brown hair pulled back in a cascade of curls, her lively blue eyes fixed on her destination, her round cheeks flushed with anticipation, she looked seventeen, which she was—not fifteen, as she claimed to be at Lincoln Grammar School. She watched herself ascending a steep path toward Miss O'Hara, who stood at the top, her face a circle of white light, her arm raised in welcome.

Suddenly, her father, his face contorted with rage, leapt out of the brush bordering the path. At his side was one of those business associates he'd been bringing home to look Frieda over, men chiefly concerned with dry goods, cut-and-cured pine board, long-horn Herefords, smeltered gold.

Frieda heard a gasp, then murmurs. Wincing, she ventured a peek. Every eye was on her.

"See something of interest?" Miss O'Hara probed gently.

"No," Frieda breathed, her eyes on her folded hands.

"Too personal?"

Frieda identified the snide voice as that of Lorraine Phelps, the group's most avid women's rightist. Lorraine championed Free Love, and with equal fervor, opposed patriarchs. What better target than Frieda's father, Abram Levie, who called Miss O'Hara a "*tsedrayte farzesseneh,*" a crazy old maid, and the Sisters, "*vilde hiyas,*" wild animals?

"I didn't see anything, I never see anything," Frieda said, her blue eyes darting like pursued fish.

"Then what made you cry out?" Lorraine pressed further.

"Time for the Circle of Yesterday," Miss O'Hara sang out, always quick to divert the aggressive impulses of her more fervent disciples.

One by one, the Sisters rose to report on their assignments at the San Francisco Fruit and Flower Mission, Ladies' Protection Society, Old Sailors' Home, Little Sisters' Infant Shelter, Civil War Veterans' Home. Frieda nodded attentively, but was too busy rehearsing her own report to listen to what the others were saying until Minnie Cohn, seated at her left, got up.

She and Minnie were Miss O'Hara's special cases that year. Frieda, a Polish Jew (the rest were Gentiles or German Jews), and Minnie, a daughter of divorce, owed their bids to Miss O'Hara's decision to widen the circle. Frieda joined in October, shortly after she entered Miss O'Hara's eighth-grade class at Lincoln School; Minnie followed in January. As the most recent initiate, Frieda had to serve as Big Sister to the newcomer. She had been as mute and watchful as an immigrant housemaid during her own initiation, and was equally uneasy about Minnie's. Each time the tiny, wire-haired girl got up, Frieda held her breath, afraid Minnie was going to make a fool of herself and shame her Big Sister in the process.

"I was supposed to help Frieda at the Perry Street Kindergarten," Minnie said, "But I had bronchitis most of the month. Mademoiselle promised me that if I...."

Why, wondered Frieda, did Minnie go on with her interminable excuses? Everyone knew she had a governess because she was too spoiled to attend public school or a girls' seminary.

"Thank you," Miss O'Hara said, rushing Minnie along before she got immersed in an irrelevant domestic tale. "Let's hope you'll be well enough to work with the Smith sisters next year."

Before Minnie sat down, Frieda was on her feet, anxious to erase the smirks her work-shy Little Sister had elicited.

"This has been the most exciting month of my life," Frieda began. "Nora and Kate Smith's charges at Perry Street come from poor, unenlightened families plagued with hunger, ill health, lice, scabies, worms. The Smiths take all races and nationalities, and many of the children arrive without a word of English." (Once a tiny greenhorn herself, a secret she guarded more closely than her age, Frieda had a special feeling for the shy-eyed, silent ones.) "The newcomers often weep hysterically when their parents leave, but before long, they don't want to go when it's time for them to leave."

Frieda began her report in a flush-cheeked whisper.
Heeding Miss O'Hara's gestured directions—head high,
shoulders back, more volume—she ended her remarks
steady-eyed and self-assured. When she was back in her chair,
the leader drew from her large, leather scrapbook a letter
from Nora Smith. Eyes fixed on Frieda, she read it aloud.

> ...Some Sisters of Service are squeamish about
> coming South of Market to work with our impover-
> ished, immigrant children. Not so Frieda Levie. She
> scrubbed walls and floors, washed dishes, chamber
> pots, diapers, and completed every task assigned her,
> speedily and without complaint, even when it meant
> staying after dark. She was especially adept with the
> younger children. We look forward to having her
> back with us next year.

"This goes in our 1875 Book of Distinguished Perfor-
mances," Miss O'Hara said, waving the letter at Frieda, who,
hands splayed on her cheeks, listened, her emotions shifting
across her face—embarrassment, pride, fear, pleasure.

She was still throbbing like a one-hundred-pound heart
when Lorraine rose—*first again*—for the Circle of Today,
words of inspiration. Lorraine adjusted her coronet of brown
braids and surveyed the room, gathering attention, before she
proclaimed in a cautionary tone: "The wife who submits to
sexual intercourse against her wishes or desire, virtually commits suicide; while the husband who compels it, commits
murder...."

For several moments Lorraine gazed around the circle,
ostensibly claiming the words as her own, before attributing
authorship to "Victoria Clarion Woodhull, speaking at the
American Association of Spiritualists, 1873."

Frieda had never heard sex openly discussed before she
joined the Sisters of Service. Now she was learning of sexual
wrongs and rights she had never dreamed of. In her inspira-

tional quote at the May meeting, Lorraine had focused on a related subject: a woman's right to reign over her own body. Heretofore, Frieda thought about her body as little as possible, and who reigned over it, not at all. Certain it wasn't her, she preferred leaving the duty unassigned. She wished Lorraine would be more discreet. Her selections invariably made Frieda think of Rudy Seiffert, and once she started, she couldn't stop.

After Lorraine came Beatrice Boaz, the group clown. Miss O'Hara and the Sisters were still laughing when Bea sat down. Frieda hadn't heard a word Bea said, but she laughed, too, and nodded accord when Miss O'Hara commented:

"Laughter can be more satisfying than honor; more precious than money; more heart-cleansing than prayer."

Frieda quickly thumbed through the six inspirational quotes she'd brought and placed the most humorous on top. Turns were going clockwise. Hannah Nathan, a slim, pretty girl burdened with huge breasts, stood up. Knots of boys, Rudy Seiffert among them, had taken to gathering around her desk at school and in front of her house. Mrs. Seiffert was once again fetching Rudy from school in her carriage, as she had soon after he'd started walking home with Frieda, who Mrs. S. disdained as "a wayward little Polack."

Hannah read a passage rebuking men for toying with women. Tears shimmering in her hazel eyes, she urged the Sisters to join her in Serving Mankind, not one man.

Amens, Frieda's among them, were still resounding when Minnie rose to read something philosophical in French her governess had prepared for her.

"That's French?" quipped one of the girls.

"Not the way Minnie reads it," another responded.

Hoping to add to the jocular mood, Frieda rendered her Thoreau quote as a stern injunction: "Avoid all enterprises that require new clothes."

The Sisters were silent.

"Is that all?" Beatrice asked.

"Yes, 'Avoid all enterprises that require new clothes.'"

"Why?" wondered Evangeline, a dressmaker's daughter.

"We've been talking about graduation dresses so much, I thought we needed to be reminded that ideals are more important than attire."

Frieda's words drew blank stares. Red-faced, she dropped back into her seat, and sat reviewing her other quotes, wondering which might have been better received.

Refreshments—cinnamon cookies and fruit punch—followed the Circle of Today. Still uneasy over the misfired epigram—the room buzzed with talk of new dresses—Frieda retreated to a window. Fog steamed through the Golden Gate, obscuring both the Presidio and the Marin shore. Her eyes picked out a sailboat skimming the water's surface, first on one side, and then as the wind shifted, on the other. She couldn't see the sailor struggling to keep his craft afloat, but she felt with him, and gasped each time the sail dipped seaward.

"What are you going to say for the Circle of Tomorrow?" Minnie's voice rang out as she pushed herself close to Frieda. Frieda pretended not to hear.

"What are you going...." Minnie started again.

Frieda would be expected to report on her post-graduation plans, but she had none. Her father had made it clear that when she completed the eighth grade she was through with school and the Sisters of Service. To avoid embarrassment, she'd prepared a general statement on Serving Mankind. But Hannah had already brought up Serving Mankind, and Miss O'Hara was a sworn enemy of *rote and redundancy*.

"Wait and be surprised," Frieda whispered.

"Everyone's going to have an interesting life but me," Minnie said. "I'd love to be a schoolteacher like Miss O., but I have a weak constitution. My mother told me to say I'm going to devote myself to Business and Civic Duty."

Frieda restrained a guffaw, but two Sisters nearby didn't bother to conceal their amusement.

"What did your father say about high school?" Minnie wanted to know.

Frieda jumped as if she'd been pinched. She looked around quickly to see if anyone was listening, then hooked arms with Minnie, and suggested they find new seats for the Circle of Tomorrow.

Amy Weisenfeld and Helen Breitbart, the future physicians, had asked to speak first. Frieda chose two chairs to the right of Helen. The one next to Helen for Minnie, who'd fuss if she couldn't sit alongside Frieda, and one for herself, just beyond Minnie. That way she'd be last, and could give her report and run.

Amy, tiny, and Helen, large, (out of earshot the Sisters called them the mouse and the moose) rose together. They'd been inseparable since fifth grade; Amy did the talking, Helen, the nodding. Amy named the high school, university, and medical college they were going to attend, then added, "and continue our training with the Sisters of Service. As pioneer women physicians, we'll need the attributes of the Elevated Feminine Spirit: the nurturing heart, the loving gaze, and the spiritual touch."

"Service to Health," Miss O'Hara said, delightedly.

Lillian Latham, fair, round, compliant, was returning to the Sandwich Islands to work with her parents, both missionaries, and to marry their young colleague.

"Service and Marriage," Miss O'Hara said. "Some of our most effective women's rightists have combined the two."

Felicia Ungarfeld, Rudy's cousin, was going to Munich. "I'm going to study piano with an outstanding *maestro.*"

"Service to the Arts. Brighten our rough path with beauty, my dear."

Evangeline Sales, Hannah Nathan, and Lettie Brown had nothing exciting to report. Miss O'Hara received their mundane plans with enthusiasm, but Frieda had no doubt as to whose undertakings genuinely interested their leader. When Lorraine announced she was going to attend Girls' High, then Emma Willard School, Miss O'Hara's alma mater, and thereafter to devote her life to the advancement of women's rights, Miss O'Hara, tears magnifying her large blue eyes, clapped her hands and crowed, "Service to Womankind."

A trace of undigested cookies and punch backed up into Frieda's mouth. She swallowed hard. Minnie was blabbering about Business and Civic Duty, and the Sisters were snickering. Frieda was measuring the distance to the door when she felt a jab in her side.

"It's your turn," Minnie said.

Quivering, Frieda stood, her eyes fixed on the Persian carpet. Remembering she was supposed to face her audience, she forced herself to look up into the circle of expectant faces. What was her opening line? She felt like a small greenhorn again, her mouth sewn shut, her heart pounding.

"After that lovely letter from Nora Smith, we're eager to hear your future plans, my dear," Miss O'Hara prompted.

Frieda's mouth dropped open, and a sob popped out. Aghast at the jagged sound, she whirled around to find the copy of her speech she'd left on her chair. Picking it up, she turned back to the group. "Standing before you, Miss O'Hara and esteemed Sisters, I pledge that for the rest of my life...." Tears flooded her face.

"What is it, dear?" the leader asked, stretching a long, thin arm in Frieda's direction.

Frieda fastened her gaze on Miss O'Hara.

"M-my f-f-father won't let me g-go to high school."

"Why not?"

"He—he doesn't w-w-want me to be a schoolteacher."

"You want to be a schoolteacher?"

"Oh, yes, more than anything."

"Have you told him that?"

"Yes, and he said I couldn't." More vehemently and at greater length than Frieda cared to reveal.

"Speak to him again. Help him to understand."

Frieda listened, dubious.

"Appeal to him openly, honestly. Show him you respect his opinion, but let him know you have one of your own."

Let her father know she had an opinion of her own? She often complained about him behind his back, but never to his face. Sometimes she went weeping to her mother, who cried with her, then pleaded for peace.

"Tell him Rabbi Bettelheim is sending his daughter to high school."

Frieda listened, unconvinced.

"Would you like me to talk to him, my dear?"

"Oh, no," Frieda responded.

"Then promise me you will."

If she promised, she'd have to do it. The girls were leaning forward, waiting for her response.

"Where there is fear, Frieda, there can be no love," Miss O'Hara told her. "You do love your father, don't you?"

"Yesss," Frieda managed.

"And he loves you?"

"Yesss."

"Then bare your heart to him."

"I'll try."

"Promise?"

"I promise."

"Say it like a Sister of Service."

"I promise I'll speak to my father," Frieda said, imitating Miss O'Hara's self-assured tone.

"Louder, stronger."

"I promise I'll speak to my father," she called out like a drum major ordering a turn.

"That's more like it."

Miss O'Hara's smile hit Frieda like a sunbeam, lighting up her countenance.

"Time for the closing song, girls."

Frieda extended one hot hand to Helen and the other to Minnie. They squeezed her hands, and she squeezed back, their voices chorusing "This World, a Better Place."

CHAPTER TWO

810 Sutter Street

FRIEDA WAS IN THE KITCHEN, feeding her little sister, when she heard the front door open and her father call, "Right this way, gentlemen."

They'd moved to Sutter Street the year before, shortly after the house was completed, and her father was still showing off the fashionable two-story Italianate.

"Would you look at mine fireplace? I bought it in Virginia City, from a mansion that burned down. The tiles show scenes from *A Midsummer Night's Dream*. That's a play by Mr. William Shakespeare."

As the voices rumbled on, her father's in the lead, Frieda noticed he sounded more vendorish than houseproud. He was touting one object after another—the twin sofas upholstered in emerald green brocade; the large, round oak table; the wall tapestry depicting Queen Esther and King Ahasuerus; the gilt-framed mirror hanging over the fireplace.

"Two hundred and fifty dollars for each of these brass chandeliers."

As he guided them to the other side of the house, to the study and the music room, their voices grew faint. When they returned to the dining room, back within earshot, Frieda heard her father say, "You know who made those cupboards for me? The same cabinetmakers who did the cabinets for the new Palace Hotel."

The visitors were genuinely interested; they asked pointed questions. How many bedrooms? When was the house built? How much did it cost? How much was the mortgage? When the group—her father and three men dressed in black business suits—reached the kitchen, Abram neither greeted her and Ida nor identified them as his daughters. After he pointed out the new Sunshine range, with six burners and two ovens, for coal or wood, the laundry stove and oak drainboard, he led the men toward the parlor. The youngest of the three, a sharp-eyed, athletic-looking fellow with ginger-colored sidewhiskers, hung back and asked Frieda for a glass of water. When she returned from the cooler on the rear porch, the man was bending over Ida, caressing her silky, yellow curls. His hand brushed Frieda's as he accepted the glass.

"Your baby, kitty?" he asked Frieda, eying her as if she were a winsome servant.

She flushed, whipped around, and peered into a pot of cabbage rolls simmering on the range.

"Smells delicious," he tried again. "Does the cook go with the house?"

Frieda fiddled with the pots, wondering what the man meant—*go with the house?*

"Bring wine," her father called from the dining room.

Tray in hand, Frieda pushed through the swinging door, eyes lowered, now consciously playing the housemaid. Her father was extolling the desirability of the neighborhood— Sutter and Hyde, just two blocks from stylish Van Ness Avenue. And bragging about their neighbors (whom he privately despised)—the Gustave Goldbaums, the Heinrich Handlers, the Emil Kleins—all German Jewish families, who denied the Polish Jewish Levies a "good day." Then their Gentile neighbors on the north side of the street—the Samuel Blythes, the Benson Taylors, Captain Henry Halsey— mainly Forty-niners, who resented the south-side *newcomers* for blocking their sweeping view of the south bay.

Sutter Street celebrated, Abram backtracked to describe his climb to this peak.

"I came to California in 1859 and went right to mine cousin, who had a Cheap John store in Grass Valley. When the silver excitement broke out, I moved mine family to Vir-

ginia City, and from there to Gold Hill. When I got to California, I had forty dollars in mine pocket and a wife and a
baby to feed. But I worked hard and I done fine in mining
and farming supplies, general merchandise, a few mineral
stocks here and there. But mine wife...." He was motioning
to Frieda to bring more wine.

Frieda knew where the story was headed. Her mother
had hated life in the interior and begged for a move to San
Francisco. But Abram had been making progress in his various ventures and wouldn't leave. In the winter of '62, when
he was away on one of his frequent selling trips, first Frieda,
then Bella, came down with diphtheria. Wing Lee, who had
just arrived from China, happened on the cabin, found
mother and child delirious with fever, and stayed to take care
of them. When Abram returned, Bella was nursing Wing,
who had come down with the disease, too. That summer the
family moved to San Francisco with Wing, who by then had
made himself indispensable as cook, nursemaid, handyman,
and during Abram's absence, protector of the household.

When Frieda returned, Abram was saying, "In San Francisco I did wonderful, wonderful, until this spring everything
fell in pieces. The silver market tumbled. I lost a lot of cattle
from the drought in the south, then a load of lumber I was
bringing from Eureka burned up. I'm going to Virginia City
for a week to sell my properties there, but first I got to cover
my loans at the Bank of California."

Several minutes later, back in the kitchen, Frieda heard
the front door slam. The men had gone, her father with
them, she deduced from the ensuing silence. Since June, in
Wing's absence (he was in Yuma visiting family), she'd nursed
her sick mother and her baby sister, run the household, and
waited for an appropriate moment to reintroduce the subject
of high school to her father, who had been operating at a
whirlwind pitch all summer. Now the deadline for enroll-
ment was a few days off, and he was leaving.

It was a little after eight when Frieda heard the front

door slam and her father hurry down the hall to his study. Ida and her mother were asleep, and she had just finished tidying the kitchen. She went into the hall and listened, hoping for a clue to her father's state of mind. A book hit the floor. Fallen or thrown, she couldn't tell. She heard a groan, a curse, then silence. He'd been hospitable, even jolly, with his guests. Whatever his mood, she couldn't wait any longer; she had to speak with her father now.

She found her father seated at his desk, bent over a stack of papers, his bald head gleaming in the light of the gas lamp. He looked up startled when she entered, then returned to his work.

"I cooked a nice supper for you, Papa," Frieda started.

"I'm not hungry," Abram said.

"Vegetable soup, cabbage rolls, *tsimmes*. I even baked a sponge cake."

"Nothing," Abram said, starting to write.

"Maybe later."

"Maybe."

"Mama is feeling better. The doctor wants her to get out of bed a little more."

"Good."

"We received a letter from Sylvia and Sammy today. The Edelsteins want them to stay another week. Is that all right?"

"All right."

"I'll drop them a note."

She felt like one of those straight-backed oh-so-efficient housekeepers in an English novel, discussing household matters with the moody master of the manor. Instead of tall, lean, and wavy-haired, her father was short, square, and bald. But he had on his best broadcloth suit, the smoke of a long, expensive cigar curled in front of him, and his expression was decidedly otherwise engaged. This distant, grim-faced man was not the only Papa she knew. Another image of him sprang to mind.

She was a toddler at the time, Ida's age now. They were still living in a tiny cabin in Gold Hill. The tinkling of horses' bells announced her father's return from a peddling trip. She remembered leaping out of bed, shouting his name and rushing outdoors in her nightgown, her mother, as excited as she, running at her side. Papa had jumped down from the wagon seat and scooped her up in one arm. With the other, he drew her mother close and, thus entwined, they had walked back to the cabin. Too ecstatic to sleep, she'd nestled in her father's lap while he ate his supper and recounted his adventures on the road.

In recent years, her father never touched her, and rarely even looked at her. *If only he'd lift his eyes and see me as I am now, an eighth-grade graduate; since June, the mistress of his household.*

"Papa, there's something I want to discuss with you," she began.

"Not tonight. I'm very busy." He did not look up.

"It's something we must discuss before you leave."

"I got to get these papers ready."

"It will only take a few minutes."

"I can't think now."

"It's very important."

"Later."

"It can't wait."

"Then speak." His eyes were still on his papers.

"I want to enroll in high school on Monday."

"No high school."

"I want to go, Papa."

"Who said you should go to high school, that tsedrayte schoolteacher?"

"Listen to me, for just a minute."

"I told you before, Frieda, no high school." He glanced up, his eyes flashing annoyance.

"Why not?" she asked in a controlled tone.

"Why not?" said Abram, glaring at his daughter. "Because a good Jewish girl don't need no high school."

"Rabbi Bettelheim is sending his daughter."

Abram jerked back the chair and sprang to his feet.

"Rabbi Bettelheim can send his daughter to Gehenna for all I care."

"I can help Mama and still go to high school," Frieda said, taking one step, then another, back from the desk.

Slapping his brow, Abram tilted his head toward the ceiling and emitted a long, rumbling groan. "I say no, she says yes." His voice cracked with anger.

"Schoolteaching is an honorable profession."

"Profession? Abram Levie's daughters don't have *professions.*"

"But, Papa, things are different in America. People have a right to improve themselves—women as well as men. With education and hard work, we can make this country a place of peace and plenty."

"What kind of plenty? Plenty *tsoris*? Trouble, that's all I got is trouble." Frieda's father wailed. "Worthless silver stocks, dying cattle, unfinished houses, and a daughter who wants to be a schoolteacher." Eyes closed, he barked, "Go away from me."

"Not until you've heard what I have to say."

"I heard enough."

"All summer long, I took care of Mama, Ida, the house, everything, now I come to you and bare my heart, and you won't even...." She stopped trying to restrain tears.

"*No high school*," her father shouted. "Jewish girls don't need high schools."

"I won't take 'no' for an—"

"*'Won't?'*" Mine daughter says 'won't' to *me*?" Abram tore around the side of the desk and seized Frieda's arm.

"I do my best to be a good daughter, but you won't listen to a—" Sobs blocked her words.

"Listen? I'm not supposed to listen. You're supposed to listen."

"But, Papa—"

"Stop, no more," Abram cried, seizing her arm.

Frieda opened her mouth to speak.

Her father jerked her so hard her hairpins flew out and

her brown curly hair cascaded down her back.

"Don't, Papa, you're hurting me," Frieda screeched.

"Quiet," he shouted, doubling his fists. "I said *be quiet.*"

"If you refuse to consider my wishes I'll go elsewhere." She threw back her shoulders and turned from him.

"You won't go anywhere. You'll do what I—"

Frieda started for the door.

Her father grabbed her shoulder and whirled her around to face him.

"Don't touch me," she commanded.

His face red and wet, his teeth bared, Abram doubled his thick fists.

"Mama. *Mama,*" Frieda cried. "Mama!"

Her screams fueling his rage, he battered her with both fists.

Frieda crouched, her arms shielding her head, until another defense occurred to her. She got as far as the open door when her father seized her by the hair, threw her to the floor, and dragged her back into the study.

"*Mama. Mama,*" Frieda wailed.

Abram grabbed her and clapped his hand over her mouth.

"Maamaa," came Frieda's muffled cry.

"Stop, Abram, stop," she heard her mother cry out. "You'll kill her."

Turning her head, Frieda saw her mother inching down the hall. Bella held a gas lamp in one hand, and used the other to support herself against the wall. Bare-footed, dressed in a white nightgown, she looked like a child who had just awakened from a nightmare.

"*Oy, gevalt,*" Abram groaned. "Now this one." He scrambled to his feet and strode toward his wife.

"Don't touch her. She's sick. Papa. *Papa.*"

Frieda pulled herself to her feet and stumbled after her father. She grabbed his shoulder and tried to pull him away from her mother.

Abram flung her hand off him in disgust.

Just then, Ida appeared at the opposite end of the hall, calling, "Fweeda, I want Fweeda."

Her face bruised and bleeding, Frieda looked from her mother to her baby sister then back to her mother. Her father had swept her up into his arms.

"Don't hurt her," Frieda pleaded.

"I'm not going to hurt her," her father hissed back. "I'm going to take her back to bed. You take the baby." When she didn't move, Abram shouted. "*Go*. Do as I say."

"Mind him, Frieda," Bella begged, her voice as limp as her child-sized body.

Ida gazed after her retreating parents, then entered the study, face distraught, arms outstretched. Frieda lifted her up and clutched her against her heaving chest. The toddler buried her face in the hollow of her sister's neck and bellowed. Her control snapping, Frieda sank to the carpet, her sister with her. Locked in each other's arms, the sisters sobbed, the little one emulating the big one's consoling pats and caresses. When at last Ida fell asleep, Frieda carried her to her crib, then, bent over in pain, tiptoed to her own bed to shed more tears.

CHAPTER THREE

Who's *Mechulah?*

The next day, her hair combed to conceal her battered face, her features arranged in a dutiful expression, Frieda greeted her mother, breakfast tray in her hands.

"Good morning," Bella managed. She held her head as if it were cracked at the top and the slightest move would cause the butterflies inside to flutter out.

Frieda set down the tray and began preparing her patient for the day, as Miss O' Hara had taught the Sisters to do for the inmates at the Kings' Daughters' Home. Offer her a bed-pan, wash her hands and face with a warm, wet cloth; change her nightdress, avoiding sudden motions; feed her slowly; and confine one's remarks to uplifting subjects.

"Another spoonful of oatmeal," Frieda coaxed. "Another bite of toast." Opening and closing her mouth on command, Bella consumed half the meal, and waved away the rest. Neither mother nor daughter alluded to the night before until Frieda was at the door, tray in hand.

"Papa went to Virginia City."

Without turning, Frieda said, "I know."

"Frieda, don't be mad at him."

She whirled around, spilling the remains of the tea over the tray.

"He's got a lot a trouble," Bella pleaded.

"Trouble is no excuse for violence, particularly against one's own," Frieda said, starting to weep.

"Sometimes a person can't stop himself."

"Physical brutality is an expression of tyranny," Frieda said, quoting Thoreau.

"Everybody makes mistakes."

"But, Mama, I *must* go to high school."

Bella tried to pull herself up again, tears starting down her cheeks. "Don't fight with him, Frieda. When he makes up his mind, it's no use."

"Lie still, Mama," Frieda said. "Don't you get upset."

"I wish Wing Lee was here," Bella said.

"So do I," Frieda responded. "I've got to go look after Ida."

Frieda found the toddler out of her white crib and seated on a white enamel chamber pot in the corner. She looked like a cherub on a wedding cake.

"Breakfas'," she cried, jumping up.

The child's renewed placability made Frieda all the more aware of her own lingering resentment. If, on his return, her father asked her forgiveness, she would grant it, but only if he agreed to discuss her future with her. Whether he apologized or not, of one thing Frieda was sure: she would never again bare her heart to her father.

All that day, and for the next two, Frieda and her charges lived as if in an eggshell. The only outsiders she saw were the tradesmen who came to the back door—Eugene, a thirteen-year-old butcher's emissary, who nodded, blushing, as Frieda gave him her meat order; Ho Long, the fish man, a fat Chinese friend of Wing Lee's, with six English words and an expressionless face as round and flat as a frying pan; and Heinrich, a German grocer, who, as he put it, had come to San Francisco to make money, not conversation.

Removed from the turbulent world, in charge of the household, Frieda calmed down, her bruises healed, and the ugly scene in the study faded. She was occupied from early morning until after nine in the evening. Each night she returned to her room tired but satisfied with her efforts. Proof, according to Miss O'Hara, that she'd spent the day in service, not servitude.

Thursday night a new problem loomed as Frieda stood gazing at the shiny bottom of the empty tin cracker box in which her mother and Wing Lee kept the household money. The tradesmen and the druggist would allow her credit for a few days, but what would she do after that? And where could she get money for her tuition?

If her father didn't return by Monday morning, she'd write a letter to the Bank of California requesting funds from her father's account to tide them over during his absence, and help Bella, who could neither read nor write, to sign it. As she replaced the box on the shelf, Frieda found herself wishing her father would stay away. The house was tranquil without his agitated and agitating presence, and she liked being in charge.

Later, upstairs in her room, she put on her blue-flowered nightgown and climbed into the double bed she usually shared with her fourteen-year-old sister, Sylvia. Luxuriating in her privacy, she adjusted the gas lamp and opened to her place in *Jane Eyre.* The spunky orphan had already survived persecution at Gateshead Hall, exploitation at the orphanage Lowood, and had just arrived at Thornfield Hall to serve a mysteriously absent master.

Frieda was repelled by Mr. Rochester's abusive first encounter with his charge's new governess, but forced herself to read on. Were she in Jane's place, she would have fled in shame. Not Jane. She held her ground and matched her employer maneuver for maneuver. Excited by the duel between the spirited servant and her surly master, and yearning to see the heroine emerge victorious, Frieda raced through Jane's tests of fire—flaming bedclothes, warnings to lock her door at night, demonic laughter in the hallway—until they threatened to undo the plucky governess's confidence. Scalp tingling, heart pounding, Frieda slammed the book closed, turned off the gas lamp, and willed herself to sleep.

She was dreaming of a parade of men in police uniforms, each holding on a leash a fierce-looking German shepherd, when a thumping sound awakened her. Frieda bolted upright, blood roaring in her ears, adrenaline shaking her limbs. The noise stopped as suddenly as it had begun. Burglaries were rampant in the new houses on Sutter Street of late. A recent story in the *Chronicle* blamed the increase on hard times and unemployment. Shivering, even with her shawl pulled around her shoulders, ears trained for strange sounds, she crept down the hall to look in on her mother and Ida.

Ida lay in her crib uncovered, her white cotton nightgown pulled up to her waist. Her legs, the spliced path between them, and her navel, were exposed to the man in the moon and anyone else capable of peering through the second-story window. Frieda quickly closed the curtains and threw a quilt over the rosy-faced child, wishing that Ida could remain forever as she was as at that moment—unblemished, angelic.

From there, she tiptoed to her parents' room. Silvered by the moonlight, Bella's sleeping face looked more than ever like Ida's. Her curls were no longer golden, and her small, fragile, thirty-three-year-old face bore the crisscrosses of uprootings, eight pregnancies (four miscarriages and four births), bewildering American children, a high-handed husband. Yet beneath the traces of suffering, the sweet beauty in Bella's face lingered. Frieda could hear her father's voice recounting the story of their meeting and marriage.

"I was on a business in Luck, a little nothing of a town. So when a poor musician made a party to celebrate his daughter Bella's betrothal to a Russian soldier, Jewish, of course, everybody in town went, and I went too. When I saw the little bride-to-be, so young, so pretty, so blonde and so shy, I right away wanted her. So with the *schnapps* I brought with me, I invited her father to a few *l'chaim*s, and began to bargain with him. 'Listen,' I told him, 'why should you marry your daughter off to a penniless soldier from the *blotes*, the swamps, when you can give her to me, a rich businessman from Lublin? You can keep the copper pots, linens, the featherbed you got for her dowry. I'll take her in the clothes she's got on.' A week later, we were married and on our way to Lublin."

Bella had a commentary to add to the tale. Lublin was

not as grand, and Abram's family was not as rich or as hospitable as he had led her to believe. His pious family, outraged that he had married without consulting them, mocked her until she wept and scolded Abram until he shouted. Less than a year later, his parents gave Abram money to go to America with his wife and new baby daughter (Frieda), where his rebellious ways would no longer disrupt the household.

Her mother's lips parted in a smile. Laudanum? Her mother rarely smiled these days. Except when she was working with Wing Lee at the kitchen table, their hands and arms in pots of dough, chattering away in their private tongue— English, Yiddish, and Chinese.

Hurrying along the hallway on the way back to bed, Frieda was passing her brother Sammy's room next to hers, when she again heard the sound that had awakened her. As she stood in front of the door listening, she heard another long, low groan. Frieda seized the doorknob and turned it. The door was locked.

"Who's there? Tell me or I'll call for a policeman."

"Go away," cried a voice, strained with anguish.

"Papa?"

There was no reply.

"Papa," she tried again, "Is that you?"

"Yeh—it's me."

"Are you sick, Papa?" Frieda waited to hear. "Do you need help?"

"Help? You can't help."

"What's wrong?" She listened for a response; none came. "What is it, Papa?"

"*Mechoooleh,*" was her father's response. A loud thump ensued. He had either thrown himself or fallen from the bed to the floor.

Frieda's heart lurched. She had heard the Yiddish word before, uttered in hushed dread. It clearly described great misfortune. A friend *mechuleh* aroused commiseration; a foe *mechuleh,* gloating.

"Papa, are you mechuleh?"

Animal-like bellows pierced the locked door. Frieda looked down the hallway to where her mother and baby sister lay sleeping. Her bare feet pinned to the rose-covered carpet, she stood guard between her crazed father and her helpless charges. After a while, his cries slipped into a guttural refrain: "Sonma bitch, I had everything," he repeated over and over. Frieda remained in place, her hand on the knob, her ear against the door, until the lament was replaced by a raucous snore.

Back in bed, her body stiff, her breath coming in short, rapid gasps, Frieda waited for daybreak.

Straining out the usual morning noises—birds twittering, wagon and carriage wheels rumbling on the cobblestones, the Sutter Street horsecar clattering in its tracks—Frieda listened for sounds from the room next to hers. Reassured by the silence beyond the yellow-flowered wall, Frieda rose and quickly dressed. Ida riding on her hip, she stopped in front of Sammy's room, tried the knob, found the door still locked, then placed her ear against it. After a moment's hesitation, she hurried down the hall.

One glimpse into her mother's room reinforced Frieda in her decision not to mention the events of the night before. Bella lay in bed, her face turned to the sunny window, watching the pigeons eat crumbs she had scattered on the windowsill. A cat lay stretched out on the limb of the sycamore tree, his narrow eyes fixed on the birds.

"Look at the murderer," Bella called to Frieda as she entered the room. "When I was a little girl in Luck, we had a yellow cat we kept in the yard to chase the rats. We called our cat Rebbitzen," said Bella, assuming a storyteller's voice. "Next door to us lived a poor rabbi who married a proud widow from Lodz. The new *rebbitzen*...."

Frieda had heard the story many times before, but she feigned interest, allowing her mother this pleasure before sorrow burst like a boil and spread through the house.

•

Frieda was in the kitchen spooning rice and milk into Ida's rosebud mouth when a clatter at the back door caused her to leap up in alarm.

"For God's sake, it's only us," Sylvia said, dropping her heavy suitcase to the floor.

"I wasn't expecting you for another few days," Frieda said, relieved.

"You don't sound happy to see us," Sylvia replied. She was a black-haired girl whose pale, high-cheek-boned face looked as though she had spent the last month in a shuttered boudoir instead of in a Lake Tahoe cabin.

"Of course I'm *glad* to see you," Frieda said, straining to sound as if she were. At fourteen, Sylvia was contesting Frieda's first-born prerogatives, and had engaged twelve-year-old Sammy, round-faced, big-nosed, and jolly as a peasant, as her loyal lieutenant.

"Mr. Edelstein had to get back to San Francisco," Sylvia said, "because of the bank."

"The bank?"

"Don't tell me you haven't heard about the bank?" Sylvia said.

"I haven't been out of the house in three days."

"The Bank of California ran out of money the day before yesterday and closed its doors. They nearly had a riot. Mr. Edelstein went wild when we got back to San Francisco and he found out Ralston was gone."

"Where'd he go?" Frieda wanted to know.

"For a long, long swim," Sammy said.

"He drowned the day the bank closed," Sylvia said. "The newspaper said fifty thousand people attended his funeral yesterday."

"Sammy," Frieda said, turning to her brother, who knew more Yiddish than she, "do you know what 'mechuleh' means?"

"Who's mechuleh?" Bella asked as she entered the kitchen. She was carrying a pigeon, its gray-pink body clutched in her hands, a broken leg tucked up against its belly.

"Us, probably," Sylvia said.

"Don't let her frighten you, Mama, we're not mechuleh."

"Yes we are. Mr. Edelstein told Mrs. Edelstein Levie's bankrupt, busted."

"Mechuleh," Bella cried, her pale face turning green. She reached out for the wall. The wounded pigeon flew out of her hands and began to circle the room.

"Get the bird, Sammy," Frieda said, jumping up to catch her mother who, one hand against the wall, was sliding to the floor.

"If you don't believe me, ask Papa," Sylvia said.

"Where is he?"

"In Sammy's room. The door's locked and he won't come out."

"Sammy, you go out on the roof and climb in the bedroom window," Sylvia said. "Frieda, you take Mama back to bed. Sammy and I will find out what's wrong with Papa."

Five minutes later, Frieda found the door to Sammy's room ajar, and Sylvia and Sammy struggling to lift their father from the floor to the bed.

"Frieda, come help," Sylvia called, irritated. "What kind of ninny are you? The poor man's lying in a stupor and you're feeding Ida oatmeal? Call the doctor, *now.*"

The doctor, a stocky, middle-aged German Jew, prematurely white-haired, listened to Frieda's account of her father's condition, wearing a haughty, sour expression. He knew about the Bank of California; he had had losses of his own, but he was not, he told Frieda, permitted the luxury of lying down like a beaten dog. "Take me to him," he told Frieda wearily.

A half hour later, he found Frieda in the kitchen removing a fragrant stew from the oven.

"Young woman," he didn't know her name, though he had treated her for several childhood diseases, "I prefer not to speak to your mother in her condition. Your father's physically sound. I checked his heart, lungs, kidneys—they're normal, and so are his reflexes. But his blood pressure's low. I think he's suffering from shock induced by an emotional trauma. During the Civil War I treated a number of soldiers with similar symptoms. Most of them recovered within a few weeks. Others remained in a dazed state for quite a while." Dr. Erlichman paused, looking past Frieda with a disdainful smile. "Joshua Norton was a patient of mine before he went bankrupt. I did all I could to help him regain his faculties, but he chose to stay as he was. He's far happier as Emperor of the United States and Protector of Mexico issuing edicts and passing out fake money on the street than he ever was as a rice broker."

Frieda's stomach lurched. Emperor Norton, San Francisco's beloved madman, rambled the city dressed in a military uniform, dogs at his heels.

"There must be something you can do for my father."

"Sedate him. I gave him some laudanum and will leave a prescription for more. The rest is nursing care. Make sure he eats to keep up his strength and drinks so he doesn't get dehydrated. Keep him quiet, clean, and toileted. Call me if there is any change. If you can't handle him, I'll put him in the county hospital or in an insane asylum," Dr. Erlichman said.

"I can nurse him," Frieda said, "I'm a Sister of Service."

"A Sister of Service? Oh, yes," Dr. Erlichman remembered, "schoolgirls." He sniffed and turned his eyes to the stew cooling on the range.

"Would you like a bowl of stew?" Frieda asked.

"I would, indeed," the doctor said. "I had only a bite for breakfast and no supper. These businessmen are falling like flies all over the city." Sitting down before the steaming stew and the bread Frieda sliced for him, he hungrily forked up the meat and vegetables and sloshed the bread in the rich gravy before stuffing it into his mouth. As he ate, his professional facade vanished and he reflected cynically, more to himself than to Frieda, who stood by like a servant. "Get rich, get rich, get rich. That's all they care about. They speculate, taking ridiculous risks, endanger their homes, their wives and children, on the outside chance they'll make a fortune. Then when disaster hits, they fizzle like punctured balloons. They make me sick to my stomach," the doctor said, shoving the bowl forward for Frieda to refill. "My brother-in-law is in the same fix as your father: busted. He was at my door last night, hat in hand, whining for refuge."

His words set off a new alarm. "What will we do?" Frieda cried, searching the doctor's exhausted features.

"Go to a relative, like my brother-in-law did," the doctor said. "Don't you have a relative in San Francisco who can take you in?"

"Aunt Chava, my father's sister. But she and my father are not on speaking terms."

"Go to her anyway," the doctor advised. "Jews are obliged to help their relatives. That's what my brother-in-law tells me."

"I don't think she'll speak to us."

"Plead with her. What else can you do?"

CHAPTER FOUR

Chasing God

THE STUNNED CONFUSION of catastrophe hung over the Levie house. Sedated by laudanum and the even more powerful narcotic—melancholy—Abram continued to lie on Sammy's bed, tapping the wall and muttering, "Sonma bitch, I had everything." Dizzy and prone, Bella had her own refrain, "I wish Wing Lee was here." With their mother and father incapacitated and their servant Wing Lee absent, the three older Levie children improvised. Sylvia and Sammy went out each day with clothing, jewelry, silverware, crystal glasses, and porcelain figurines to pawn for money to buy food and medicine, while Frieda looked after Ida, the household, and her ailing parents.

Her father remained limp and vacant-eyed; his body hers to wash, feed, medicate, and, given the right signals, lead to and from the W.C. She performed these tasks with care, but warily. Her father's brooding demeanor reminded her of a wounded lion who'd caught her eye once at Woodward's Gardens. Rear and front legs wrapped in bloody bandages from knee to ankle, the cat lay curled up in a corner of his cage, his eyes closed. When she stretched her hand through the bars to pat the lion's flank, a keeper lunged at her.

"Get your hand out of that cage, girlie. Charlie may have sore legs, but there's nothing wrong with his teeth."

On the fifth morning of what Frieda thought of as "Papa's trouble," two representatives of the bank appeared at the front door. One was dark, burly, with an insulting smile. The other was sandy-haired, with squinty blue eyes magnified by wire-rimmed spectacles. Flashing authorization from the bank, they went to work listing the contents of the household. Frieda ran to find her brother and sister.

"Ask Aunt Chava what we should do, but don't let her come here," Frieda instructed Sylvia and Sammy, remembering the last tumultuous meeting between her father and his sister. They'd moved from room to room for hours, shouting, slamming doors and banging things. Abram had finally seized his sister's arm, pulled her to the front door, shoved her through it, and locked it behind her.

An hour later, Frieda was in Sammy's room preparing her father for the day when she heard the front door slam. She'd just finished washing Abram's hands and newly-shaven face, and was combing the fringe circling his bald pate. Her father was absently caressing her free hand, as he often did—to Frieda's pleasure and embarrassment—when Aunt Chava's deep, grating voice assaulted her. Hurrying to the hall, she leaned over the balustrade and saw her aunt grilling the appraisers.

Frieda slammed the door to the sick room, and stationed herself in front of it. Listening to her aunt clump up the stairs like a peg-legged pirate, she girded herself for battle. But when she faced her aunt eye to eye, Frieda caved in. Chava was a head shorter and twenty-five years older, but she had superior weaponry—vile insults, hysterical fits, murderous threats, the determination of the angel of death.

Her wide, Slavic face framed by a black Orthodox matron's wig, lips pressed together, jaw set, small brown eyes gloating, Chava shoved Frieda out of the way, and charged into the room with a loud "ah-hah." On legs shaped like tree trunks terminating in feet gnarled as roots, she clumped toward the bed, her gaze harpooning her fallen brother. "Ah-hah," Chava repeated.

Through his melancholic stupor thickened with laudanum, Abram seemed to sense the presence of his older sister and shuddered in alarm. She stood alongside the bed and gazed down at him like a policeman apprehending a wrongdoer. Frieda saw her fallen father flinch.

"Look at the big man," Chava cried. "What did I tell you? A good Jew is supposed to chase God, not gold. Running up and down the state like a *meshugener*, a crazy man. Silver in Virginia City, cattle in Los Angeles, houses in San Francisco. Borrowing money from the *goyim*, working on *Shabbes*, letting the children run wild in the streets. Did I tell you where it would end? I told you."

Stiff and white as a dead man, Abram's face rolled toward the wall.

"Aunt Chava," said Frieda, hoping to break into the diatribe.

"Leave Lublin, go away from your mother and father, your grandparents, your aunts and uncles, your cousins, you told me. You'll make a better life in America, in California where the fish *spit* gold. Some life. Mine Chaim, a cantor with a voice like a *malach*, an angel, you took to the mines so he should fall down a shaft and kill himself and leave me a poor widow to raise a wild boy."

"Please, Aunt Chava, not so loud," Frieda said, taking her aunt's elbow.

Chava yanked her arm from Frieda's grasp. "I swallowed mine pride and I came to you, begged you, we should live like a family, all together. We should make a kosher boardinghouse. And what did you say? 'Nobody wants a kosher boardinghouse in San Francisco. Don't mix in mine life, Chava. I got no time for you; I got no money for you. I got to give mine wife a Chinaman in the kitchen—a Chinaman in a kosher kitchen, *feh*. Not a thought about your nephew who ran away from his poor mother, about your sister alone in a big house falling to pieces without a man to take care of her. What kind of a brother is that? What kind of a Jew is that?

"Not now, Aunt Chava," Frieda pleaded. "Can't you see he's sick?"

"Sure he is sick. He should be sick. I told God to make him sick, to punish him."

Abram's eyes rolled back, showing the whites.

"Mechuleh," Chava spat. "Penniless. And you the *ganse macher*, lays like a dead one on a bed. So now your wild animals remember their Aunt Chava, who lives with the poor people South of Market. Chava, the horse, who can drag her troubles, and yours too. In a few days, they're going to come and throw you out on the street. What should I do? Should I take you in? Did you take me in? No. So why should I have pity on you? I'll tell you why, because I'm a good Jew."

"Easy, Aunt Chava," Frieda said, trying to sound firm.

"Easy, easy, nothing in life is easy. Oy, mine feet. Bring me a chair and I'll sit down and explain to my *bruderle* what is going to be."

Chair in hand, Frieda approached her aunt. Sitting down, Chava leaned close to her brother. "So, Abram, look at me."

At the sound of his name, without opening his eyes, Abram began to move his lips, struggling until he shaped the words, "Sonma bitch, I had everything."

"You had everything, now you got nothing. So you will listen to me."

Aghast, Frieda looked on as her aunt switched to her graveside voice. As a small girl, before her father and his sister had their falling out, Frieda had been loaned out weekly to accompany her aunt on the long horsecar ride to the cemetery to visit her husband's grave. Frieda remembered being caught between tears and giggles as Chava addressed Chaim. In a voice tuned up to reach the other world, she apprised her dear departed of the problems and pleasures of the preceding week and the events she was looking forward to in the week to come.

Now, face tilted ceilingward, she spoke to God in the same voice, "*Gottenu*, look down on Abram where he lays like a dead one. Have mercy on him, and on me now that I have to take him and his family on mine back and *schlep* them down from their fancy hillside to mine poor house where they will be a lot better off. How will we live? We will make a kosher boardinghouse, earn a living and do a lot of *mitzvos*, good deeds, in Your Name, for a lot of good Jews wandering around without a woman to make a kosher house for them."

Except for an occasional fluttering of eyelids and quivering of lips, Abram appeared to be deaf to his sister's plans.

"Bella and Abram I will give my room, and I will sleep in the pantry next to the dining room. A space big enough for a cockroach, but what kind of room does a poor widow need? The girls will sleep in the crow's nest, and Sammy will share a bed with a boarder. With a few changes, we can make eight bedrooms and two more in the basement. Two to three men to a room, we can have maybe twenty boarders, and if another poor luckless one comes, we'll squeeze him in too. Charging two dollars a bed, two dollars for food, we can gross up to eighty dollars a week, maybe more with a little luck." Bending closer to Abram without lowering her voice, she added, "I decided to call it Levie's Kosher Boardinghouse, Abram Levie, Proprietor, so everyone should know we got a man in charge."

Abram spread a hand over his face.

"Bella will help me, may God give her a *pahtch* on her backside to scare her out of her lazy ways. Frieda, Sylvia, and Sammy will do their share. Then when Abram is better, in thanks to You for sparing him, he will become a real Jew. Three times a day in the parlor he will make a *minyan* to say prayers. Then You will forgive him for the way he treated You and his sister."

Her message delivered, Chava leaned back in her chair, and began to move her lips in silent prayer. Frieda watched the grim, oblong face soften as tears washed the wrinkled cheeks. Though Abram's eyes were closed, and he still gave no sign of having heard any of Chava's words, a thread of tears slipped out of the corner of one eye and slid down his cheek.

"Abram," said Chava, addressing her stricken brother tenderly. "Tomorrow I will go find the rabbi and ask him to say a prayer for you after reading the Torah on Shabbes. Now you must say the *Tefila L'Chola*, the prayer for the sick."

When he did not respond, Chava lay her work-worn hand on his pale, cool one and shook it. "You must, Abram. God has to hear it from you, Abram," she commanded softly, her hand moving up to shake his shoulder.

Frieda saw her father's eyes open and close. She moved to her aunt's side, ready to intercede if necessary. Chava rose, her joints cracking, and bent over her brother. Seizing his shoulders she pulled him, as if he were a sack of flour, into a sitting position and propped a pillow behind him. Then she sat down alongside him and took his face and turned it toward her.

"I will say the words, then you will say them after me. I can't say it for you. You will have to talk to God yourself so he will know you are sorry."

Abram's face crumbled like a little boy's about to sob. A jolt of shame shook Frieda. She wanted to turn and run from the sight of her father's helpless anguish, but she dared not leave. Chava was determined to extract repentance from Abram, even if she killed him in the process.

"*Adonoy Ro-i*, the Lord is mine shepherd, say it, Abram. Adonoy Ro-i." Chava shook Abram's shoulders again, then she slapped his cheeks, first the right then the left.

"Don't force him," Frieda cried in alarm.

"I have to force him," Chava answered, matter-of-factly. "He's ashamed to speak to God after ignoring him for such a long time. Adonoy Ro-i, say it, Abram," Chava commanded.

Abram's lips parted, trembling. He cleared his throat as if trying to make way for the words.

"Adonoy Ro-i," Chava repeated.

"I had everything," Frieda heard her father whisper.

"Now you got nothing. God is the judge. Praise him, Abram, praise him and live. Adonoy Ro-i. The Lord is mine shepherd. Adonoy Ro-i."

Frieda saw her father's wet eyelids part. He gazed at his sister for a long time before he opened his lips and said, "Adonoy Ro-i."

"*Lo echsar. Lo echsar*, I shall not want. Say it, Abram."

Aunt Chava's voice had turned gentle and persuasive; Frieda was perplexed. She was coaxing the prayer words out of her brother the way she talked a free transfer from a horsecar conductor. But why, Frieda wondered. For her father's sake, or for her own?

"Lo ech...ech-sar," Abram said lifting his head from the pillow, struggling to find the words in his befogged brain and force them through his lips.

Frieda watched in awe as Chava pulled her father through the rest of the prayer. When he uttered the final word, both brother and sister fell back exhausted—Abram, head on pillow; Chava, chin on chest. Frieda and the rest of the family had hung back afraid. Not Chava. She'd plunged in after him and fought his resistance the way a lifeguard struggles with a swimmer bent on suicide. After several moments of rest, Chava, mustering new energy, wiped the perspiration from her brow and leaned forward, seizing Abram's hand. Her eyes glowing, triumphant, Chava confided her plans. "I will go right to work. By next Shabbes you and your family will be in mine house."

His eyes closed, Abram weakly nodded his assent. Frieda felt Chava's net drop over them. *Run while you still have time,* her instincts prompted.

After seeing her aunt onto the cable car, Frieda stood exhausted looking down the street. The late-afternoon fog was gone and the evening sky was bright and clear. Illumined by the gas lamps and the full moon hanging above the onion-domed Temple Emanu-El four blocks down the hill, Sutter Street glowed with a golden tranquillity.

Except for the Goldbaums, who had lined up at their windows to watch Aunt Chava noisily depart, the rest of the neighborhood seemed oblivious to the crisis unfolding in the Levie household.

Frieda gazed at the other houses, all glowing with light. She could see her neighbors seated at their supper tables—the master at the head, the mistress at the foot, the children in their seats—being served a well-prepared meal by an Irish or Chinese cook. Afterwards the family would adjourn to the parlor or music room to enjoy a peaceful evening at home. Her father had worked so hard to get them to this place. The residents of Sutter Street occasionally had neighborly disputes, and wisps of rumors—rarely substantiated—circulated about one family or another. But on the whole, life on Sutter Street was orderly, gracious, up-to-date, American.

South of Market was impoverished, dirty, noisy, overcrowded. It was where poor newcomers stayed until they could find a way out. Her family had lived there from the time she was three until she was eight. Once they had moved, Frieda had never returned until she joined the Sisters of Service. The first time she went back was when the group held a Christmas party for poor children in the iron-fenced South Park. She'd moved along as wide-eyed as a tourist through the narrow, people-choked, garbage-littered streets that reeked of beer, urine, horse manure, and the foul-smelling smoke that billowed from the surrounding factories. She could feel the eyes of the diverse inhabitants—they came in all colors and costumes—scrutinizing her and the other Sisters. The more anxious girls hurried along, eager to dispense their benevolence and get back to the safer, cleaner, prettier side of Market Street. Emulating Miss O'Hara, Frieda tried to appear fascinated with the colorful immigrant quarter.

A horsecar jiggled to a stop a few feet away from where Frieda stood. The conductor waved and called:

"You going downtown, Miss?"

Frieda looked up puzzled.

"Going downtown?" he repeated.

"No," Frieda cried, jumping back from the curb. She hurried up the front steps and slammed the door behind her.

CHAPTER FIVE

Assignments

THAT NIGHT, UNABLE TO SLEEP, Frieda buried her face in her pillow, curled her hands into fists, and reconsidered the offer Mrs. Cohn, Minnie's mother, had made to her just before she and her daughter had left for Monterey.

"In September, how would you like to come live with us, Frieda? You and Minnie could attend Girls' High together, do your homework, go to Sisters of Service meetings, attend parties, everything together, the way girlfriends your age love to do. In exchange for a few household duties, I'd pay your school expenses and a small stipend."

What she meant was live as a servant in the Cohn household and wait on Minnie twenty-four hours a day. Frieda assured Mrs. Cohn that her offer was tempting, but her father would never permit her to live away from home. Now, given the choice of Aunt Chava and a kosher boardinghouse or Minnie and Girls' High, the Cohn mansion at the corner of O'Farrell and Van Ness radiated like a beacon in a storm. Sylvia would say it would be selfish of her to leave her poor family in the clutches of Aunt Chava. Was it?

Church bells were ringing seven o'clock when Frieda reached Miss O'Hara's two-story, bay-windowed, dove-gray house, the next morning. Was it too early to disturb Miss O'Hara? A noisy bluejay on the branch of a twisted Monterey pine in the front yard appeared to be warning her it was. Just as she was starting back down the hill, the front door swung open and out stepped the tall, white-haired teacher, wearing a blue school dress and carrying a large, canvas book bag. She greeted Frieda as if she customarily came by to walk with her to school. They strolled a block, exchanging pleasantries, before it occurred to Miss O'Hara that Frieda had graduated.

"I don't have to be at school today, either," Miss O'Hara told her. "I want to speak to the principal about subscribing to the *Overland Monthly*. When I was on vacation in Monterey, I met the new editor. We walked on the shore together, and I lectured him on the need to acquaint our young with the scenic grandeur of the West, and to awaken in them a sense of stewardship...."

Six feet tall and energetic, Miss O'Hara stepped along like a parade marshal as she outlined her mission. Instantly drawn into her leader's thoughts and gait, Frieda hurried along at her side, forgetting the purpose of her visit until Miss O'Hara thought to ask.

Frieda struggled to verbalize her anguish without revealing the pitiful state of the Levie household. As they passed a vegetable peddler arguing with a competitor and spraying his wares, an ill-directed shot of water splashed the side of her dress. Frieda threw her arms into the air and screamed.

Her reaction brought curious stares from the peddlers and passersby, and from Miss O'Hara, instant concern. She consulted the watch pinned to her bodice, then took Frieda's arm, saying, "Don't say another word, until we find a bench at Union Square."

Miss O'Hara's hand clamped under Frieda's arm, they hurried along in silence. As soon as they were seated, Miss O'Hara looked at her watch again, then urged Frieda to speak. After several lame starts from Frieda, Miss O. took the lead.

"I met the Cohns on the train coming up from Monterey. Minnie told me your mother had been ill all summer and you were looking after her and your baby sister."

Frieda nodded. Leave it to Minnie to blab.

"I was also sorry to hear your father had suffered business reversals."

Her family's troubles aired on Union Square took Frieda's

breath away. She felt like a hill giving way in a rainstorm.

"The Bank of California fiasco caught me short too."

Frieda ventured a glance at Miss O'Hara. She'd seen her more distraught reading aloud *Oliver Twist*.

"Mrs. Cohn said your father suffered physical as well as financial collapse."

The word "collapse," calmly pronounced by Miss O., lost its catastrophic ring. No longer in danger of tears, Frieda met her teacher's gaze and answered candidly when she was asked, "How's your family managing?"

In less than two minutes Miss O. had the facts out and Frieda bemoaning Aunt Chava's club-fisted plans.

"She says we'll all work together, but my mother and father can't do anything, and my sister and brother go to school, and she talks to me as if I were her char girl."

"At least you'll have a roof over your heads. Lots of destitute San Franciscans are living on the street."

"But, Miss O'Hara," Frieda cried, "I don't want to work in a kosher boardinghouse, I want to be a schoolteacher and Serve Mankind. If I don't go to Girls' High now, I'll never...."

Miss O'Hara clasped Frieda's shoulders and turned her around to face her. "Now listen to me, young lady, Service to Education isn't the only way to Serve Mankind. I began with Service to Family, too. How old are you?"

"Seventeen," Frieda responded, forgetting to say fifteen as she usually did.

"Exactly my age when I left school to care for my mother and father. I know how painful it can be. When my father had his first stroke, I was in my second year at the Emma Willard School, working with some of the most forward-thinking women in the United States—women who were planning the first Women's Rights Convention.

"My mother had been suffering a heart ailment for years and was unable to care for him, and my brother and sister, both much older than I, lived some distance away and had

their own families to look after. My father was a Congrega-
tionalist minister in Pitney, a village about fifty miles from
Boston. Most of his earnings came from a small farm he'd
inherited from his father...."

Frieda watched her teacher's pale oval face tighten, recalling the travails of her youth.

"I came to Mrs. Willard in tears, and she talked to me
much as I'm talking to you. 'Mary Ellen,' she said, 'Serving
Mankind is a noble endeavor, but we must never squander on
the common good the care due our near and dear.'"

Miss O'Hara's fervent eyes sought Frieda's bereft ones.

"I thought I was the most unlucky girl alive when I said
goodbye to my classmates and co-workers and returned to
the farm. For weeks I did little but weep and write letters.
But with the help of our hired man, Old Ned, a runaway
mulatto slave and a strong, willing worker, I learned to do
what had to be done. I nursed my failing parents, and once
my rebelling spirit quieted, did what I could to ease their
suffering.

"My mother died when I was twenty. I found her
stretched out on the kitchen floor one morning, stiff as an
icicle. My father lingered on for another ten years, suffering
three more strokes, a heart attack, and ulcers, before pneumonia released him. I watched the keenest, most life-loving
man I have ever known transformed into a speechless, twisted
wraith. For two more years, I kept alive a skeleton that knew
no one, including himself. I refused to give up until he did,"
Miss O'Hara said, her face darkening with the recollection of
sorrow.

She lowered her chin, stared at her lap, then looked up,
her face washed clean of pain and bright with zeal. "We must
go where we are called, accept the assignment we are given."

"And not become a schoolteacher?" Frieda said, her
shoulders drooping with disappointment.

"One assignment at a time," Miss O'Hara intoned. "I was
almost thirty when I sold the farm, completed my education,
and moved west to make a new start. But I assure you, my

dear, the days I spent giving Service to Family were not wasted. Washing bedpans, sitting up night after night with an anguished sufferer, pushing food into a slack mouth with a dropper, holding the hand of a loved one twisting in agony...."

Frieda's face contorted with distaste.

"Learning to do unto others as you would have them do unto you is not an easy lesson."

Frieda nodded, she knew. Home nursing was hard work, boring, at times nauseating, and rarely gratifying.

"Of course, I continued to study," Miss O. said. "I read, wrote letters to friends, and reflected at length on what I was learning about the feminine nature. Few men would have, or could have, done the work I did. It's essential to the future of the human race to cultivate these gifts and spread them, not only in the home, but in the workplace." Miss O'Hara wrapped her large hands around Frieda's. "Don't you agree, my dear?"

Frieda nodded. She agreed, more about the future of the human race than about her future. "A kosher boardinghouse, south of Market, Miss O'Hara...."

"Better that than an isolated farm, fifty miles from Boston." She fixed a loving gaze on Frieda. "You're one of our most dedicated Sisters, my dear. I *know* you can do it."

"Without you and the Sisters?" Frieda said, unable to fit the Sisters of Service and Levie's Kosher Boardinghouse into the same picture.

"With me and the Sisters. We'll help you, and you'll help us."

"How?"

"By sharing your experiences, reporting on your progress."

"At the boardinghouse?" Tell the Sisters about her stupefied father, her pushy Aunt Chava, her childish mother, her rivalrous sister?

"Yes, of course. We'll want to know about your organizational and operational problems. Your relationships with the residents and fellow workers. Residents of a kosher boarding-house," Miss O'Hara reminded Frieda, "need lovingkindness as much as the inmates of the Old Sailors' Home or the Kings' Daughters' Home."

"That's true," Frieda said, sounding more sure than she felt.

Miss O'Hara consulted her watch again. "I can't be late. Walk with me to Lincoln School."

Arms linked, the two hurried toward Fifth and Market, Miss O'Hara suggesting aims for the boardinghouse: to provide clean, comfortable surroundings and well-prepared kosher meals for homeless Jews; to encourage Jewish newcomers to observe Jewish laws in their adopted homeland; to help immigrants become knowledgeable, healthy and happy Americans.

"What a boon you'll be to your fallen family," Miss O'Hara told Frieda as they approached the school. "And what an inspiration to the Sisters."

Heartened, Frieda responded, "Thank you, Miss O'Hara. I hope so."

"You've given me reason to be proud of you this year, Frieda, and I know you'll give me more reason in the future," Miss O. told her. Then, spotting the principal walking toward her, she waved, and rushed toward him.

Walking home, Frieda composed her first report. *The collapse of the Bank of California forced my family to find new means....* By the time she'd crossed Market and started up Sutter, buoyancy borrowed from Miss O. had begun to evaporate. Her feet dragged as she approached the Levie house, which from a distance appeared to throb with sorrow.

CHAPTER SIX

Levie's Kosher
Boardinghouse

TEETERING ON ITS FOUNDATIONS like a loose tooth, the tall clapboard house at 535 Tehama Street had, indeed, been too much for Aunt Chava to keep up alone. Outside, a jungle of weeds reached the windowsills and, inside, the rooms were so littered it was hard to get from one to the next.

For the first few days, Chava, with Frieda in tow, moved through the maze, discussing renovation plans. Frieda kept expecting laborers to turn up, but it soon became clear that she, her aunt, and her aunt's two boarders, Berl and Schmerl, aging twins and unemployed cigar makers from Warsaw, were the crew.

Dressed in a ragged wrapper, Frieda scrubbed floors, white-washed walls, helped repair broken windows, put doors back on their hinges, and built partitions. She accompanied Chava to the cobwebbed attic and the wet-walled basement to drag forth pieces of scarred furniture, and followed her aunt through dark, dust-coated junk shops on Second Street, where from seemingly monolithic piles they untangled bedsteads, chairs, and tables. Then she stood by while Chava talked them out of the shop on credit.

One afternoon, two weeks after the refurbishing began, Abram, to Frieda's great relief, joined the effort. He appeared on wobbly legs at the door of the dining room, where he stood watching Berl and Schmerl argue about the proper way to rehang a chandelier.

"No, no, no," Abram said, exasperated. "Don't you men know nothing?" He pulled at Berl's pants leg until the cigar maker stepped down from the chair and allowed Abram to mount it and do the job himself.

Thereafter, the work was divided into men's, with Abram in charge, and women's, with Chava. Frieda and her boss moved into the kitchen. On Sutter Street, Bella had maintained the dietary laws, more or less. Aunt Chava was adamant and exacting; deadly sins could be committed in the kitchen. The culinary and eating utensils brought from Sutter Street were set aside for purification. They were not simply unclean, they were contaminated. Aunt Chava refused to touch an item. Wing Lee had had the run of the Levie kitchen, and he ate pork and other kinds of revolting *trayf*, foods forbidden to Jews. Under Chava's vigorous direction, Frieda scoured and re-scoured everything. Then she divided the pots, utensils, and tableware for meat meals, and the pots, utensils, and tableware for dairy meals into two vats of boiling water. "Separate, separate, *meat and milk*, separate," Chava kept repeating. Ignorant of the spirit of the law, Frieda, fearing castigation, kept to the letter of her aunt's orders.

Before the month was out, Chava pronounced the crudely assembled boardinghouse ready for business. Chava had Berl, once a scribe's apprentice, make a large sign with the words in English and Yiddish, LEVIE'S KOSHER BOARDING-HOUSE. That same day Abram placed an ad in the newspaper, *The Jewish Observer*. Chava then stationed herself on the front porch, ready for the parade of good Jews to appear. Day after day, she waited impatiently, first on the porch and then on the sidewalk.

Reb Chaim Blatner was the first new boarder. He was born in Lodz, he said, of a long line of *shochtim*, ritual slaughterers. When his wife died, he decided to join his only surviving son in San Francisco. But his son was married to an American girl, Jewish but impious, sloppy, impudent, and ugly. Blatner would not live in a house that wasn't kosher, even if his daughter-in-law wanted him, and she didn't.

Frieda could see why. His odd attire, full, wiry black beard
and sidecurls gave him the unsavory look of a medieval ma-
gician. His arrogant manner, aggressively protruding stomach,
and intrusive eyes made Frieda draw back with a shiver.

Not Chava. She received him as though he were a long-
awaited relative. And so did Abram, when he came in from
the yard. Within moments the two men were discussing the
construction of chicken coops and a shed where the *shochet*
could practice his skills on behalf of the residents of the
boardinghouse and other observant Jews.

Noting Blatner's entrepreneurial skills, Chava instantly
offered him a choice room—second floor front—and a business proposition. She would give him a dollar off his rent for
every boarder he brought in. Blatner promptly agreed. The
next day, taking Sammy as a guide, he tracked prospective
boarders at local Orthodox synagogues. He repeated the tour
daily, until by the end of a week, Levie's Kosher Boardinghouse was a limping operation, and a week later, a running
one.

Cleaning rooms, scrubbing linens, cooking and washing
dishes, Frieda worked as long as she could stay awake and on
her feet. She had counted on slipping away to the Sisters of
Service meeting but was unable to get away in September or
October. Beside herself with loneliness and agitation, Frieda
described her desperate state in a note to Miss O'Hara. Her
reply came by return mail. Get a change of scenery, if only
for an afternoon.

After lunch on the second Sunday in October, Frieda put
on what she'd come to call her North of Market attire,
slipped out of the boardinghouse, and took a streetcar to the
new Golden Gate Conservatory in Golden Gate Park.

She was standing before a massive exhibition of fall chry-
santhemums, oohing and aahing over the brilliance and variety of the blooms, when a man paused at her side. She gave
him a quick glance, noting nothing more than a tan Stetson
and a long cigar. Swept away by the magnificence of the dis-
play, she dropped to her haunches and pressed her face into

the ochre, rust, and yellow flowers.

A noisy sigh caused her to look up. This time the eyes under the tan Stetson met her eyes.

"Never seen anything so beautiful in my life," he said.

"I *adore* fall flowers," she answered.

"I've never seen anything as beautiful as *you.*"

Embarrassed by the man's brash words, Frieda buried her face in the flowers again. Out of the corner of her eye, she saw brown cowboy boots alongside her. Too flustered to rise and meet the man's gaze again, she kept her face buried in the petals.

A finger tapped her back, but she didn't stir until a stern voice chided, "Lady, you're not allowed to touch the flowers."

"I'm sorry," Frieda cried. Looking up, she saw a uniformed guard standing over her. "I'm sorry," she repeated, jumping to her feet. As she rose, she collided with the man in the Stetson standing next to the guard.

"If everybody handled the flowers, we'd soon have nothing left to show," the guard continued.

Frieda blushed. "I'm afraid I no longer know how to behave in public."

"*Tú y yo,*" the man in the tan Stetson said, white teeth glittering in his sun-weathered face.

"*Tú y yo?*" Frieda questioned.

"You and me," he translated. "Spanish, and familiar at that. I've been down on the border so long, I no longer know whether I'm speaking English or Spanish, much less formal or familiar."

"The border?" They started down the aisle.

"The Arizona-Sonora border, a tiny outpost...."

He was a Californian, he told her, who now made his home in the Arizona Territory. Every few months he was taken by an irresistible urge to see trees, grass, and flowers, and to feel the sea air on his skin. She knew the feeling, Frieda responded. San Francisco was her home, but in recent months she'd been confined to the house. At that point, he had thought to introduce himself.

"Bennie Goldson, Goldson, A.T."

Frieda laughed and countered, "Frieda Levie, Levie's Kosher Boardinghouse." She'd never identified herself in that way before. It didn't feel as bad as she thought.

She'd expected disdain, at best, indifference.

The man appeared to be impressed. "A house full— imagine that. My brother and I are the only Jews south of Gunsight and east of Yuma. A stray member of the tribe passes through from time to time, but not often."

They walked on side by side, exclaiming over the flowers and the tropical plants, the moist, warm air, the light filtering through the glass dome. After completing the tour they left the Conservatory together. As they rode back downtown on the streetcar, they discussed their life goals. His was Civilizing the West; hers, Making the World a Better Place. Their goals, they noted, actually were quite similar. Which was why, they also noted, they both had this strong feeling they'd met before.

"Once we've got a good water supply, and some good business prospects, we'll be looking for good women. What would you think about making *our* world a better place?"

"*Your* world?" Frieda asked.

"You bet. As Mrs. Bennie Goldson." His loud, flirtatious tone caused passengers to turn.

"In Goldson, Arizona Territory?" Frieda asked, ignoring the curious glances.

"My home, now and forever."

"San Francisco's my home, now and forever," she said, matching his fervency.

"I could never live in San Francisco."

"I could never live in Goldson."

"If you change your mind, let me know," Bennie said, with an engaging smile.

"If you change *your* mind, let me know," Frieda said, astonished at her brazenness.

When they parted, they shook hands and wished each other the best of luck. Each urged the other not to give up, no matter how rough the road. Both promised they wouldn't.

She asked him to send her a letter from Goldson, Arizona Territory, for her exotic postmark collection. He said he would.

She returned to the boardinghouse, uplifted by the outing, but several arduous days at the boardinghouse soon had her down and gasping for air again. By November, Frieda was ready to kill rather than miss the Sisters of Service meeting. The night before, she had stayed up until one in the morning cooking lima bean soup, cabbage rolls, and rice pudding for supper. (By the third month, Frieda was doing most of the cooking; Chava, the shopping and supervising; and when she was well enough, Bella helped out. Sylvia and Sammy hurried off to school each morning and did not return until almost dark.)

The next day, after washing the midday meal dishes, Frieda set the tables for supper, then rushed to the crow's nest to change into her Sisters of Service uniform. Her attire concealed beneath a huge black shawl, she went down to her parents to tell her mother she was going out. Bella was resting quietly on her bed, sewing with elegant stitches bedroom curtains of cheap calico. Ida—the family member least disconcerted by the move from Sutter Street—sat on the floor cheerfully hosting a tea party for her dolls. Frieda patted her mother's wan cheek, explaining that she had to pay a call on a very sick girl. Bella looked up alarmed. A very sick girl? She hoped it was nothing contagious. Frieda assured her it was not. Promising to be back before suppertime, she left.

Downstairs, Reb Chaim called to her. He had just come from slaughtering chickens, his hands, beard, and apron splattered with blood. She pretended not to hear. Streaking past the dining room, where her father and some boarders were studying Scriptures, she slid out the front door.

Nervous after so long an absence, Frieda hurried along. She could see dark clouds steaming in from the west, but refused to consider a rainstorm on her second afternoon out of the boardinghouse. The downpour caught her as she was mounting Powell Street, several blocks below Pine. She darted into the doorway of a jewelry store, where she stood gazing out at the emptied sidewalk and the traffic-snarled street. A clock in the window read three-forty-five. The meeting had begun at three-thirty. She studied the wall of water, then hitched up her skirt and sprinted into the rain.

A little after four, she stumbled into Miss O'Hara's parlor drenched to her drawers. The Sisters, seated in their circle, hooted with pleasure, and Miss O'Hara jumped up to greet Frieda with an impulsive embrace. Leading her toward the stairs, she clucked about getting her out of her wet clothes so she could dry them before the fire. In her bedroom, Miss O'Hara rummaged through her wardrobe until she found an embroidered apricot kimono and matching slippers for Frieda to put on. "Hurry," said Miss O'Hara, as she was leaving to allow Frieda to change. "We want to hear your report."

"Pretty, pretty, Frieda-san," cried Beatrice Boaz, when Frieda reappeared.

The Sisters chorused their praise as Frieda, holding up the long kimono and shuffling along in the big slippers, shyly entered the parlor. Her long, curly brown hair, towel-dried, framed her head like an aura; her pale face, tinted by the delicate, fruit-toned cloth, glowed; and her blue eyes sparked with excitement. She gathered in the warmth coming at her and beamed it back.

"We just completed the Circle of Yesterday when you arrived," said the leader. "Take as much time as you require, my dear."

Heart swelling but suddenly shy, Frieda straightened the kimono, brushed back her hair, then raised her eyes.

"Praised be our dear leader," Frieda started softly. "Were it not for her, I would have shunned this assignment."

The Sisters shifted their eyes from the radiant disciple to her beaming leader.

"I wanted to go to high school with some of you." Frieda's gaze circled to find Helen, Amy, Andrea, Lorraine, Harriet, Hannah, and Beatrice.

"And was disappointed when circumstances denied me that privilege. But Miss O'Hara has made me see the value of starting with Service to Family." Frieda stopped, laughing nervously. "So I am pleased to tell you that after three months Levie's Kosher Boardinghouse has thirteen boarders and can accommodate seven to ten more."

The Sisters applauded.

Andrea Bates, a passionate horticulturist, raised her hand. Interested as ever in genus and species, Andrea wanted to know, "How is a kosher boardinghouse different from an ordinary boardinghouse?"

"Jewish dietary laws are observed. Milk and meat products must never be cooked or eaten together. Only certain meats are permitted, and then only if slaughtered properly. One of our boarders is an authorized animal slaughterer. He kills and butchers all the animals, then we salt and soak the meats until no blood remains...."

Minnie and a few of the other more squeamish Sisters wrinkled their noses with distaste.

"What exactly does 'kosher' mean?" asked Amy Weisenfeld.

"Ritually fit, clean," Frieda answered, glad she'd prepared with a peek in the dictionary.

"By whose decree? Are these practices considered modern and scientifically sound? What I mean is, are they hygenic?" Amy probed deeper.

Frieda paused, silenced by the images of the litter-strewn rear yard; the coops stuffed with chickens and the small shed, paved with straw and manure; her aunt's gnarled hands diving in after a chicken's rainbow-colored innards.

"We're Jewish, too, but my father doesn't have the slightest interest in dietary laws," Amy said. "He's a pharmacist and he says...."

Miss O'Hara interceded.

"The Jewish dietary laws were set down in the Old Testament, in Deuteronomy and Leviticus. 'Do not seethe a kid in it's mother's milk,'" Miss O'Hara quoted. "At the core of these laws lies a tender concern for all living creatures. The slaughterer is ordered to work with a steady hand, using the sharpest instrument and the greatest speed possible. He who is assigned this duty must be a God-fearing individual, a person who destroys life only with the greatest reluctance."

Blatner? With the bloody hands and the ravenous eyes? Frieda thought.

"Only four-footed animals that chew their cud and possess a cloven hoof, and only fish that have both scales and fins may be consumed," Miss O'Hara continued.

Frieda listened with the others, eager to learn the logic and the lore of the Jewish laws diligently practiced but rarely explained at the boardinghouse. Miss O'Hara made the observances sound quaint, charming, high-minded.

"The ancient Jews accepted earthly appetites as part of human nature, and designed laws that acknowledge and control them. Everything, but in moderation, is their ruling principle. For Jews, lovingkindness and self-control go hand in hand."

"Does the lovingkindness and the concern for fellow creatures extend to women?" Lorraine Phelps wanted to know. "I mean, what about women's rights? I've been told that Orthodox Jewish girls are forced to marry early; men their fathers choose for them."

"No one is going to force me to marry," asserted Frieda. "I am now, as before, pledged to give Service to Mankind, not one man." The Levie elders and some of the boarders were showing concern about her single status, but Frieda saw no point in mentioning that.

"Agreed that you can preserve your heritage and help to provide a good home for poor, lonely men, but what can you do at Levie's Kosher Boardinghouse to advance as an Elevated Feminine Spirit?" Lorraine asked.

Frieda was stuck. Miss O'Hara rushed to her rescue once more. "I'm surprised, Lorraine, you failed to perceive that Frieda has in her own home opportunities aspiring young Elevated Feminine Spirits travel halfway around the world to find—souls in need of the nurturing heart, the loving gaze and the spiritual touch."

Lorraine listened, but when Frieda sat down, Lorraine leaned over to Harriet Biddle and whispered, "I'd still rather go to high school."

Halfway through the Circle of Tomorrow, Frieda was agreeing with Lorraine. Harriet was starting a drawing class; Beatrice had a role in a high school play; Amy and Helen were excited about dissecting frogs; Evangeline was sewing a ball gown for Mrs. James Fair; Minnie was going on a cruise with her mother if she was well enough; and Lorraine Phelps was helping to make arrangements for a lecture by Elizabeth Cady Stanton at Platt's Hall.

CHAPTER SEVEN

Jewish Girl Marries

LATE ONE AFTERNOON, Frieda was returning to the boardinghouse after a quick trip to the greengrocer on Second Street. Hurrying along, she rehearsed a Swinburne poem she planned to recite at the March meeting of the Sisters of Service the next day. As she approached Howard Street, she saw a crowd singing and jigging behind a brass band. The men wore black suits and stovepipe hats; the women, bright-colored dresses and black shawls. The foaming buckets of beer sloshing in their hands made the street smell like a saloon. When the band swung into the "Wearing of the Green," Frieda realized it was St. Patrick's Day, March seventeenth, her eighteenth birthday. No one at the boardinghouse, including Frieda, had remembered. Her response was dismay, rapidly followed by relief. Mention of her age invariably brought to mind a related subject: marriage.

Frieda's parents and some of the more pious boarders were concerned about her single state; her aunt was frantic about it. Almost daily, Chava thought of new reasons why her niece "should have been married for a long time already." Frieda had argued that at seventeen she was still too young. Not seventeen, almost eighteen, Chava corrected her. And she was not too young—she was too old. Youth, strength, and industriousness were the only bargaining points a girl with a poor father of ordinary learning and two younger sisters had. Especially a girl like Frieda, with other drawbacks. According to Chava, she was too educated, too American, and had been allowed too much freedom. No really desirable Jew would want her. She'd have to be satisfied with a lesser light, and as quickly as possible.

Each time Chava brought up the subject, Frieda politely told her aunt she didn't want to discuss it. Chava persisted. To her, the issue was as impossible to ignore as a dead body on the kitchen floor. One day, Frieda's patience snapped. Banging pots and flailing the broom, she told her aunt she was wasting her breath. She was not going to marry soon— or ever.

Chava listened to her niece, quietly, acknowledging that Frieda's reluctance to wed was not unusual. Lots of girls in Lublin had not wished to marry, Chava among them. But her family had pressured her and she had succumbed, as had most of the others.

"Jewish girl marries," Chava explained. "Except a few who…" she stopped to think of the right description, "don't count."

No explanations, tears, shrieks—nothing short of murder—would keep Chava or her parents from trying to marry her off. The only way to keep her temper and her sanity was to pay no attention. Some days their words slid over her like brook water; other days they exploded in her ears like firecrackers. The more annoyed she became, the more she looked forward to the Sisters of Service meetings. But she was not always able to attend, and when she did go, she did not always come away reassured.

Instead of the meeting in December, the group had attended a performance of *A Midsummer Night's Dream*, and in January they visited Muir Woods. Frieda had been unable to join them for either outing. At the February meeting the girls were still bubbling over Muir Woods. The hit of the Circle of Today was Hannah Nathan's latest poem, "God in the Woods." Miss O'Hara had shown it to her friend Ina Coolbrith, a prominent local poet, who suggested Hannah submit it to one of the local newspapers.

During the Circle of Yesterday, Frieda reported on recent developments at Levie's. They had twenty boarders and were operating at near capacity. Her father had also started three small moneymaking enterprises—a soda pop factory, a winery, and a backdoor bakery. (The first two were still draining rather than producing income, and the bakery orders brought a great deal of work and only a little profit.) The Sisters listened but asked no questions and, as soon as she sat down, returned to panegyrizing Muir Woods and Hannah's poem. Miss O'Hara followed Frieda to the door. Gazing down at her, she took Frieda's hands. "Poor little hands," she crooned. "You're working terribly hard."

Frieda nodded, her eyes brimming with tears.

"This assignment is not forever, Frieda. Bring an inspirational quote on spring to the next meeting. That will help you keep an eye on the sky."

"'For winter's rains and ruins are over, and frosts are slain and flowers begotten,'" Frieda recited, as she turned up Tehama Street.

She was working twelve to fourteen hours a day, seven days a week. When she did get away from the boarding-house, it was on an urgent errand that left her no time to attire herself properly. When out, she scurried through the streets on guard, wary of meeting her friends dressed in her South of Market drudge clothes. The boardinghouse routine was demanding and isolating, but she could contend with it—her body was strong and her hands were able. What was wearing her down was the friction.

Marriage talk was only a small part of the conflict in the kitchen. Chava and Bella irritated each other until both were ill. Each saw herself as a culinary *artiste*. They disagreed without end on recipes and techniques, particularly in baking.

Chava could not bear to watch Bella as she painstakingly measured and mixed the ingredients.

"*Schnell, schnell*, you got to make it fast," Chava chided her sister-in-law.

And when Bella rolled out pie or strudel dough, "so thin you could see through it," Chava went wild. She'd try to seize the rolling pin out of her hands. In this situation, as in no other, the fragile Bella defended her herself against Chava, who, with her heavy hands and slapdash ways, would ruin *everything*. Ignoring her sister-in-law, Bella performed the task step by step, just as Wing Lee had shown her. Once the pastries were out of the oven and cooling on the table, Bella would wrap her aching head in a vinegar-soaked cloth and take to her bed.

Chava was physically stronger than Frieda's mother, but she had her ailments too. Her varicose veins often forced her off her feet; hot flashes left her gasping and soaked with perspiration; and high blood pressure, particularly when she got excited, made her light-headed and dim-eyed. What each woman could not do for herself, she looked to Frieda to accomplish for her. If she did as Chava told her, Bella wept. If she did as Bella told her, Chava shouted. To her humiliation, Frieda often found herself alternating between weeping and shouting.

Her father's ways also pained her. He was as busy chasing God as he had been chasing gold, and equally irascible. Three times daily the minyan met to pray. In the evenings and on Saturday afternoons, Abram and some of the boarders studied the Scriptures and the Talmud and discussed the small synagogue they hoped to start nearby. The rest of the time, Abram was occupied making soda pop and wine, and soliciting orders for the beverages, bakery goods, and the poultry Reb Chaim slaughtered and butchered. To deliver the orders, he had bought an old, splintery wagon and a nag with a sagging belly and bony joints he called *Yerushalayem*; both were frequently in need of repair. Most of his instructions came to Frieda via her aunt or her mother. Only when something went wrong did he speak to her directly. From time to time, he turned up with a potential suitor and stood with the man looking at Frieda as though she were a chest of drawers. Otherwise, he shunned her. Were it not for the envious tears that sprang to her eyes at the sight of her father scooping up Ida with a groan of delight, Frieda would have believed that she cared for him no more than he seemed to care for her.

Her relationships with the boarders were no more amiable than those with the Levie elders. In the beginning, she had treated Berl and Schmerl with the solicitousness she had offered the men at the Sailors' Home. But the brothers, long cowed by Aunt Chava, whom they called "the Missis," fled when Frieda approached. A terrifying Angel of Death in her dreams, by day Reb Chaim was an intolerable nuisance. He hung around the kitchen and was constantly pressing his big stomach against Frieda's arm or breathing on the back of her neck. She dared not look at him, but she could feel his black eyes swinging at her like meat hooks. Old man Baum's son, who was six feet, three inches tall and weighed two hundred and fifty pounds, hid under the backstairs to see her ankles and more. In the dining room, in front of everyone, he stared at her as though she were a golden-brown chicken breast waiting to be speared, as did other boarders, who were supposed to have better sense and higher morals.

In numbers alone, they stifled her. Their masculine presence filled the dining room, parlor, halls, porch—the entire house. Most of all, she disliked going into their private quarters, touching their soiled, hair-strewn sheets, and picking up their dirty underwear. The intimacy of her contact with them nauseated her. Particularly knowing that they thought of her as a marriageable girl in need of a husband.

Occasionally, late at night when she was up baking, or lying in her bed too exhausted or upset to sleep, that man from the Arizona Territory came to mind. Minutes after they met, they were chatting like longtime friends. She wasn't a man-hater—not at all. Nothing would please her more than to meet an attractive, intelligent, idealistic young man who would pluck her out of Levie's Kosher Boardinghouse and whisk her off to the highest hill in San Francisco.

"And time remembered is grief forgotten," Frieda recited as she climbed the boardinghouse steps.

CHAPTER EIGHT

A Matter for the Sages

FRIEDA HURRIED TO THE KITCHEN, grocery bag in hand. Seated at the work table, back to the door, was a small figure clad in black cotton.

"Wing Lee!" Frieda cried out in delight.

The man did not turn. Bella was standing at the stove filling a bowl from the steaming kettle, a towel draped over her arm. She shot her daughter a long, anguished look. Frieda hesitated in the doorway, watching Bella wash her servant's hands and face. Was her mother making a great fuss over a small injury? Bella's stiff movements, the blood-soaked towel that came away from Wing's face, and Wing's hunched shoulders and shaking body, warned Frieda that that was not the case.

On shaky knees she moved across the floor to her mother's side and looked down at the deep gashes around Wing's narrow eyes, the huge welt on his forehead, and the bleeding cuts on his swollen mouth. When his lips parted to greet her, Frieda saw that one of his front teeth was missing and the other broken into a triangle. He was holding his bruised and bloodied hands—several fingers were twisted and swollen—out in front of him like crushed claws. His usually immaculate coat and pants were torn and mud-streaked.

Lips trembling, stomach churning, Frieda patted Wing's arm, and turning, cast a questioning look at her mother.

"The Irishers got him," Bella said in a grim monotone.

"Why?"

"Do the Irishers need a why?"

"No like Chinese. They crazy men." A tear streaked

blood down his face.

"Where did this happen?"

"On Second Street," Bella said. "I hate South of Market."

"I come back San Francisco work for Levie family," Wing whistled through his broken teeth.

"He took his sick brother from Yuma to Los Angeles, he should die with his people. The brother passed away last week, so he came back to me."

"How did he know where we were?"

"He went to the Sutter Street house and when he didn't find us, he asked Oh Lee at the Goldbaum house where we went."

"I work for Levie family. No good for Chinese in Los Angeles," Wing Lee told Frieda, his body convulsing.

"Miz Bella need Wing."

"Oh, yes, Wing Lee, more than ever," Frieda assured him, tears spotting her bodice.

"I good worker."

"And a good man," Bella added.

Ida, carrying her rag doll, drifted into the kitchen. Recognizing her beloved Wing—he had cared for her from birth, as he had Sylvia and Sammy—she ran to his side. In mute commiseration, she placed her doll in Wing's lap, then she stood on her tiptoes and patted his thin black-and-gray hair, cooing comfort. Frieda stood by watching her mother wash Wing Lee's wounds and rub them with a balm Wing himself had mixed for the family.

Next Sylvia and Sammy rushed into the kitchen, keyed up and panting. Billy Flaherty, one of the Tehama Street boys, had told them they would find a bloody Chinaman at their house, and they had raced home to see.

"How did Billy know?" Frieda wanted to know.

"He saw the beating," Sylvia said.

"What did he see?"

"A bunch of fellows were hanging around the Frog's Head Saloon after the St. Patrick's Day parade when Wing Lee passed by. They yelled at him to get his yellow *you-*

know-what out of the neighborhood, but he just kept walking," Sylvia reported.

"Who were they?" Frieda wanted to know.

"Just some fellows full up on beer and down on the Chinese," Sammy said. Gritting his teeth, he turned and headed for the door. "I'm going out there and I'm going to...."

"Get your head busted," Sylvia said, angrily grabbing his arm and yanking him back into the kitchen. "We're going to the police. I want those hoodlums arrested."

"No police, no police. Send me back to China. No police."

"This is a democratic country," Sylvia said. "The Chinese have just as much right here as the Irish. We can't let them get away with this. Get Papa," she ordered her little brother.

"Get away with what?" Aunt Chava asked, as she entered the rear door. She was carrying two freshly-plucked chickens, her black wig askew and dotted with feathers. Spying Wing Lee, she stamped to Bella's side demanding to know, "What's *he* doing here?"

Bella quickly handed the jar of balm to Frieda and signaled her sister-in-law into the corner. Slapping down the chickens on the drainboard, Chava followed Bella to the corner, where she confronted her in a belligerent stance—arms folded over her chest, legs astride. Frieda continued to medicate Wing's wounds, her ears tuned to the argument between her mother and aunt.

Chava wanted no Chinese in her kitchen, in her house, on her street, in San Francisco, in the United States. She'd heard the Irishers making speeches against them and agreed with what they said. The Chinese took jobs away from white men. Good Jews like Berl and Schmerl were unemployed because of the Chinese. They were dirty, sneaky; they smoked opium, gambled; and they had women with whom they did terrible things. Still worse, they stole little white girls, used them until they were worn out, then cut them up and buried them in their basements.

Not Wing Lee, Bella assured her sister-in-law. He was

like a brother to her, better than a brother. He'd done more for her than her own family. They had to take him in now, and protect him against those Irish hoodlums.

Chava would not budge. No Chinamen in her house. She repeated all of their abhorrent practices, and added one more hideous sin—they eat *chazzer*, pig. The argument circled three times before Sammy returned to report that his father would come as soon as he and the boarders finished their evening prayers.

Several minutes later, Abram arrived flanked by the two most learned residents of the boarding house, Max Finkelstein, a cantor from Belz, who was as diminutive as Wing Lee and looked remarkably like him, and Samuel Kahane, a tall, portly English Jew with a long nose, large ears, and wire-framed glasses. Finklestein drew back alarmed, tears filling his eyes at the sight of the wounded Chinaman. Kahane, who claimed to have been a judge in a Jewish court in London, scrutinized the victim, asking for the details of the attack. Abram, to Frieda's surprise, remained calm. He greeted Wing Lee with the compassion due an old friend in trouble. Then he quietly questioned him, extracting the facts and passing them on to Kahane and Finkelstein. As the investigation proceeded, some of the younger, more assertive boarders, hearing of violent assault—a pogrom, perhaps—had found weapons—sticks, broom handles, hangers, a buggy whip— and stood in the doorway, waiting for a signal to defend the household.

Chava restrained herself until Wing Lee's story was told, then pushed between Finkelstein and Kahane to stand alongside her brother.

"I want him out *now*. Out."

Abram gave his sister a long, reprimanding look. "You call yourself a pious Jewish woman, yet you would throw this poor, suffering creature to the Irishers."

"Madame, we are trying to determine our moral obligations in this matter," Kahane stated. "We are not heathens."

Of the boarders, he was least intimidated by "the Missis."

On the contrary, in most matters, she bowed to his greater learning and wisdom. He was, after all, a *Kohen*, of priestly lineage, while her family were Levites, their assistants. But this matter was clearly too crucial for hierarchal deference.

"This is mine house, and he can't stay here," Chava repeated, shooting Kahane a scorching look.

"Indeed, this is your house, but that in no way mitigates our responsibility to assist this oppressed creature. Remember, Madame, we are enjoined to have *rachmones* for the suffering stranger."

"And who will have pity on us?" Chava flashed. "Must we borrow suffering from the Chinese? Don't we have enough of our own?"

"Don't listen to that heartless woman," Bella said, rushing to her husband's side and seizing his arm.

Kahane beckoned to Abram and Finkelstein to return with him to the dining room, where they could discuss the matter without further interference.

From these hysterical women, Frieda mentally completed Kahane's sentence. Trembling with resentment, and still more with fear of the men's assumed omniscience, she searched the kitchen for calming work. The dead chickens on the drainboard. She'd plucked chicken feathers hundreds of times; now, as never before, the task sickened her. Shelter and feed the chickens until they were full-grown, then snatch them from their fellow creatures in the coop to slaughter, cook, and eat them? How cruel. Yet even as she puzzled over this heartless human practice, she poked the fat, yellow fowls, thnking what a rich soup they were going to make. The boarders would drain their bowls, beg for seconds. Would the men determining Wing Lee's fate be any kinder to him than they were to the chickens?

When the men finally returned from the dining room, Abram moved directly to Wing Lee. He pulled up a chair, sat down, and patted Wing's knee.

"This neighborhood, Wing Lee, is not like Sutter Street. These Irishers are thirsty for blood. Me and mine family, we got bad times. We're poor people now. We had come to live here with mine sister because we got no place else to go. If this was mine house on Sutter Street, you could come to me like a member of the family."

"I come back San Francisco work for Levie family," Wing Lee said.

"I am very sorry, Wing Lee. Mine sister doesn't want you, and this is her house."

"I love Levie children. I good worker. I no eat chazzer no more."

Chava had taken a position behind Abram's chair and stood there, solid as a wall. Abram stood up, picked up his chair, and waved her away with one hand as he moved closer to Wing Lee.

"What can I do? Nothing. Mine sister is mine sister. She's afraid. She's got good cause to be afraid. Bad things happened to her. She thinks the Irishers will drive away her boarders, and burn down her house if she lets a Chinese live here. Maybe she's right."

"No," Bella cried, tears flying from her eyes. "Don't send him away."

"It's too cruel, Papa. Good Jews are supposed to—" said Frieda, rushing to her father and taking his arm.

"You, *sha*," Abram shouted, pulling out of Frieda's grasp. "And you too, Bella," he added, casting a searing look at his wife.

Bewildered, Wing Lee turned from Levie to Levie pleading, "I good Jewish cook. I make *knaidel*, I make *lokshen*, I make *challah*, I say *broches*. I no eat chazzer no more."

Wing was a wonderful Jewish cook. His matzo balls, noodles, Sabbath bread were superb. And he did recite all the Hebrew blessings. He was even willing to give up pork. Poor Wing. Frieda's eyes blurred with emotion. She listened as her mother continued to protest the men's decision. When her father, his features set, turned away, Frieda put her arm around her mother's quivering shoulders, and called after her father, "Papa, Wing's a member of our family, we can't send him away."

Abram whipped around, face inflamed, fists doubled, and started toward her.

"I make no trouble. I go. I go," Wing Lee said, trying to rise. "I go fast."

"But where, Wing?" Frieda asked.

"I got cousin. He fish peddler. Very poor but he take me. I work hard make money. I go away San Francisco. I go Yuma work on Colorado River boat. I good cook."

"Don't send him back out on the street," Bella pleaded. "They'll kill him."

"Don't worry," was Abram's sharp answer. "I'll take care of him. Later tonight, I'll put him in the back of the wagon, cover him with a tarpaulin and drive him to Chinatown."

"No pogroms, no murderers—a free country," Bella upbraided her husband. "Some America you gave me." She was standing close to Wing Lee, her hand on his slight shoulder.

"I all right, Miz Bella," Wing Lee said. "You no cry."

"What kind of all right?" Bella wanted to know, exchanging a long, abject look with her Chinese servant.

"I work river boat. Nobody want work Arizona Territory. Arizona hot as hell."

"Poor Wing. Poor us," Bella grieved.

The matter settled, Kahane approached Wing Lee. "Nothing personal intended. We are all strangers in a strange land. This time it's the Chinese, the next it could be the Jews. There's no getting away from the *yetzer ha-ra*."

"*Yetzer ha-ra?*" A puzzled look spread over Wing's face.

"The evil inclination."

"I no evil. I good worker—cook, wash, watch baby," Wing said.

"Don't despair, old chap. We must go on in spite of it all," Kahane said. Signaling to Finkelstein, he led the way out, palms pressed together on his chest.

Shortly after midnight, the tarpaulin-covered wagon was ready to leave. Abram sat at the reins with Sammy alongside him, a buggy whip in his hand. Frieda went down the back steps into the cold, black night to say goodbye, a basket of food on her arm for Wing Lee. There she found her mother wrapped in a shawl. Bella had dragged a box to the rear of the wagon, stepped up on it, and stood conversing with Wing, the edge of the tarpaulin pulled over her head. When Bella stepped down, Frieda climbed up on the box. As she was saying goodbye, she noticed Bella's gold-framed cameo brooch resting on the wagon bed in front of Wing. It was her mother's last piece of valuable jewelry; she'd promised Sylvia she'd save it for her.

Back in the house, Frieda joined Bella, who was sitting on her bed still wrapped in her shawl. She looked up at her daughter and patted the spot alongside her on the bed. Except for intermittent sighs and groans, she and her mother sat in silence, the weight of their misery too deep for words. Bella finally turned to her daughter to beg, "Don't ever leave me, Frieda. I got nobody but you now."

"Poor Mama," Frieda said, slipping her arm around her mother's girlish shoulders. She drew her close, offering her comfort but no promises.

When Frieda heard the wagon enter the yard, she rose quickly to avoid seeing her father again that night. The swiftness with which he and his wise men had disposed of Wing Lee had carved a niche of terror in her.

CHAPTER NINE

Loving Everyone

ON SATURDAY AFTERNOON, Frieda stood at Miss O'Hara's door, rubbing the tips of her worn graduation shoes against her mended stockings. Her nerves still twanged with the strain of getting out of the boardinghouse. She had slapped Ida, chased Sammy with a broom, borrowed Sylvia's dress in her absence, and lied to her mother, Aunt Chava and four boarders who, one by one, had asked her where she was going as she hurried toward the front door.

Frieda rapped the brass knocker once, twice, then pounded it against the door.

The bedroom window on the second story opened and a hoarse, plaintive voice called, "Who's there?"

"Frieda Levie. You invited me to tea."

"Today?" Miss O'Hara said.

"This is May ninth, isn't it?"

"Is it? I've been sick in bed most of the week." That said, Miss O. gazed down at her, as if weighing her options.

Frieda crossed her fingers and held her breath, silently begging to be let in. When Miss O. called, "I'll be right down," the girl undid her fingers and exhaled.

Miss O'Hara appeared in the doorway, her white hair disheveled and her usually glowing face clouded with sleep. She wore a faded rose-colored wrapper and smelled of menthol and brandy.

"Don't look at me," she cried. "I'm a sight. Wait for me in the parlor. Put the kettle on."

Frieda had never been in Miss O' Hara's parlor when it was not filled with laughing, chattering girls. Without them the room looked dark, shabby, forlorn. She threaded a path through the gilt-framed Queen Anne chairs, the rosewood Chinese tables, and the potted palms to the green love seat, which had been turned to face the window framing a view of San Francisco Bay.

The sky was mottled with streamers of fluffy clouds, lit by the sun and glowing like lanterns. Moving patterns of light and shadow played over the plodding steamers, fishing boats trailing seagulls, and sailboats bouncing on the choppy water. This was the San Francisco she loved and hoped never to leave.

"Frieda," Miss O'Hara called, searching the room for her guest.

Frieda sprang out of the chair and went to meet her.

She'd changed into a soft coral gown and long, jet earrings, but her eyes were red-rimmed and rheumy, and medicinal odors lingered beneath her flower-scented toilet water. She extended her hand to Frieda, then, seized by a fit of coughing, raised both hands, one with a handkerchief in it, to her mouth. The upper half of her body rocking back and forth, tears wetting her cheeks, waving off her alarmed disciple, Miss O. hacked away. When at last the coughing subsided, she wiped her face and extended her hand again.

Frieda took it; it was hot and dry. "I could come back another day," she offered.

"Oh, no, stay, stay. I could use some company. Did you put on the kettle?"

"I'm sorry, I didn't," Frieda apologized, her eyes turning back at the bay window. "I stopped to look at the view, and—"

"Ah, the sea and the sky," Miss O. said, stepping to the window. "How they reflect each other's moods. Enjoy it, I'll get the tea things."

While Miss O'Hara was in the kitchen, running water, clinking china and silver, Frieda considered topics of conversation. Mark Twain's recent speech in San Francisco on women's suffrage? The coming Centennial celebration? The article in the *Overland Monthly* on the grandeur of the High Sierra?

She was favoring Twain when Miss O'Hara glided into the parlor with a black lacquer tray loaded with an orange-and-gray oriental tea set and a platter of cinnamon cookies. She placed the tray on the table in front of the sofa, sat down, beckoned Frieda to her side, and poured the tea. After several long draughts from her cup, Miss O. cleared her throat, wiped her nose, then turned a penetrating gaze on her guest. Frieda bounced her crossed leg and sipped her tea, avoiding her hostess's eyes.

"You're paddling through white water," Miss O'Hara told Frieda.

Eyes still averted, Frieda edged toward the corner of the sofa. She'd written to Miss O'Hara saying she wanted her advice on some problems at the boardinghouse. "We've been terribly busy with the spring festivals—"

"It's *you* I want to hear about, Frieda," Miss O'Hara said. "You look peaked, unhappy, melancholy. What happened to that ambitious, vivacious girl I knew last year?"

Frieda looked back at the seascape. Miss O. cupped the girl's chin, and turned her head until their eyes met.

"What's troubling you, my dear?"

"I'm not rising, I'm falling," Frieda blurted. "I hate the boardinghouse more every day. There's so much bickering. Things quiet down on Shabbes, then poof, the squabbling begins again."

Miss O'Hara brushed back Frieda's flyaway brown hair, her fingers dropping to linger for a moment on the girl's flushed cheek. "Listen to me," she said, her urgent tone underlining the importance of what she was about to say.

Frieda attended, tears forming.

"Family life is a training ground for life in the world. Learn to get along at home, and you'll get along everywhere."

"I can't spend another day in that kitchen with my mother and aunt. One's always shouting, the other, crying."

"Do you know why you were put in that kitchen?"

"No."

"To stay the lion, and coax forth the lamb."

To stay the lion and coax forth the lamb? "Me?"

"You can be of great help to your people, Frieda. You must know that."

"There's too much work and too little help. My sister Sylvia won't do a thing, and my brother, Sammy—he's in the sixth grade—has already found a job at Carmody's Saloon so he can make money instead of working for nothing at the boardinghouse."

Her voice had grown shrill, resentful. These unspoken grievances had been weighing her down for months. Once she began to speak of them she couldn't stop. Nor did she feel the need to, not with Miss O'Hara urging her on with sympathetic nods.

"Sylvia's already warned me that as soon as she graduates, she's going to work for her music teacher giving piano lessons."

"It doesn't seem fair," Miss O'Hara said. "But look at it this way, some people will never know the rewards of putting other people's needs before their own." Miss O'Hara's hand gripped Frieda's knee. "Should we let the most selfish among us set our standards?"

"I want to give Service to Family," Frieda cried, "but it's too hard."

Miss O'Hara took Frieda's hands into her own. "When you find yourself sliding, I want you to stop what you're doing, and if you can't stop, stop in your head, and think to yourself, I give thanks for the challenge of obstacles and for the strength to overcome them. Say it."

"I give thanks for the—"

"...challenge of obstacles and for the strength to overcome them."

"...challenge of—obstacles—and for the—the strength to—overcome them," Frieda said, stumbling over the words as if speaking an unintelligible foreign language.

"It will help, I promise you."

Miss O. coughed, blew her nose, then leaned back exhausted. Silence thickened between them. Frieda was about to leap to the safer ground of Mark Twain's lecture, but Miss O. spoke first.

"Something else is troubling you," she said.

Frieda's gaze flew back to the window.

"This is no time for shame, dear."

Frieda turned to look at the clock on the mantel. "It's getting late," she said, starting to rise.

"Is it one of the boarders? Have you fallen in love with one of the boarders?"

"No," Frieda protested.

"It's perfectly natural for a girl of your age to fall in love...."

"Quite the opposite."

"Quite the opposite?"

"The boarders make me sick."

Miss O'Hara leaned closer. "How so?"

"I hate living with all those men. They're always there, watching every move I make, some openly, others, on the sly. Sylvia says she wouldn't do what I do for anything." Frieda crossed her arms and sealed her lips, sorry she'd said as much as she had.

"What *do* you do?" When Frieda didn't answer, Miss O'Hara added, "that Sylvia wouldn't.*" More silence. "You can tell me."

"Clean the men's rooms. Pick up their dirty clothes, change their sheets." Frieda bowed her head. "I feel like a slave serving a houseful of masters."

"Religious Jews have rules of conduct in relation to women," Miss O'Hara remembered.

"All kinds of rules. They're not supposed to look right at a woman, or accept an object from her, because she might be...." Frieda stopped, choking with shame.

"Menstruating."

"They make me feel dirty, inferior," Frieda's face

scrunched up with distaste. "And I feel the same about them. They disgust me, Miss O'Hara," Frieda cried, swatting her tears as if they were burning her face.

"Look at me, Frieda," Miss O'Hara said sharply.

Frieda lifted her head, expecting to be reproached. Instead, her teacher's face radiated approval. "I congratulate you," Miss O'Hara murmured. "You've taken a giant step."

Frieda peered at her, her brow furrowing.

"Most of the Sisters of Service won't get to where you are for years. The thin-blooded ones never will."

"I don't understand."

"What you are expressing is a youthful fear of the opposite sex."

"The opposite sex?"

"Occasionally, you find a boy appealing, but on the whole, you're uneasy with them. Do you agree?"

Frieda agreed. Rudy Seiffert was the only boy she really liked.

"Most of us start out feeling uncomfortable with the opposite sex, also with the alien, the infirm, the colored, the aged."

Frieda nodded again. Visiting hospitals, old folks' homes, jails, and insane asylums with the Sisters of Service had often filled her with aversion. And after living South of Market for more than year, she still half-expected some foreign-looking passerby to leap at her with a weapon or an indecent proposal.

"To become a truly Elevated Feminine Spirit, you must recognize this revulsion and master it. Until you have, the nurturing heart, the loving gaze, and the spiritual touch are only words." Miss O'Hara lowered her voice to an awed whisper. "Learn to feel, to look, to touch, Frieda. When you do, you will know true lovingkindness, given and received."

Frieda had often watched Miss O'Hara, her face aglow, move among the very old and the very sick, caressing their skeletal hands, their sunken cheeks, murmuring words that brought light to their faded or pain-wracked eyes. Negroes,

Chinese, Mexican, Polynesians, and Jews, too, she treated as she did her own kind. Frieda had always thought of Miss O'Hara as *giving*, but she was *receiving* too, wasn't she?

"Don't get the wrong idea," Miss O. went on, "I'm not speaking about Free Love. I agree with Victoria Woodhull that our bodies are as constrained as our intellects, and as much in need of liberation. And I do concur that a woman must avoid enslavement to one man, but on the theme of female sexuality, we part company. There Woodhull veered off the track and missed the whole point. Our saving grace lies not in sexual love but in spiritual love. Most people can't tell the difference, and that poses a real danger. But dangerous as it is, we must try to love everyone—man, woman, rich, poor, healthy, ailing, virtuous, wicked, straight, twisted, black, white, brown, yellow, clean, dirty. Frieda, can you imagine what it's like to love everyone?"

"Not really," Frieda said.

"Is there a young man you like, a man you'd be happy to embrace?"

Frieda nodded.

"Close your eyes and visualize meeting him."

Frieda's lids closed and she saw Rudy, tall, dark-haired, chocolate-brown eyes, wide brow, slim nose, full lips, standing under a tree.

"Go to him and embrace him."

As she approached him, Rudy spread his arms to receive her. Their two forms blended, becoming one shadow.

"Feels good, doesn't it?"

Frieda nodded, flushing.

"Open your eyes and look at me."

Frieda obeyed.

"Now think of the man you would least like to embrace."

Frieda hesitated.

"Close your eyes and find him."

Reb Chaim. He was standing over her, swinging a dead chicken in one hand and a bloodied knife in the other.

"Put your arms around him," Miss O'Hara instructed.

Frieda tried to imagine embracing the fat shochet. Distaste pinned her arms to her sides.

"What are you feeling?" Miss O'Hara asked.

"Disgust, fear, anger," Frieda admitted.

A sly smile rippled across Miss O'Hara's mouth. "An Elevated Feminine Spirit embraces everyone."

Even Reb Chaim? Frieda's face darkened.

"Don't be discouraged, it takes effort and time. When you see that man, in the flesh or in your mind, think this: If I could embrace this person, the World Would Be a Better Place. Can you do that, my dear?"

"I'll *try*," Frieda said, uncertain.

"I know you can, dear."

Frieda jumped up. "I have to go now. Thank you for seeing me, Miss O'Hara."

"I should thank you, Frieda. You're good for what ails me." When they reached the door, Miss O. spread wide her long, thin arms, and whispered, "Come here, my dear."

Frieda looked at her, uncomprehending.

"Let me embrace you."

She never had before. But there she was, open-armed, waiting for her. Frieda inched forward. Miss O'Hara reached out, closed her arms around her, and drew Frieda against her angular body. The top of Frieda's head reached the woman's nose; the teacher's breasts pressed against her shoulders. Unaccustomed to touching and being touched—Ida and her mother were the only people she ever hugged—Frieda stood still, arms hanging at her sides. After the first shock of contact receded, she felt the warmth of Miss O'Hara's body and inhaled the unusual, but no longer distasteful, smells emanating from her. Frieda's arms circled Miss O' Hara's thin back, and she gave her a long hug.

"Ah." Miss O'Hara sighed, "I needed that." Then she dropped her arms and stepped back to look at Frieda, "You see how nice it is?"

Frieda nodded, she did see.

"Come visit whenever you can, my dear. Think of my

parlor as your sanctuary."

Sanctuary. The word brought to mind a quiet, secluded, relaxing spot, as unlike the boardinghouse as a place could be. She wanted to throw herself back in Miss O'Hara's arms and blubber about friendship and gratitude. Instead, she murmured some courteous words of thanks, wished her hostess a speedy recovery, and fled.

After the door shut behind her, Frieda closed her eyes, flung open her arms, crossed them over her shoulders, and squeezing herself tight, rocked to and fro, grinning with relief. A moment later, arms swinging, she strode down Pine Street, taking in the sights she'd been too troubled to notice on the way up. The brow of the hill was covered with half-completed urban palaces she'd read about in the newspapers and had heard the boarders discuss.

Months before, Miss O'Hara, in a rare breach of magnaminity, lambasted the Johnny-come-lately railroad and silver moguls who'd bought lots on Nob Hill after the California Street Railway went into construction. On the subject of the new millionaires and their mansions, residents of the boardinghouse held diverse opinions. Chava sided with the unemployed workingmen who rallied on sandlots against the new rich, claiming they'd taken the city's wealth and brought in cheap Chinese labor. The ultra-pious boarders, who dwelled in San Francisco and dreamed of Jerusalem, dismissed the showplaces with a wave of the hand and a quote from Koheleth, "Vanity, vanity, all is vanity." Brotman, a carpenter, skilled and unemployed, daily climbed Nob Hill to study the construction and, who knows, find a job. While Shapiro, a student of the prophet Isaiah and the Single Taxer Henry George, cursed the rich for being rich: "May they all hang and burn like their new chandeliers."

In Frieda's elated state, the rising palaces inspired a new thought. What if she were suddenly lifted out of bondage at the boardinghouse and enthroned in one of these mansions? San Francisco abounded with stories of cooks turned queens. It would be wrong to strive for riches, Frieda decided, but if wealth were thrust upon her, she would make good use of it. An Elevated Feminine Spirit with the wherewithal could ease the pain of countless suffering souls. Before her rose the Frieda Levie Kindergarten, the Frieda Levie Old Folks' Home, the Frieda Levie Foundling Home.

Near the bottom of the hill at Sutter and Powell, Frieda found herself walking to the sound of violins. The Saturday Afternoon Sampler was in full swing at Union Square. She moved toward the music as if by hynoptic command. On a small stage in the middle of the crowded square was an offering from the California Theater, Gypsy Violins—six men and two women fiddlers—bodies swaying, feet tapping. Frieda stayed to see them, then Professor and Clara Baldwin, Debunkers of Spiritualism. "See How They Do It," read their placard, "Human Agency, Transmutation, Handcuff Test, Clairvoyance." After the Baldwins came the Vienna Gardens offering: "The Japanese Troupe—Equilibrists, Jugglers, Contortionists, Conjurers, Top Spinners."

As George Ciprico, who was appearing in *Carmen* that night at the Wade Theater, mounted the stage, Frieda tore herself away, head turned to hear the opening strains of the toreador song. If Sylvia got back to the boardinghouse before she did, she'd make her take off her dress on sight. (The last time she caught her in the front hall, and Frieda had to run to the crow's nest in her petticoat.)

CHAPTER TEN

Independence Day

FRIEDA PULLED A PALE, blue faille dress, a hand-me-down from Mrs. Edelstein, over her head, then smoothed the feathery bangs on her forehead.

Ida was sitting on Frieda's bed watching her. "Where are you going," she asked.

"To a party," Frieda said, brushing once more the curls cascading down her back.

"Where?" Ida wanted to know.

"At my friend Minnie's house."

"Why?"

"It's America's birthday; our country is one hundred years old."

"That's old."

"Not for a country. There are going to be parades, picnics, races, fireworks; they're even going to have a sham battle."

"What's a sham battle?"

"Soldiers or sailors pretend they're fighting a war."

"Why?"

"Oh, for God's sake, Ida, I don't know. I'm in a hurry," Frieda said, picking up her black shawl and starting for the door.

"I want to go with you," Ida said, her blue eyes filling with tears.

"I'm sorry, baby, I can't take you. But I'll bring you back some sweets, and maybe a little flag."

"I don't want to stay here," Ida said, her face puckering.

"What's bothering you, baby," Frieda said, sitting down

alongside her little sister.

"Why are they sitting on boxes in the parlor singing sad songs and crying?"

"Because it's the saddest Jewish holiday of the year, *Tisha B'av.*"

"What's tishy bob?"

"It's when the Jewish people remember all the terrible things our people have suffered, the destruction of the first temple, the second temple, when they were chased out of Spain...."

"Who chased them, the Irishers?"

"No, the Spaniards."

"I'm hungry," Ida whimpered. "I didn't have breakfast."

"No one did. Jews are supposed to fast on *Tisha B'av.*"

"Fast?"

"Not you, baby. Come down to the kitchen, I'll get you something to eat," Frieda said, wrapping herself in her old black shawl to conceal her party attire.

On the stairs, the sound of lamentations emanating from the parlor—the worshippers were wailing like mourners at a funeral—summoned a second plea from Ida. "I don't want to stay here. I want to go with you."

Frieda picked her up and carried her to the kitchen, her sister's face buried in her shoulder, her fingers plugging her ears.

A few of the less pious boarders were seated around the work table listening to Shapiro read a newspaper account of the Centennial celebrations the previous night at some of the local synagogues. "The rabbi then offered a prayer for the welfare of the country," Shapiro read, "giving thanks for the discovery of a land where Jews, despised and persecuted, driven from land to land, found refuge."

Frieda set an apple, milk, and cookies in front of the child, who ignored the offering and sat, lips sealed, tears streaming down her cheeks.

"So young and already mourning for Tisha B'av," Shapiro teased.

"She wants to go out and celebrate," Frieda said.

"We're going out later; we'll take her with us," Weinstein said.

"Where are you going?" Frieda asked.

"To the cemetery. We always go to the cemetery on Tisha B'av."

"Eat something, baby, you'll feel better," Frieda urged the little girl, as she rose to leave.

"I don't want to stay here," Ida shrieked. "I want to go with you." She jumped out of the chair and ran to wrap her arms around Frieda's legs.

Frieda looked around the kitchen for a consolation offering. Finding none, she caught Weinstein's eye and signalled him to detach her squalling sister from her leg.

By the time Frieda got to Market Street, the funereal mood of the boardinghouse had evaporated and she felt part of the high-spirited celebration in progress wherever she looked. The day was unusually bright for July, and the red-white-and-blue flags, banners, and bunting decorating the street and every establishment, flapped in the light wind. Music originating in a variety of places blended into one exhilarating beat. Smiling San Franciscans, dressed in their holiday best, filled the sidewalks and spilled into the streets. Frieda removed her black shawl, stuffed it into a cloth bag, and jumped onto a crowded cable car. Clutching the overhead strap, Frieda rode down Market Street, happy to be an American, happy to be a San Franciscan, happy to be alive, happy to be away from the boardinghouse.

She was the first guest to arrive at the Cohn residence. Sally, the Irish maid, attired in a gleaming black-and-white uniform, threw open the door. She led Frieda to the kitchen, where Mrs. Rosamund Cohn, resplendent in a red satin dress and a chestful of pearls, was arguing with the cook. Her face wet and rosy as a split peach, the cook grumbled, "She doesn't like the crab sauce. She doesn't like the Duchess potatoes. She doesn't like the string beans *à la meunière*, the shrimp casserole, or the rice pilaf. Now she wants me to file the turkey in slices you can see through, and me having to ice the Lady Baltimore cakes, and decorate the petits fours and fill the eclairs."

"Is there something I can do to help?" Frieda asked.

Mrs. Cohn whirled around, her expression shifting from murderous to entreating. "Frieda, dear, I am so glad to see you. I hired two assistants for the cook. One didn't show up at all, and the other arrived so drunk I had to send her home. I don't know what's wrong with the workers in this city. All I ever hear about is the plight of the poor, but give them a chance to earn an honest dollar and this is what happens. You can slice the turkey thin, I trust?"

Frieda could.

On the way upstairs to find something for Frieda to wear in the kitchen, Mrs. Cohn explained about poor Minnie. She had been suffering from an asthma attack all week and was still wheezing so badly she could not leave her room. "I'm counting on you to console the poor little thing. Do plan to spend a little time in her room, won't you, Frieda?" said Mrs. Cohn.

Frieda assured her she would.

"Shush," said Mrs. Cohn, as they approached Minnie's door. "If she hears you, she'll want you to stay with her now. She's been complaining all day about being neglected. I tried to explain that Mademoiselle and I had no time to amuse her, not with seventy-five guests coming. But you know Minnie."

Minutes later, Mrs. Cohn deposited Frieda, dressed in work clothes, in front of a turkey and a carving set. "Oh yes," she remembered. "How's your penmanship?"

"I always got ones in school."

"Good. When you finish the turkey, I want you to write the guests' names on the dance cards. You'll find them and the guest list in the cupboard behind you," Rosamund said.

When Frieda was through with the turkey, she took the dance cards and the guest list out of the cupboard. Before starting, she scanned the list, curious to see who in San

Francisco befriended a bold and independent divorcee like Rosamund Cohn. Arthur, Alvord, Blake, Becker, Baum, Carpentier, Goldman, Grant, Frieda skipped ahead, Reese, Sacks, Seiffert—Rudy Seiffert. The paper fluttered from Frieda's hand. Her gaze flitted from the front door to the cards on the table before her to the stairway leading up to Minnie's room, then back to the cards.

Thirty minutes later, she was back in her blue dress and on her way to spend some time with Minnie before going to the party. The musicians had come and were tuning up with "Yankee Doodle Dandy." Looking over the bannister, she scoured the entry hall, by then aswarm with guests. Unable to spot Rudy among them, Frieda hurried to Minnie's door.

"Come in," called the girl in a mournful wheeze.

She was propped up against the pillows wearing a filmy cambric nightgown embroidered with yellow flowers, her unruly black hair pulled back in a mass of curls in the latest style, just like Frieda's. On the night table to the right of the bed stood a vase of long-stemmed red roses, a stack of books, and a large box of chocolates.

"Frieda," Minnie said, "Where have you been? My mother and Mademoiselle decked me out like a corpse at a wake then abandoned me here with nothing to do. Just look at you, all done up like Lotta Crabtree. My mother had this gorgeous white satin dress made for me, thinking we'd make a beautiful pair—her in red and me in white. Now Mademoiselle says I'll have to save it for my wedding." Minnie broke out into hysterical giggles.

She gasped, then broke into a fit of coughing. Her thin chest heaved and her breath came in short, desperate snorts. She waved Frieda to her bed and patted a spot alongside her, then she pointed to the inhaler tube on the table. Her eyes squeezed shut and tears running down her cheeks, she applied the inhaler to her nose.

"Shall I call your mother or Mademoiselle?"

No, Minnie shook her head. "They'll get mad at me for bothering them," she said, placing her hand on her wheezing chest, as though she were trying to still it. When the attack at last subsided, Minnie whispered hoarsely to Frieda, "Hand me my medicine."

"Which?" asked Frieda. There was a cluster of bottles on the chest of drawers.

"The brown—" Minnie choked.

"Echol's Australian Auriclo?"

"Yes."

Minnie downed two spoonsful, then lay back against the pillows, her eyes closed, her breath still labored.

"Frieda," Minnie said, "go downstairs and bring me a big glass of sherry. Tell the cook it's for me."

Frieda leaped up and ran downstairs, stopping for several moments to peer at the women in bright-colored silks and satins and men in black-and-white suits in the parlor and dining room. The musicians were playing a quadrille and some of the guests were dancing. Still no Rudy.

When she returned, Minnie, her chest purring audibly, had a checkerboard arranged on the bed alongside her. She downed the sherry in quick gulps and set down the glass, announcing, "The gardener taught me how to play checkers. You know how to play, don't you?"

Before Frieda had a chance to say no, Minnie ordered, "You take the blacks." Eyes fixed to the board, yelling triumphantly, "I jump you," and "King me," Minnie quickly won three games. Frieda moved her pieces in turn, trying but failing to feign interest. By the time Minnie was setting up the sixth game, she had regained her color and was gossiping happily between moves about the Sisters and Miss O'Hara.

Minnie had been out of the house as little as Frieda that spring. Yet, by gleaning the newspapers, pumping the hairdresser, modiste, and shoemaker who came to the Cohn house, and interrogating her peripatetic mother, she knew what was happening everywhere. She was able to tell Frieda that Beatrice Boaz was engaged to a widower with two small children, the owner of the store where her father clerked. Lettie Hanover's mother had given birth to her thirteenth child, and Lettie was planning to run off with an Australian sailor. Evangeline Sales' mother had died suddenly and Evangeline was staying with Miss O'Hara. Lorraine Phelps was preparing to leave in the fall for the Emma Willard School in Troy, New York. And Harriet Biddle was planning to marry an Indian agent working on a reservation in the Oklahoma Territory.

With a winning leap and an exultant cry, Minnie scored another victory. "My seventh in a row," she told Frieda, setting up the board again. "How many Sisters of Service do you think will be married by the end of the summer?"

Frieda didn't know.

"Lettie, Liliana, Harriet, and Beatrice," Minnie counted.

"Two are just plain marriages, but two are Marriage and Service," Frieda noted.

"My mother thinks I should be thinking of getting married. Your turn," Minnie prompted.

Frieda made her move.

"She invited three young men here today just to meet me. One is Rudy Seiffert, Felicia Ungarfeld's cousin."

Frieda's eyes turned to look at the door again.

"My mother met him at a musicale last week. Go on, Frieda. You know him, don't you."

"Who?"

"Rudy Seiffert."

"Yes, he was in my seventh- and eighth-grade classes."

"Is he handsome?"

"Some people thought so."

"For goodness' sakes, Frieda, why don't you watch what you're doing. You've left yourself open for a triple jump."

"I'm doing the best I can, Minnie."

"This is my eighth win in a row," Minnie cried. "You're not concentrating."

"I'm hungry," Frieda said, swiveling her head to look at the door.

"It's too early to eat."

"I haven't had a bite all day."

"It's not time yet."

"When I went down for the sherry, some of the guests were already at the buffet table," Frieda fibbed.

"They were?"

"If we wait too long, the best food will be gone."

"You're just saying that," Minnie said.

"I'm not. They're heaping their plates with turkey, crab, spiced beef, even the desserts."

"The desserts?"

"The Baltimore cake, the angel food cake, the pecan pie, the petits fours."

"Then go down now. I don't want to miss the desserts. Bring me one of each and another glass of sherry, in case I start coughing again."

Frieda was about to close the door behind her when Minnie called her back. "See how my mother is doing. She invited all her beaux, hoping they'd fight over her."

Minnie and Mrs. Cohn often spoke of their tragedy— Rosamund's divorce from Leopold Cohn and his subsequent marriage to his French Catholic mistress, who had borne him five children while he was still married to Minnie's mother. Rosamund seemed to have no difficulty supporting herself or attracting gentlemen friends. Still, she, and Minnie in emulation, could neither forgive nor forget the injury he had inflicted. Even to someone as inexperienced as Frieda, Rosamund's flirtations seemed more retaliative than amorous.

Frieda had no trouble spotting Mrs. Cohn. She was standing in the reception hall surrounded by a group of men. Her horselike eyes travelled the circle, her white teeth flashing, her fan snapping like a guillotine. Rudy Seiffert was standing on the outer rim of the circle. Frieda turned, about to run back upstairs, then whirled around, hand gripping the bannister, to have one more peek at him.

He had grown several inches and had a moustache, a feeble one that barely covered his lip. In his sack coat and striped pants, he looked older than seventeen. His dance card was extended tentatively toward Rosamund, but his eyes were fixed on the floor. Frieda impulsively started toward him, then, remembering that they had not exchanged one word in the eighth grade, she stopped. His gaze turned toward her. He looked at her without a flicker of recognition, then turned away. Stricken—they had been inseparable for almost a year—she left the bottom stair and walked past Rudy to the buffet table in the dining room.

She had two plates piled high with food, when a voice said, "Hungry, Frieda?"

Her face flaming, the plates in her hands clinking one against the other, she turned.

"You are Frieda Levie from the seventh grade?"

The two plates touched Rudy's white vest. Nodding, she responded with a questioning look.

"Rudy, Rudy Seiffert," he said. "I didn't recognize you, either, at first."

"Rudy," said Frieda, feigning surprise. "You look so grown up."

"So do you, and pretty, too."

Frieda blushed with pleasure, the pain of his betrayal forgotten.

"You must be very hungry," Rudy repeated.

Frieda's blush deepened. "One plate is for Minnie, Mrs. Cohn's daughter. She's upstairs sick in bed."

Other guests were bumping against them, trying to get to the buffet. Frieda was unaware of being jostled until a portly gentleman in a black coat and checkered pants tapped her arm, saying, "Please, Miss...." His arm was extended, clearing a path for her.

Rudy followed her as she made her way out of the crowded room. At the stairs, she turned and, to her embarrassment, gushed, "It was *so* nice to see you, Rudy."

"Nice to see you, too, Frieda. Aren't you coming back downstairs?"

"Minnie's all alone and bored. I've been playing checkers with her."

"I was thinking I might leave soon to go see the fireworks at Woodward's Gardens. Come with me."

Go to Woodward's Gardens with Rudy? The prospect dizzied her. "I'd love to, Rudy, but…."

His face was inclined toward hers, waiting for her response. "Say yes; I don't want to go alone."

"It may take a few minutes. Minnie can be insistent. But don't leave without me."

"Good," Rudy crowed. "I'll wait for you at my house. You know where it is, down the street. I have to get out the buggy—it's a crusher, brand new."

"Where's your mother?" Frieda thought to ask.

"In Santa Cruz for the week."

"I'll be there as fast as I can."

CHAPTER ELEVEN

Fireworks

RUDY WAS WAITING in front of his house, perched on the driver's seat of a shiny black buggy, its top sportily folded down.

"Ready to go," he called as she approached.

As soon as Frieda was settled alongside him, Rudy loosened the reins and flicked the horse's flank with his whip. The trim chestnut mare balked, and he brought the whip down harder.

"This is my first time out in this rig," Rudy said, his voice vibrating with nervousness. "I don't even know this nag's name. Giddy-up, giddy-up. There she goes," he said, seeming surprised the mare took his orders. "Isn't this grand?" he asked Frieda as the buggy rolled down Van Ness.

"It certainly is," Frieda said, trying to sound as if she rode in smart, new buggies everyday.

"I was thinking we should have taken the cable car, but now I'm glad we didn't. I wanted to have a go at this buggy before I go back to Munich."

"When are you leaving?" The late afternoon July fog had rolled in, and she was shivering.

"In two days."

"So soon?" There were goose bumps on her arms, but she refused to cover her pretty blue dress with her shawl.

"I'm not happy about it," Rudy said. He reined in the horse and shouted, "Calm down, mare."

They had entered Market Street, and the din of the traffic, the firecrackers popping and the music thundering out of the saloons spooked the mare. Tense-faced, Rudy sat on the edge of the seat trying to control the animal and steer clear of adjacent vehicles. Frieda sat at his side silent, trying not to distract him. Inwardly, she felt as skittish as the mare.

The fireworks were already exploding in the darkening sky above Woodward's Gardens when they arrived. Rudy drove the buggy into a sandlot crowded with vehicles next to the Gardens. He jumped to the ground, hitched the horse, then came around to help Frieda down. Hand in hand, they ran through the swarms of people toward the entrance.

The wooden grandstands were packed with roaring spectators. Frieda and Rudy squeezed in, making seats for themselves between a fat, frizzy-haired blonde woman drenched in sweat, and an Irish grandfather holding a red-haired toddler, who reeked of urine. Moments later, they lost themselves in the crowd, ohhing and ahhing, gasping and applauding each new spray of fire. In between the fiery displays, acrobats, clowns and cyclists dominated the arena, drawing easy laughs and ready applause from the spectators.

An hour and a half later, they rushed out of the grand-stands to see what else Woodward's Gardens had to offer. Uninhibited as toddlers, they ran up and down the gravelled, gas-lit paths to the conservatory, the zoo, the freak show. Finally exhausted, they fell on to an isolated bench near an artificial lake, fed by rushing waterfalls and dotted with lily pads, ducks, and swans.

Frieda inhaled the pungent aroma of fog-dampened eucalyptus leaves mixed with the lingering smell of the fireworks. Cutting through the voices of the crowd came the sound of a departing organ grinder turning out a song.

"*Il Bacio*," said Rudy. "My cousin Felicia sings it."

"The Kiss," Frieda translated, with a sigh.

She gazed out at the silver streak of moonlight reflected in the water. A cool breeze rustled the leaves. Frieda was shivering again. Rudy took off his sack coat and put it on her. The garment hanging on her shoulders still bore the heat of its owner's body. Frieda trembled with pleasure. Conscious of his arm brushing her arm and his leg only inches away from hers, she moved a bit closer.

Rudy turned to face her. "Still cold?"

His arm dropped around her shoulder and drew her against him. Frieda nestled into the curve of his arm. If I turn, she thought, he'll kiss me. I won't let him kiss me. He didn't speak to me all through the eighth grade—after we'd been so close. She slipped her hand under Rudy's jacket and settled it under her left breast, as if to muffle the sound of her pounding heart.

"Isn't this nice," Rudy murmured.

Frieda nodded. Tears filled her eyes. Maybe it was his mother's fault he'd stopped speaking to her. Their thighs were touching. Was he as thrilled at being with her as she was with him?

Rudy's hand took hold of her chin and shifted her face to meet his. His eyes glowed like twin lights in a dark mask. His breath singed her cheek for a moment before his mouth found hers. His lips were warm and wet, and his moustache tickled her nose. She might have laughed were it not for the currents of sensation surging from her mouth through her throat and breasts down to her belly. They had kissed before. But they were children then. Now, she was a woman; he, a man.

Frieda drew back to look at him, expecting to see some regard for her in his eyes. What she saw instead was the hypnotized gaze of an aroused animal. More excited than offended, she lowered her lids and pulled Rudy's head toward her until their lips met again. Wrapping her arms around him, she allowed one kiss to inspire another.

When a round of giggles cut through the darkness, Rudy and Frieda sprang apart. The suddenness of their movements triggered more laughter. Frieda peered into the night at the noisy party on a nearby bench. No one she knew, she hoped. It'd be so embarrassing to be caught kissing in public like one of those girls in Dupont Alley.

"How do you like Munich?" Frieda asked.

"Not as much as I expected."

"I thought you'd find Germany fascinating."

"It takes some getting used to. I've been living with my mother's brother's family. He owns a big department store, and he and his wife are awfully stuffy."

"Living with family can be difficult," Frieda agreed.

"There's a constant round of parties to attend and a lot of bowing and card exchanging. They laugh at my German and call me the *Amerikaner*, and I hate the cold."

"Are you at school?" Frieda asked.

"Yes and no. I am hoping to get into the Munich Academy. It's one of the leading art centers in Europe. But I have a lot of work to do before I can even apply."

"What kind of work?"

"I take private classes—German, pen-and-ink drawing, watercolor, the fundamentals of oil painting, things like that." Rudy's down-turned lips curled in a sly smile. "My mother thinks I'm studying art as part of my cultural adornment, not as a life work. She expects me to go to the university, and from there to medical school."

"But you prefer art?"

"By far."

"You were the best artist in the class."

"I was, wasn't I?"

"You were also outstanding in mathematics and science."

"You're right," Rudy responded, unsurprised that Frieda recalled his proficiencies. "But drawing and painting come naturally—I'd rather draw than eat."

"Then you should be an artist," Frieda said.

"When you begin to study art, it becomes a lot harder."

"Dedication grows on difficulty as babies grow on milk," Frieda said, quoting Miss O'Hara.

"But I feel like such a fathead in Munich. Everyone is ahead of me in the classes, and my cousins treat me as if American was a synonym for idiot."

"You felt the same way when you came from Fiddletown in the seventh grade and you were behind in all the subjects. But by the time we were in the eighth grade, you were one of Miss O'Hara's most promising pupils."

Rudy nodded.

"You were lonely then, too," Frieda reminded him.

"Was I?"

"When you first arrived, I was your only friend," Frieda said, looking into Rudy's self-absorbed brown eyes. They'd rushed at each other like countrymen meeting in a strange land. "But you made other friends."

"I guess I did."

"Do you know what I think of you, Rudy?"

He waited to hear.

"I think someday I'll be bragging that Rudy Seiffert and I were friends when we were in the seventh grade."

He laughed, frankly pleased. "I'm certainly glad I ran into you, Frieda. I've been lower than a garter snake since I got home. That's why I didn't go to Santa Cruz with my parents. We've been arguing for two weeks. I didn't want to go back to Munich and spend another year in my relatives' house. I hate being ordered about and teased."

"Rudy Seiffert, I know a lot of young people who would be more than willing to put up with a little personal discomfort to get the education you're getting." Frieda stopped, forced to deal with the lump in her throat. "If you think you can become an artist, then do your best to become a great one."

"I'll swallow those words and blow them on my frostbitten fingers this winter," Rudy said, abruptly.

"I mean it, Rudy, you're very special, and you—"

"Thanks, Frieda," he interrupted her.

By the time they started for home, the crowds had thinned and the chestnut mare was subdued and obedient. The reins draped over his fingers, Rudy directed her through the streets with a light tug, a cluck, and a tap of the whip. They were traveling along Van Ness Avenue when Rudy asked, "You still live on Sutter Street, don't you?"

Frieda neither agreed or objected.

Rudy brought the buggy to a stop in front of 810 Sutter.

Frieda waited on the seat, hoping he would kiss her goodbye, but Rudy no longer appeared to be in the mood. Unwilling to leave him, she tried to think of something else to say, something engaging.

"I'll have to have my jacket back," Rudy said.

"I forgot I had it on," she said slipping it off.

"It was nice to see you again, Frieda," Rudy said, absently flicking his whip.

"Nice to see you, Rudy. I hope you find your stay in Munich more pleasant this year."

"I'm sure I will," Rudy said, as if he'd forgotten his confession at the Gardens. "I know German better now, and I'm beginning to catch up in my classes. Also my cousin Felicia is coming to stay at my uncle's house this year. So there will be two Americans to stand up to the German cousins. You know Felicia, don't you?"

"Yes. She and I are in the Sisters of Service together," Frieda answered stiffly.

"She's wonderful company and a talented musician."

"She plays the piano and sings beautifully," she said, trying but failing to match his enthusiasm.

"I have to go now. My parents may return tonight and I didn't ask permission to take out the buggy."

"*Auf Wienersehen,*" Frieda said as she started out of the buggy.

Rudy's head flew back in laughter. "Not *auf Wienersehen, auf Wiedersehen.*"

Frieda stood on the sidewalk, looking up at Rudy. "*Auf Wiedersehen.*"

"Goodbye, Frieda," Rudy called, as he turned the buggy around and started back up Sutter to Van Ness.

Her eyes filling with tears, Frieda watched him disappear into the night. She turned to look at the beautiful house where she used to live, aglow with another family's lights. She felt like a child cast out into the street. Taking her black shawl out of her bag, she draped it over her head and, keeping her distance from drunks and mashers, hurried through the dark streets.

When she got back to the boardinghouse, the Tisha B'av grieving was over and the rejoicing had begun.

"Frieda," her mother called, as she passed the parlor, "Come sit."

"I'm too tired," Frieda said, climbing the stairs to start her own lamentations.

CHAPTER TWELVE

Unmarried Girls

THE NEXT MORNING, Frieda was at the drainboard, drying the dishes, when Aunt Chava, businesslike as a bailiff, came to announce that her father wanted to see her in the parlor.

Abram stood alongside the scarred oak table and Bella and Chava were seated side by side in the threadbare love seat. Frieda took the kitchen chair assigned to her by her father.

"Where were you last night?" he asked, his voice controlled and solemn.

"I told Mama I was invited to a Centennial celebration at a friend's house,"

"What kind of a friend?" The words were icy with suspicion.

Frieda's eyes flew to her mother's face. "Minnie Cohn, a sick girl I visit. I told Mama about her. Rosamund Cohn's daughter."

"Mrs. Rosamund Cohn?" Abram asked after a long silence. "The divored *deutschke* who lives on Van Ness?"

Studying her father's scowling face, Frieda remembered that Mrs. Cohn had been one of his creditors.

"Is that who you let your daughter visit?" Abram demanded of his wife.

"Her girl is sick, what should I say?"

"You should say don't go."

"But she's doing a mitzvah, a good deed."

"Would the big businesswoman Rosamund Cohn send her daughter to do a mitzvah for Frieda?"

"Rosamund, Shmosamund," Chava cried, "Ask her about the gentleman in the buggy."

"What about the gentleman in the buggy?" Abram echoed his sister.

"What gentleman?" Frieda asked, her eyes searching her father's.

"The gentleman Roth saw you in the buggy with."

"Where was he when he saw me?" Frieda's voice was steady, her eyes unwavering.

"*Where* was he, she asks. He was riding on a Market Street cable car when he saw you go by in a buggy with a gentleman. The buggy top, he says was down, and you had on the gentleman's coat."

"What time did he say it was?"

"What time?"

"I was at the Cohn residence until nine o'clock."

"He didn't say what time. Were you in a buggy with a gentleman last night?"

"If it was a little after nine, the answer is yes."

"What gentleman?" demanded Abram rushing at Frieda, and seizing her arm.

"Abram, calm yourself," Bella whimpered.

"I don't know his name."

"You don't know the gentleman's name?" Chava moved to her brother's side.

"No, Aunt Chava, I don't know his name."

"American girls," Chava spat. "She goes riding in a buggy on Tisha B'av night, with a man she doesn't know."

"Where did you find this man?" her father demanded.

"At Mrs. Cohn's house."

"At Mrs. Cohn's house," Abram mocked. His face was red, perspiration beaded his bald pate. "Where did you go with him?"

"He drove me home, Papa."

"Why did you let a strange man drive you home?"

"He's Mrs. Cohn's liveryman. It was late and Mrs. Cohn didn't want me to return home unescorted."

"She looks sweet as cream, but she tells plenty lies," Chava informed her brother.

Abram's eyes narrowed as though he were trying to see into Frieda's head. "Are you lying to me, Frieda?"

"Ask Mrs. Cohn, she'll tell you."

Abram grimaced.

Just as she thought; he'd never go to Rosamund. She was home free, or was she?

"Why were you wearing the liveryman's coat?"

"I was cold, and he didn't want me to get a chill."

Frieda's reply clearly irritated Abram. "Don't you have better sense than to wear a man's coat in public?"

"I didn't think."

He studied her like a high wall he had to climb.

"Is there anything else?" Frieda asked, pleased with the progress of the interrogation. "If not, I have work to do," she said, starting out of her chair.

"Sit down," Abram ordered. "I've got a lot more to say."

"Yes, Papa."

His eyes avoiding hers, he started, "I want to talk to you about Sammy."

"What about Sammy?"

"You know what kind of trouble I have with him? He don't want to study for his *bar mitzvah*." Abram was pacing in front of her. "Am I wrong to want him to have a bar mitzvah?"

"No, Papa. I've tried to talk to him."

"So what does he say?"

"He won't listen to me. He has other things on his mind." Sammy would rather hang around at Carmody's Saloon, running errands and playing the saxophone with the band.

"As important as his bar mitzvah?"

"Not nearly as important."

"You think it's important mine only son, named after mine father, and mine father's father, should learn to read from the Torah and have a bar mitzvah?"

"Yes, Papa, I do. If I were a boy I'd be happy to please you in that way."

"You'd be happy to please me?" Abram asked.

"Of course, Papa."

"So why don't you please me?"

"I do my best, Papa. I work at the boardinghouse day and night. I clean, cook, bake, wash the dishes, keep the books. What more can I do?"

He was hanging over her, glaring at her. "You don't know what more you can do?"

"No, I don't," she murmured, her eyes turning from him.

"You can stop making me crazy. You and Sammy are making me crazy," her father shouted. "He's supposed to have a bar mitzvah and you're supposed to get married. So why don't you?"

Frieda sought help from her mother and aunt. Their eyes posed the same question. She lowered her eyes, pressed her lips into a straight line, but she could not make her heart stop drumming.

"You're getting older, pretty soon no one will want you. Terrible things can happen to an unmarried girl."

He was not going to make her cry. If he wanted her tears he would have to hack them out of her, Frieda thought, her features hardening.

"The whole minyan keeps after me. 'When are we going to hear a *freilach*, Abram? With three daughters, Abram, you'd better get going with the wedding music.' You make me look like a *schlemiel* who don't know how to take care of his business."

She was merchandise he had to unload and couldn't.

"I'm a poor man, busy with wine, with chickens, with a bakery, with soda pop, with the minyan. I don't have no money for no big dowry." He turned to his wife and sister for corroboration. Three pairs of eyes accused her.

Her vision dimmed and white spots danced in front of her as she stared at her apron.

"How many real Jews do you think there are in San

Francisco? Eight suitors I brought already to Shabbes supper. I tell them about mine wonderful daughter, a good girl, capable, smart, everything but not rich, rich she is not. I talk to them, compliment them. Chava talks to them, compliments them. And Bella, poor Bella, she does her best. But what do you do? You look at them like they were tax assessors. I ran out of real Jews. No one who wants to come see you. They all know about Levie's oldest daughter, the *stuck-up* American girl." Abram stopped to appraise the effects of his words on her. "What do you say for yourself?"

Frieda squared her shoulders and narrowed her eyes at her father. "Nothing. I have nothing to say."

"First we are going to have a bar mitzvah, then we are gong to have a *chasseneh*. Do you hear me, Frieda?"

She peered at him as if he were far away, and nodded.

"Good. Kahane told me I should call a *shadchan* to make a match for you—Mrs. Nussbaum, a very high-class woman. I told your mother she should buy you a new dress. You have to look nice. And more important, you have to act nice." He studied her stony face, then threw up his hands. "You talk to her," he ordered the women, and he fled.

Bella sighed, relieved that the ordeal was over. "Don't worry, Frieda," she told her daughter. "We will tell Mrs. Nussbaum she's got to find a man who lives in San Francisco. You shouldn't have to go far away."

"Like mine son Harvey, the wanderer," Chava said.

"If you will excuse me," Frieda said, "I have a great deal of work to do."

"Don't be mad on us, Frieda," Bella said. "We want you to be healthy and happy. Someday, you'll thank us."

"Don't wait, Bella," Chava said. "From American children you get no thanks. They'll eat out your insides, that will be your thanks."

"Don't aggravate your father, Frieda. You'll make him sick again," were Bella's parting words.

Frieda's throat clogged, so she could hardly get out her words. "I'll be in the henhouse collecting the eggs."

Frieda often went to the small, dark shed, thick with the primitive smell of dank straw, chicken feathers, and manure, to cry. This time her anger was too cold and impacted for tears. Gathering eggs, she answered her elders with her own recriminations.

Her parents and aunt always spoke as if they knew what was best for her. How could they? Frieda raged. They knew little of what she was and nothing of what she could become. To them, she was their *Yiddishe tochter*, Jewish daughter, a disappointment from the day she was born, even to the Jewish daughter who bore her. Born the wrong kind, she was obliged to redeem herself in the only way possible, by presenting her cheated parents with a replacement, a grandson. Frieda pushed aside a squalling hen to get the egg beneath it. "Are you a boy or a girl," Frieda asked the egg. "A girl?" She flung the egg against the shed wall and watched the yolk hit the wood, splatter, then drip mournfully to the ground.

She was not only a disappointment, as a female she was an irrational animal. Left to her own devices, she'd run wild and bring shame to the household. Trained and governed by a shrewd master, she could be made to be useful. A muffled crow came from a rooster perched in the corner of the shed. Frieda picked up a stick and flung it at the bird. It squawked a shrill protest, fluttered its wings menacingly, then settled back on its perch to stare at Frieda with bright, angry eyes. "You think I ought to get married too," Frieda cried at the puff-chested bird.

A babylike whimper passed through her lips. Her father would give her to any real Jew who would have her. The suitors he brought were *unsuitable,* couldn't he see that? What did Miss O'Hara's most dedicated Sister of Service have in common with a wan shoemaker with a limp and two children, a lusty-eyed, bloody-aproned butcher, or those unemployed greenhorns who saw her as a ticket to free room and board? Moreover, she'd rather stay single forever than marry a man who daily thanked God he wasn't a born a woman.

Tears trickled from Frieda's eyes like water from the

seams of a rock. Let them bring their matchmakers, their suitors, their pleas and their threats. Let them hurl their accusations: Frieda, you're making us crazy; Frieda, you're making us sick; Frieda, you are making fools of us. She'd give thanks for the challenge of obstacles and the strength to overcome them. And when she'd accomplished all she could at the boardinghouse, she'd move on to her next assignment, far away, very far away.

Her basket brimming with eggs, Frieda dried her tears with her apron, left the henhouse, and ran up the back stairs. She was about to enter the kitchen, when she heard an unfamiliar voice. She eased the door closed and backed into a corner of the rear porch, propping the egg basket on the railing, wary of another surprise attack.

"She's a good girl, a quiet girl, a real *berriah*," her mother was saying. "In all San Francisco there's not a girl more capable than Frieda."

"But she's very stubborn, Mrs. Nussbaum," Aunt Chava added. "They sent her to the public school through the eighth grade. They even let her join the Sisters of Service."

"A Sister of Service? That's not good," said the visitor, concerned.

"We didn't let her, she went," Bella said.

"Not anymore she don't," Chava assured the guest.

"I know these San Francisco girls. I been doing business here twenty years," Mrs. Nussbaum said. "When a girl says she doesn't want to marry, I say, so don't get married. I let them sit. Pretty soon, their girlfriends, their cousins, their neighbors, all the girls their age, begin to get married. They go to one wedding after another. They see for themselves: the parents are happy; the guests are happy; the musicians are playing a freilach and everyone is dancing and singing. The bride has a beautiful dress, and everyone tells her how pretty she looks. If she's lucky, she has an adoring husband, who can't take his eyes off of her. She has a place of her own, and pretty soon she gets pregnant. Everyone is waiting for the baby. When it comes, if *Baruch Ha Shem*, it's a boy, there's another celebration, a *bris.* The grandmother is busy baking and the grandfather is walking up and down the streets like the town crier inviting his friends to come to the circumcision. Then the girl has a beautiful baby to wheel around town. Pretty soon Miss Independent begins to notice something, the good Jewish men are nearly all gone. Who's left for her? The leftovers. Fools, tricksters, beggars, dimwits, sick ones—without jobs, without dollars, without sense."

"That's right, I told Frieda myself," Chava said.

The mention of her name made Frieda shudder, but she could not pull herself away.

"Listen, the real Jewish girls are taken too. The only ones left are the crazies, trouble-makers, bums, ugly ones." Mrs. Nussbaum grunted with scorn. "So pretty soon Miss High and Mighty comes running to me. 'Mrs. Nussbaum, maybe you know a nice fellow for me?' She's older, a little worn, she's not expecting the Prince of Wales no more. She's polite, and she is interested in the men I have—a single man, a widower, maybe with a couple of children, a fellow from the interior...."

"No," Bella begged, "not the interior."

"Listen, Mrs. Levie, I'm not going to lie to you. With a girl like your Frieda, a Sister of Service, a girl with a reputation for being stuck-up, a girl with a little nothing dowry, you'll be lucky to get any real Jew."

On trembling legs, Frieda hurried down the wobbly rear stairs, ran around to the street entrance, and up the front stairs to the crow's nest. She threw herself on the bed, pummeled the mattress with her fists, then jumped up and paced around the crowded room bumping into furniture. Wringing her hands, tears washing her crumpled face, her body tossed with agitation. To hear them talk, she was lower than the least of God's creatures, a cockroach, an ant, a fly, a mosquito.

"You don't want to marry, so don't marry, I tell her," Mrs. Nussbaum's words echoed. "Pretty soon she comes to me, Miss High and Mighty."

"Hah," Frieda said, "Hah. I'd rather die." She stopped

in front of the door, slammed it closed, opened it, then slammed it again. Then pressing her head against the door, she pounded it as if she were hammering a nail.

"Frieda, Frieda," Chava called from the second landing. "Mrs. Nussbaum is here and wants to meet you."

Frieda seized the doorknob and held the door closed.

"Frieda," Chava called again, at the locked door, turning the knob. "I know you are there. Let me in."

She stood panting, her cheek smashed against the wood.

"Frieda, open the door."

"I'm not dressed," Frieda shouted.

"Get dressed," Chava shouted back. "You'll meet Mrs. Nussbaum. She's a nice woman."

"I don't want to meet her."

"You got to meet her. Get dressed." Chava rattled the doorknob.

Frieda pressed her body against the door. "I can't come now."

"You'll like her. She'll find a good husband for you."

"Are you sure, Aunt Chava? Are you sure she can find a husband for me? Even for me?"

"Even for you. Get dressed up so you look nice."

"You want me to look nice for Mrs. Nussbaum, Aunt Chava," Frieda said through gritted teeth.

"Nice, yes. I'll wait for you."

"It'll take me a few minutes to get ready. I'll be there as fast as I can."

"You're sure?"

"I swear it, Aunt Chava, I'll be right down."

Frieda stood listening to her aunt clump away. Then she flew to her laundry bag and pulled out a filthy wrapper she had worn several days before to clean the chicken coop. She took off her dress, put on the wrapper, then loosened her stockings so they dropped to her ankles and hung over her shoes, which were clotted with straw and manure. Next she seized her curly, brown hair and pulled it into a tight knot at the top of her head. The smelly wrapper hanging unbelted, she went to the cracked, yellow-tinted mirror to prepare a dimwitted, cross-eyed, nasty-tempered expression. Then she headed for the stairs, practicing an ungainly limp.

About to enter the kitchen, she heard Mrs. Nussbaum say, "So where is she, your beautiful, intelligent, capable daughter?"

"H-h-h-here I-I-I-I- a-a-am," Frieda stuttered.

CHAPTER THIRTEEN

The County Assessor

"DID I TELL YOU come quick, Frieda?" Weinstein cried, rushing through the kitchen door. "I told the Missis the man wasn't from the taxes; he was from Langley's City Directory. But she don't care. She locked the front door, anyway, and told him to wait on the porch. Shapiro and Glutsky are watching him like he was a Cossack, while she runs through the house hiding things—silver, crystal, the tapestry. Over the piano she throws a sheet. He'll make a mistake and think it's a stuffed elephant, maybe?"

Frieda was grating onions at the sink, a peeled onion perched against her topknot to draw the fumes from her eyes—with little success. "I told you I'd be there in a few minutes, Mr. Weinstein. I have to get these onions grated now so I can get the potato *latkes* done this morning. I have a million other things to do this afternoon. I'll be finished in a minute."

"He'll think we got some kind of bad business at Levie's Kosher Boardinghouse. A diamond mine in the basement or an opium den, maybe."

"Mr. Spiegelman knows our house."

"It ain't Mr. Spiegelman. It's a new fellow. It's cold as ice out there on the porch and he's getting impatient."

"Go tell him I'm coming." She ducked her head, dropping the onion into the bowl with a plop. Wiping her tear-streaked face on her soiled, gray Mother Hubbard, she crossed the smoky kitchen to the huge old coal stove and closed the grate beneath the pan of bubbling chicken fat. She whipped around just in time to seize Weinstein's arm, forcing him to drop a handful of latkes back on to the pile cooling on the work table.

"Aren't you ashamed of yourself, stealing latkes? It's the third day of Chanuka and you've had latkes three nights in a row."

"Is it my fault you make the best latkes in America?"

"If you have a stomach ache tonight, you'll wake Mr. Shapiro, then you two will start arguing and I'll have to come downstairs to quiet you so you don't wake the entire house. Besides, I'm far too busy to stand here making latkes all day."

"Today uphill, tomorrow downhill. Give the man a few minutes, Frieda."

"I said I was coming," she answered, stuffing a latke in her mouth. Sliding past Weinstein, she hurried toward the porch, pushing back her straggling hair. "What can I do for you?" she asked the man, dressed in a business suit, standing with his back to her.

When he turned to face her, the just-consumed latke leaped back into her throat. It was Twitch Sanford, one of her eighth-grade classmates.

"Good morning, ma'am. Langley's sent me out to gather information for the 1880 directory."

"I'm too busy today," Frieda snapped. She kept her head bowed, hoping he wouldn't recognize her. Dressed as she was and reeking of onions, she was too embarrassed to speak to anyone from outside the boardinghouse—even Twitch Sanford—the eighth-grade class dullard.

"Perhaps I could talk to Mr. Levie."

"He's out making deliveries."

"Or the woman who answered the door?"

"Out of the question." Chava couldn't read the records, which Frieda kept in English, and if she could, she'd never reveal boardinghouse business, particularly for public use.

"But this is my only day on Tehama Street, Mrs. Levie."

Mrs. Levie? Was that what she looked like? A middle-aged boardinghouse proprietress? Frieda winced. "I told you, I have no time."

"Just five or ten minutes, ma'am. Not being in Langley's is like not being in San Francisco."

"Come with me," she ordered, leading him to the darkened parlor, away from the nosy boarders.

Frieda seated Twitch in a chair at the oak table and went for the register, kept in the desk against the wall. Standing behind him, she opened the book and began reading off the names and occupations of the residents, as she did each year for Mr. Spiegelman.

"Excuse me, Ma'am, we'll get to that in a few minutes. Federal officials are preparing for the 1880 Census next year and have asked us to make a few additional inquiries."

Frieda listened, impressed with Twitch's poise and smoothly flowing speech. No stammer, no stumbling over the long words, even the facial tics that had earned him his name were gone. Life after school agreed with him.

"What would you like to know," Frieda said.

"How many people are in residence?" started Twitch.

Frieda counted the names in the register. Boarders had been moving in and out a lot lately. "Thirty-two boarders this week, and six members of the family. No, seven," she corrected, deciding to include Sylvia, who was now living at the home of her music teacher, Mrs. Tyler.

"How many are employed?"

"Not as many as would like," Frieda said.

The visitor commiserated with a nod. "This has been a hard year."

But not so hard that Twitch Sanford is out of a job, thought Frieda. Miss O'Hara had helped him get the position, she recalled.

"Can you give me a figure?"

Frieda counted, "Twenty-one."

"Only twenty-one?" Twitch asked, shaking his head. "Poor devils, how do they manage?"

Frieda restrained the litany of related misfortunes suffered that year by the residents. Deaths—Berl, and one month later, Schmerl; insanity—Mr. Dershowitz and his attacking blankets; suicide—a man rented a room and cut his wrists the same night; emigration—three unemployed immigrants gave up and returned to Europe, and others would have gone too had they the passage money; crime—one man was arrested for arson, and the police came to question her brother, Sammy, about smuggled goods; and illness—half the boarders suffered at least one chronic ailment.

"Are there any more questions?" Frieda asked.

"I need the names and occupations of the residents."

Frieda read from the register: "Abrams, Harry, glazier; Baum, Itzak, and Baum, Yossel, old sacks and bottles; Blatner, Moshe, animal slaughterer; Finklestein, Immanuel, book-binder and cantor...."

Back in the kitchen, Frieda picked up the grater and bent over the bowl. Tears streamed down her face, and her chest heaved with the effort to hold back her sobs. "Ouch," she cried, thrusting her cut and bleeding finger into her mouth. How dare that idiot Twitch Sanford burst in on her? In her four years at the boardinghouse, this was the first time one of her North of Market acquaintances had come to the board-inghouse, except for Minnie Cohn. And she visited only when her mother pressured her to practice making a social call. Minnie, at least, gave her ample warning.

Frieda took pains to keep her North of Market and South of Market lives separate. North of Market (in her own mind, at any rate) she was still Frieda Levie, a dedicated Sister of Service. While still giving Service to Family, she was ex-pecting at any time to be called to a new assignment, one worthy of her long and arduous apprenticeship.

South of Market, she was an old maid, a *farzesseneh*, an object of pity and scorn. Even the Levie elders had given up on her, convinced, at last, that she was not only unmarried, she was unmarriageable. Gradually, her mother had stopped weeping, her aunt had stopped threatening, and her father had stopped bringing home suitors. Resigning themselves to God's will, they had wrenched from their hearts the fondest hope of every Jewish parent: to live long enough to accom-

pany their child to the bridal canopy. For their Frieda they
would prepare no chasseneh; dance no freilach; receive no
mazel tov. There would be no multiplication of milestone
celebrations in Frieda's life, nor in those of her children, nor
her children's children. With heavy hearts, they accepted their
misfortune. Their first-born daughter would not add a single
seed to the long parade of Levies advancing to meet the
Messiah.

What had happened, they could not say. Their lovely
daughter had simply disappeared. In her place stood a
maimed offspring, a rebuke from God, a punishment for co-
vert crimes their friends and neighbors could speculate upon
with delight. As long as they were alive, she would be a bur-
den to them, like a diseased or demented child, a bone in
their hearts.

Frieda regretted that they suffered on her account, but
her pity was tinged with spite. She'd proven herself as single-
minded as her parents, as dogged as her aunt, as loyal to her
beliefs as they were to theirs. Having abandoned hope of
their approval, she no longer sought it. Let Sylvia, Sammy,
and Ida give them the *nahas fun kinder,* pleasure from children, they so ardently desired, thought Frieda, with a vindic-
tive smile.

The first time the Levie elders mentioned marriage to
Sylvia, she sat them down and set them straight. She did not
intend to marry until she was at least twenty-five, and when
she did, she would select her own mate. She was now living
North of Market with her music teacher, Mrs. Tyler, and
came home for Shabbes supper when she was free. Once a
month she contributed five dollars toward the mortgage pay-
ment. If her parents or aunt did or said anything to displease
her, she threatened to stop the visits and financial help. In her
absence, the Levie elders clucked over her strong-minded
American ways, but no one lamented over Sylvia as they did
over Frieda. Sylvia had several desirable suitors: the son of a
prominent Reform rabbi, the conductor of the Temple
Emanu-El choir, and a wealthy Jewish stockbroker. None

practiced Eastern European orthodoxy—in her father's esti-
mation the only genuine Judaism—but they were all Jewish
San Franciscans of position and property.

Sammy gave the Levie elders more cause for concern.
Summoned to the parlor to discuss his future, he owned up
that school, most of all Hebrew school, bored him silly. His
after-school job as clean-up and delivery boy at Carmody's
Saloon was no crusher, but he liked it. He was bringing
home much-needed money, learning a business, and he even
got to play his saxophone at night for extra change. So why
waste his time at school?

Face reddening, Abram lunged at him. Sammy ducked
under his father's raised fist and fled. Heartsick, Abram sought
Kahane's advice.

"Blood will out," the Englishman opined. "You can't
make a *ben tamid* out of a *klezmer*."

Chava overheard the exchange, agreed with Kahane's response, and added her commentary. An ignorant son was
Abram's punishment for failing to consult his learned father
before marrying into a family of easygoing musicians.

Ida, a first-grader, was their last and best hope. At six
years old, she was the undisputed darling of the boardinghouse. Golden-haired, dimpled, an ever-willing performer,
she moved from lap to lap, singing songs and reciting poems
in Yiddish, Russian, Polish, and Spanish, taught to her by the
Levie elders and their homesick boarders.

Frieda dumped the onions into the bowl of grated potatoes, added beaten eggs and stirred. At the stove, she re-
opened the grate and threw another spoonful of chicken fat
into the frying pan, then jumped back to avoid the splatter-
ing grease. Twitch was bad enough, Frieda thought as she
ladled out the pancake batter, but what if the visitor been
someone she really cared about? Someone like Rudy Seiffert?
She'd rather die than have Rudy see her wearing the menial
attire and grim expression she affected to discourage her
family's hopes and the boarders' advances.

She hadn't seen or heard from Rudy since Centennial

night. Since thinking of him made her feel inferior and
desolate, she tried to keep him out of her thoughts. What
little time she had to herself she devoted to exercises in Loving Everyone. When drained and disheartened, she put on
her North of Market clothes and fled the boardinghouse. A
chat with George, the postal clerk, or Mr. Smithley at the
Free Library, the friendly glances of the mashers in front of
Pickens Drugstore, or John Cole's Billiard Room always gave
her a lift. Helping Harry, a bartender at Carmody's, with his
night school homework also elevated her spirits. As did
chance exchanges with people in Golden Gate Park and
Woodward's Gardens.

Letters were helpful too, especially from exotic places.
She prized the occasional communiques she received from
Liliana in the Sandwich Islands and Evangeline in Malaysia,
and missed hearing from that man in the Arizona Territory.
He and she had exchanged several letters, mostly about Making the World a Better Place and Civilizing the West, before
he stopped responding. After two letters went unanswered,
to avoid humiliating herself further, she wrote no more. He
said business was poor and he was thinking of moving on.
She kept hoping to hear from him from a new place, and
when she didn't, she began to fear he'd found someone to
marry or had met with some misfortune. She hoped neither
was true. Strangers—and she thought of him as a stranger—
sometimes leaped over social conventions and spoke to each
other soul to soul. Frieda was gathering her thoughts on the
subject to share at the December meeting of the Sisters of
Service.

CHAPTER FOURTEEN

Reports

SEVEN OF THE SISTERS OF SERVICE I attended a re-
union at Miss O'Hara's house in May, 1879, all but two in
uniform. Hannah Nathan Goldmark had on a loose pink
smock, and Felicia Ungarfeld, a royal blue velour trimmed
with ecru lace. Eight months pregnant, Hannah, her
breasts—once large, now enormous—and her abdomen—
formerly flat, now bulging—had long since outgrown her
black-and-white uniform. Felicia had packed hers away when
she left for Germany, and had forgotten where she put it. The
absence of nearly half of the Sisters diminished Frieda's delight only slightly. They hadn't met as a group for two years,
and she'd sorely missed the company of women of like ideals.

A week before the meeting, Miss O'Hara wrote each
member a note suggesting that in light of economic conditions they confine their reports to one subject: "Coping with
Hard Times in San Francisco."

Due to the weightiness of their subject, Miss O. proposed
they bypass their usual rituals and pick lots to determine the
order of their reports. Only Felicia demurred, asking to be
last. She'd just returned from Munich, and couldn't comment
on local conditions, so she'd arranged with Miss O'Hara to
serve tea Munich style, and after the tea, to share some personal news.

Frieda began. "Like most San Franciscans, we've had our
share of hard times at Levie's in the last few years. More than
a third of the boarders have been out of work and unable to
pay their rent at one time or another, and the management
has had to cut corners to make mortgage payments. But I'm

pleased to say we've never evicted a boarder for non-payment." (They had tossed out one man for excessive drinking, three for stealing, and one for hiding a woman in his room, all of which Frieda chose to bypass in her report.)

"Our system is based on our ancient charitable traditions. When a boarder can't pay his rent, he's asked to move to a cot in a communal room down in the basement and to help out in the chicken yard, the wine shed, and the soft drinks factory. But few of the boarders remain in the communal room for long," Frieda was pleased to report.

She did not explain why. Der blotes, as the boarders called the basement, was cold and damp, and reminded the natives of Minsk of the swamps in their homeland. Its inmates were known as *downstairsers*, as distinguished from the rent-paying *upstairsers*, who got clean bed linen and a room-cleaning once a week, choice seats in the dining room (close to the proprietor), and the same fresh, tasty food the Levie family ate, while the downstairsers cleaned up after themselves and ate leftovers every day but Shabbes.

"Our needy also have other Jewish charitable institutions to draw upon," Frieda said. B'nai Tefila, the synagogue founded by her father and some of the boarders, maintained a sick fund and a burial society. When those monies were exhausted, a delegation of boarders called upon a representative of one of the numerous better-heeled Jewish benevolent societies or appealed to a wealthy Jewish businessman, who, if not already a philanthropist, was encouraged to become one.

"On rare occasions, when the need is great or prolonged," Frieda said, "we draw on public institutions. But no resident has ever moved from Levie's Kosher Boardinghouse to the alms house." The food wasn't kosher.

Amy and Helen were next. Their topic was "Sex and the Poor Female." The pair would be graduating from the University of California in June, and expected to enter the Medical College of the Pacific in September 1880. In the interim, they were serving as volunteers at various local charitable clinics and hospitals for women: California State

Woman's Hospital, San Francisco Lying-in Hospital and Foundling Asylum, and Pacific Dispensary for Women and Children.

"The plight of poor females would tear your heart out," Amy started. "Ravaged by baby after baby, with no respite for their overworked reproductive organs, by the time they're twenty-five, their malnourished bodies are stretched out of shape, their faces pallid, their spirits devastated."

Frieda stole a peek at Hannah, spilling over the sides of her chair.

"And for what?" Amy demanded. "To bring more doomed creatures into the world to be raised in dark, cramped quarters on an inadequate diet, destined for more of the same for the rest of their miserable lives?"

Helen, who stood at Amy's side, nudged her friend, then bent down to whisper in her ear. Amy listened, nodded, then transmitted Helen's message.

"I've been speaking of married women. But what of the reviled, statusless women of the streets? Women who sell themselves for a few pennies, and contract every form of venereal disease in existence. It's heartbreaking to see them lined up in the charity wards, rotting with syphilis, gonorrhea, lymphogranuloma venereum, yaws."

For nearly an hour, the pair dwelled on female maladies: abortive pregnancies, excruciating labors, freak births, toxemia, hemorrhoids, varicose veins, tumors, and cancers of the reproductive organs, until their listeners grew so restive, Miss O'Hara interceded. Amy ended the report with a plea for volunteers.

"I promise you, Sisters, join us, and you'll learn what it really means to be female."

The future doctors sat down, and Hannah lumbered to her feet to speak on "The Chinese Family." Her husband, a young attorney, was a member of a municipal committee formed to investigate the local Chinese problem. She and her family, Hannah noted, had always been pro-Chinese, but the facts the committee had unearthed were appalling. Health conditions and morals in Chinatown were vile, and Chinese immigrants were taking jobs away from Caucasian working-men. What bothered her most, though, was the erosion of the most venerable of Chinese institutions, the family. The majority of Chinese in San Francisco were males, some single, many with wives and children in China.

"My heart goes out to the women and little ones without husbands and fathers to look after them. And we can guess what kind of lives their men lead on their own in the United States." She ended her report with a poem she had been in-spired to write, entitled "A Woman Weeping in Canton."

The images were up to the poet's high standards, but the viewpoint struck Frieda as shockingly anti-Chinese. She was still pondering how much marriage had changed the once-humanitarian Hannah, when Evangeline and Miss O'Hara rose to give a joint report. (Now that the members of the Sisters of Service I were all over eighteen, Miss O'Hara asked to be treated as one of the group.)

The two, as ever, were an incongruous-looking pair but were growing less so. After three years of living together Miss O'Hara appeared shorter, Evangeline, taller; Miss O'Hara, more skittish, Evangeline, more composed. They consulted in whispers, then Evangeline stepped forward, en-couraged by her mentor to practice speaking in public.

"I've been helping Miss O'Hara oppose proposed cuts in teachers' salaries and...."

Frieda watched Miss O. lean forward, right ear turned to catch her companion's every word. What did Miss O'Hara see in Evangeline? She was as common as a housefly. But even an Elevated Feminine Spirit has earthly needs. Miss O. had visibly aged; new wrinkles mapped her once smooth face; she'd developed an arthritic limp and had grown hard of hearing. She needed Evangeline, and would need her more as time passed. After all Miss O. had done for others, she de-served to be cared for, Frieda thought, aware the assignment was not one she coveted.

Off the mark, as usual, Minnie's report was called "Bank-

ruptcy, Foreclosure and Loan Societies." It shrieked of Rosamund Cohn's shrewd business practices and Mademoiselle's
frenchified English.

"In con-cloo-see-yon," Minnie read, "the clever capitalist
can earn as *grande* a profit on his investments in bad times as
in good."

Frieda's eyes traveled from the puny Minnie to the stately
Felicia, who glittered like a diamond in a circle of black-and-
white pebbles. Between speakers, Felicia had gone to the
kitchen to put on the kettle. She was sitting now with her
slender white hands folded in the lap of her blue dress, her
eyes sliding from Minnie to the ornate German tea service,
which sat glowing on the Chinese lacquer table.

Frieda studied Felicia's long, pale face. She was not beautiful, but she had style, poise, breeding—qualities harder to
achieve and of greater endurance than beauty. How pleased
she would be to be Felicia's friend. She was well-educated,
trained in the arts, and, above all, a dedicated and serious
musician. Her announcement, Frieda decided, concerned her
musical career. Had she been admitted to the Munich Academy of Music? Entered an international competition and won
a prize? Been invited to give a concert? How clever of Felicia
to think of an elegant conclusion to a grim discussion. Frieda
watched her rise, excuse herself, and move to the kitchen.

"Let me help you," Frieda called, jumping to her feet.

In the kitchen, Frieda and Felicia arranged the pastries on
a silver tray, discussing the recipes for the *hazelbluzen*,
pfeffernuesse, *lebkuchen* and *strudel*. Back in the parlor, Felicia
filled the tea cups and Frieda passed them. When all the Sisters were sipping the dark, pungent brew, Frieda served the
cookies, discussing the names and ingredients as though she
had baked them herself. Then she accepted a cup of tea,
took a cookie, and returned to her seat. As Felicia rose to
speak, Frieda's heart raced with vicarious excitement.

"My dear Sisters," she began, "some of you have been
sweet enough to tell me that I look happier and—no im-
modesty intended—more attractive than when last seen.

These comments delighted me because they corroborate my conviction that inner contentment beautifies." Gladness poured from Felicia, filling the room. Frieda was saturated with it. "The reason for my happiness and the happiness of my entire family is that on December thirty-first, in the Regency Room of the Palace Hotel, I shall become the wife of Rudolph Seiffert."

An outcry of delight greeted the announcement. Felicia looked on, radiant and triumphant, as the Sisters recalled that Rudy had been in Miss O'Hara's class, was Felicia's cousin, was intelligent, well-to-do, handsome, artistic, and was studying to become a doctor.

It was Minnie who broke through the hubbub, screeching "Somebody, quick, Frieda spilled hot tea all over herself."

Frieda sat pinned to her chair, her face stunned and tear-streaked, her empty hands held out over her steaming skirt, an overturned teacup resting in her lap. Amy and Helen got to her first.

"You'd better come out to the bedroom, where we can take a look at you," Amy said in a calm, professional tone. "Burns on the abdomen and genitals can be nasty."

Moving across the room, supported by Amy on one side and Helen on the other, Frieda turned to Felicia to stammer, "F-for-give me, F-Felicia, I'm so c-clumsy."

Miss O'Hara followed the threesome saying, "I'll get a burn ointment and something for Frieda to put on when she gets out of that wet skirt."

The last thing Frieda heard as she left the parlor was Minnie's voice exclaiming, "Poor Frieda. Rudy was her sweetheart in the seventh grade."

CHAPTER FIFTEEN

Someone Special

FRIEDA FLED MISS O'HARA'S with her wet skirt in a bag and Minnie at her side.

"Slow down, Frieda," Minnie cried. "I told my mother you wouldn't want to walk me to the Palace Hotel. I told her you'd be in a hurry. You're always in a hurry." Minnie reached forward, linked her arm through Frieda's, and pulled her to her side.

The pair moved down Pine Street in silence, the five-o'clock wind from the Golden Gate stabbing their backs.

"I'm freezing," Minnie complained. "Aren't you?"

Frieda nodded, shivering in Miss O'Hara's thin summer skirt.

Minnie pressed closer. Frieda never disliked Minnie more, but she did not pull away. With Minnie glued to her, she was warmer than with the wind blowing between them.

"Walk a bit faster, Minnie" Frieda urged. "They need me in the kitchen at suppertime."

"I have a pain in my chest. I think I'm getting bronchitis." Minnie forced a dry cough. "My legs hurt too. See if you can find a cab."

"Do you have money for a cab, Minnie?"

"No, do you?"

"Where would I get money? Come on," Frieda said, "you can walk."

"Then talk to me. You're sullen as a bear with a sore tooth."

"What do you know about bears?"

"It's just a saying."

"Whose?"

"Oh for heaven's sake, Frieda, we won't feel so cold if we talk."

Frieda pressed her lips against her teeth. "What do you want to talk about?"

"The meeting. I can't stand Amy and Helen, can you? They think they're so smart just because they graduated from the university. My mother says they make a lot of their learning because they're motherless and ugly."

Frieda made no comment.

"My mother says that they're lucky they found each other and had better stick together because no one else would want either of them."

Frieda was mentally mapping the shortest route to the hotel. When they got to Powell Street, she guided Minnie south.

"Wouldn't you hate to have either one of them as a doctor? They'd make you take off your clothes, then prowl all over hoping to find some horrible disease. Mademoiselle says they probably sleep together like a man and a woman."

"Minnie, that's disgusting."

"'Then you'll be apprised of what it really means to be a female,'" Minnie mimicked Amy. "My mother says a clever woman can get anything she wants from a man if she knows how to keep her head and turn his." Minnie was doing her best to emulate Rosamund's throaty voice.

Frieda had heard that one before; it was one of Rosamund's favorite maxims.

"And that Amy reminds me of a witch, rubbing her hands and reciting curses. I don't think she's washed her hair in a...."

Frieda had thought the same, but she refused to encourage Minnie's outspoken malevolence.

"Miss O'Hara and Evangeline are getting on my nerves too. What Miss O'Hara sees in that little half-wit is beyond me. Between her dear Evangeline and the Sisters of Service II, Miss O'Hara has no time for our group."

Frieda lunged ahead. "I told you not to walk so fast," Minnie complained, tugging at her arm. "You're just like my mother, you don't care about me."

"I have to get home, Minnie."

"A few minutes won't make any difference," Minnie said, setting her own pace and holding Frieda to it.

"Hannah used to be so pretty," Minnie whined, picking up the thread of her jeremiad. "I've never seen such gigantic breasts." She laughed wildly. "I can imagine the look of delight on Al Goldmark's face when he nestles into them. They look like advertisement balloons: 'Recline in comfort and refresh yourself with a drink.'"

"Minnie!" Frieda cautioned.

"Have you ever thought about what it would be like to breastfeed a baby? I see poor women on the street with their babies nipping away at them like pups sucking on a dog's teats."

Frieda looked around to see who else was in earshot. "What's got into you, Minnie?" she whispered.

Minnie laughed. "Mademoiselle says I'm in heat. She thinks it's quite natural for a woman of my age."

Minnie's governess had been catering to her charge's more prurient interests of late, Frieda noted.

"Were you breastfed, Frieda?"

"I suppose so," Frieda answered shyly.

"I had a wet nurse. A great big German woman with the udders of a cow, my mother said. I drank like the town drunkard and was a roly-poly baby until the wet nurse's common-law husband caught her with another man and shot her. My mother tried one kind of milk after another, but none agreed with me. I got so sick I almost died."

Frieda thought she had heard all of Minnie's stories, but that one was new to her.

"I already knew about Felicia's engagement," Minnie told Frieda, "but she made me swear not to tell anyone before she did. She said she wouldn't let me come to the wedding if I did. We're invited, of course. My mother and hers grew up

together. I don't even want to go. I hate Felicia. She acts like
the Infanta Isabella in public but she's worse than I am at
home. Everything has to be just so—her clothes, her food,
her bed, and the whole house has to come to a standstill
when she practices piano. She's not that good, either. My
mother says she lacks both technique and fire."

One of the rocks piled on Frieda's heart tumbled, leaving
her chest a bit lighter.

"My mother says Rudy's marrying her for her money."

"Don't the Seifferts have money?" Frieda asked. (That
was what she liked best about Minnie, she answered questions, however indelicate.)

"Not as much as the Ungarfelds. Mr. Seiffert lost a lot of
money last year. My mother says that was probably why
Rudy proposed."

Another rock gave way.

"My mother says she would have spoken to Rudy's parents about me, but Mrs. Seiffert disapproved of her because
of the divorce."

Frieda laughed.

"Don't laugh," Minnie said. "My mother says, and Mademoiselle agrees, marriage is as much about business as pleasure."

When they got to Geary Street, they turned east.

"Of course, there's *it* too. You can't have a marriage without *it*. Mademoiselle says men are not the only ones who
want *it*. And then there's the babies. A woman can't have a
baby without doing *it*."

Frieda lowered her head. Minnie was talking so loud, and
there was no stopping her.

"Mademoiselle is not really a mademoiselle, if you know
what I mean. She says *l'amour* is as natural to human beings as
it is to animals. She doesn't mean love, though, she means
sexual intercourse. She was telling me yesterday how people
do *it*. It starts with a glance."

The loving gaze?

"Then one of the lovers, either the man or the woman,

touches the hand of the beloved."

The spiritual touch.

"Then they embrace and touch each other all over."

"Please, Minnie, please keep your voice down."

"You know what happens next?"

"Yes," Frieda said.

Minnie drew back and gazed up at her friend.

"You do?"

"Yes."

"How?"

"I can read."

"They don't put what Mademoiselle told me in books."

"How many books have you read on the subject?"

"None. They don't tell what really happens when a man and a woman get into bed together."

"If you don't keep your voice down, I'm going to leave you right here," Frieda said, picking up her pace and fixing her sight on the seven-story Palace Hotel, towering to the south.

"Mademoiselle says a clever lover can make a woman scream with delight."

Actually scream with delight? Frieda wondered.

"Don't you wish there was someone who wanted to be with you more than with anyone else in the world?"

They were standing alongside Lotta's Fountain waiting to cross the street. Frieda knew what Minnie meant, but she wasn't going to talk about it in a street full of strangers.

"No one wants to be with me. Except maybe Mademoiselle, and she has to, to earn a living. I wish there was one person who really thought I was special."

"No one thinks I'm special either."

"Miss O'Hara did."

"But now she has Evangeline."

"What about that man you met in Golden Gate Park? The man from the Arizona Territory?"

Frieda had read Minnie one of his letters years ago, and thereafter Minnie counted him as Frieda's lover.

"Has he written to you lately?"

"I haven't heard from him in years," Frieda responded abruptly. "I think he moved to Mexico."

"How about the masher in front of Picker's Drugstore? The one who always tips his hat and says 'Good day, Miss Pink Cheeks. How is Miss Pink Cheeks today?' no matter how many times you pass?"

"He's just lonely. He probably doesn't know another human being in San Francisco."

"What about George at the post office and Mr. Elbert at the Mercantile Library?"

"George is only eighteen and Mr. Elbert is too fresh." Mr. Elbert had arranged for her to have a library card, then he had tried to make her pay in the stacks. Frieda switched to the Free Library. The librarian there, Mr. Smithley, was as attentive as Mr. Elbert but more genteel. Frieda hadn't mentioned him to Minnie, nor did she intend to.

"My mother says she saw you in Union Square with a tall blond man. She says she's worried about you."

Harry, Frieda thought. "Why is she worried about me?"

"She says you've got the look."

"What look?"

"You glow like a gas lamp whenever an attractive man is within ten feet."

"Minnie, that's ridiculous."

"She says when a young woman begins to look like that, she's headed for the wedding canopy or the primrose path."

Frieda's mouth dropped open, then snapped shut. What was the use of arguing with Minnie or her mother? The poor man was trying to improve himself. She considered it a privilege to help him with his night school homework.

Frieda led Minnie across Market Street.

"You're going to get married soon and I'll be the only Sister without a husband or a career."

"I'm not getting married," Frieda hissed.

"You'll see. My mother knows what she's talking about."

They were standing in front of the hotel. Frieda unfastened Minnie's hold on her arm. "I have to go now."

"I don't want to go inside alone," Minnie said. "Maybe my mother won't be there, and what will I do then?"

Frieda peered into the Grand Court. "Look, there's her carriage. Ask her liveryman to find her for you."

"I want you to come with me."

"Minnie, dear," Frieda said, with an exaggerated show of patience, "I can't go into the Palace Hotel dressed in Miss O'Hara's cast-off skirt. I look like an apple vendor."

Minnie scrutinized Frieda. "You *do* look like an apple vendor," she decided, turning and rushing into the crowd.

Frieda stood in front of the hotel for several moments; she was too upset to return to the boardinghouse yet. Maybe she'd stop at Carmody's and talk to Harry. She wouldn't look like an apple vendor to him. Harry had told her more than once that she looked like a princess whatever she wore.

CHAPTER SIXTEEN

Fortunes Told Here

ON THE FIRST SUNDAY after the New Year, Minnie sent her mother's driver to bring Frieda to the Cohn house. In a dismal mood that rainy afternoon, and desperate to get out of the boardinghouse, Frieda went. When she arrived, she found Minnie home alone with the cook and waiting for Frieda to join her in a visit to the clairvoyant, Madame Angelica.

Frieda didn't want to go. She didn't believe in soothsayers and, even if she did, she had no money and couldn't allow Minnie to pay for her. (In Cohn arithmetic, one treat was good for three favors, and Frieda disliked both paying and being in arrears.)

"I'm dying to go and I can't go alone," Minnie said.

"If you want, I'll play checkers," Frieda said, willing to indulge Minnie that far, but no further.

"Don't you want to hear what the future holds for you?"

"I don't think I can bear it," Frieda said testily.

"She told my mother her sorrows were all behind her."

"What else?"

"That the road ahead glitters with gold. I'm dying to hear what she says about me. Come with me, pleassse."

"Oh, all right," Frieda said, knowing Minnie had her trapped. "But I refuse to have a reading."

"I can't, unless you do too."

"Why not?"

"I don't want to be the only one with a terrible future."

"She's not going to say you have a terrible future."

"How do you know?"

"She wouldn't have any patrons if she did."

"How can you be so sure she's a fake? My mother is an intelligent, sophisticated woman, and she thinks Madame Angelica is remarkable."

"Then she *must* be," Frieda said.

"I'm so bored I could kill myself," Minnie whined. "Lots of girls do. That's all I read about in the newspapers these days—murders, bankruptcies, and girls killing themselves. Every day some girl in San Francisco takes strychnine, slashes her wrists, or shoots herself."

Frieda had noticed.

"One of these days, Frieda, it's going to be me. I can't stand any more of this lonely, empty life. I'm so miserable, I could die." Minnie started to cry.

"Enough, Minnie. I'll let Madame Angelica read my fortune. But if I hear one more word about committing suicide, you won't have to take your own life, I'll do it for you."

A half hour later, the Cohn carriage pulled to a stop in front of Madame Angelica's. The ten-foot-wide establishment was squeezed between a pet shop and a second-hand store at the rundown end of Kearny Street near the Barbary Coast. In the dirty, rain-streaked window hung a sign reading: MADAME ANGELICA, CLAIRVOYANT. PAST, PRESENT, FUTURE.

Frieda and Minnie reached for their umbrellas, stepped out of the carriage, and leaped over the flooded curb. Promising to return in an hour, the driver drove off on an errand. The girls stood for several moments, peering into the window while the rain poured down around them. Then, turning to face each other, they shrugged their shoulders and went inside, Frieda in the lead.

The room was dimly lit and smelled of incense and chicken soup spiced with a touch of ginger. A rockingchair stood in front of a tattered Japanese screen. Pinned to the screen was a sign which read ONE PATRON AT A TIME. An arrow pointed to the rear of the store.

"You go first," Frieda said.

"You first, I'm afraid," Minnie said.

Frieda demurred.

"Why should you care? You think she's a fake."

"Shush, Minnie, she'll hear you."

"Then *go*," Minnie said, stepping behind Frieda.

On the other side of the screen, in near darkness, a stout, swarthy, middle-aged woman sat at a rickety table. An equally unstable chair awaited her client on the opposite side. She was wearing a long-sleeved blouse and a black skirt; a red satin band restrained her kinky, gray-streaked hair. Spread on the table was a black velvet cloth. Alongside it rested a cracked white cup steaming with what appeared to be hot tea. A brazier standing on the floor, close to the woman's feet, cast a smoky, infernal light.

"Sit."

Frieda eased herself into the wobbly chair, bracing herself with her feet.

"Hands."

Frieda pulled off her worn gloves and rubbed her cold fingers.

"Hands," the woman repeated, impatiently.

Without looking up, Frieda laid her work-roughened hands on the velvet cloth.

Madame Angelica's meaty hands enveloped Frieda's fingers.

"Cold," she noted.

"It's been raining all day, actually all week. The newspapers say we're in for the wettest season in twenty years. I was just telling my friend...."

"Shush," the woman commanded, her eyes closed, her head tilted ceilingward. "I see something."

An eery otherworldliness emanated from Madame Angelica. Uneasy, frightened, Frieda shuddered and wiggled her fingers.

The woman tightened her hold. "Be still," she hissed, "I feel something."

Leaning back into the chair, Frieda surrendered to Madame Angelica's hot clasp. Gradually, the heat of the woman's hands penetrated her chilled fingers, and her anxiety receded to a bearable apprehension.

"You," the woman said, "have worked very, very hard for one so young."

A tear spurted from Frieda's eye like blood from a pricked finger.

"And your efforts have not been appreciated."

Two more tears appeared.

"You're tired, disgusted, depressed, fed-up."

Frieda's tears streamed. She wanted to wipe them away, but Madame Angelica held her hands. Frieda closed her tear-rimmed eyelids, allowing the woman's words to wash over her like warm water, thawing her chilled limbs and relaxing her muscles. She opened her eyes and closed them again, Madame's lined face distracted her. In the dark, she sensed the woman knew everything about her—the work, the pain, the friction, the loneliness, the sorrow.

"Am I speaking the truth?" the clairvoyant asked.

Frieda nodded. How did she know?

"Your sorrow will soon be behind you."

Frieda's heart leaped.

"That makes you happy."

"Yes, oh yes," Frieda whispered.

"Open your eyes and look at me."

Frieda lifted her eyelids and blinked.

The woman leaned toward her. "Good fortune is on its way."

Only a few minutes before, her leathery face looked alien, menacing. Now Madame Angelica looked warm, benign.

"I have good news for you." Madame's mouth spread wide in an exultant grin. "An able, handsome man is hurtling toward you."

New-born hope tinted Frieda's cheeks.

"Yes," Madame crooned. "And with him, love, money, respect, admiration, a mansion, servants."

That voice, with its German accent—Frieda had heard it before. Madame Angelica's face was familiar too.

"Would you like that, *liebchen?*"

Frieda's lips parted in a smile. She'd detected a familiar scent on the woman's breath soon after she'd begun speaking. Brandy. Madame Angelica had apparently been communing with some earthly spirits, as well.

"Sorrow, sadness, poverty, all behind you," Madame Angelica whispered.

Mrs. Weintraub—Bessie. The Weintraubs had lived one house east of the Goldbaums on Sutter Street. Childless, Mrs. Weintraub often invited her neighbors' children to her house for cookies and lemonade, then played the piano and sang for them. Frieda used to go to her house to bring Sylvia and Sammy home. Last fall, Frieda heard that Mr. Weintraub had died of a heart attack, and Mrs. Weintraub was beside herself with grief. Had she recognized her? Frieda wondered. She didn't think so.

"Enough of the scullery, my dear," Madame Angelica was saying, rubbing Frieda's chafed hands.

Sylvia had told Frieda Mrs. Weintraub had come to Mrs. Tyler's several months ago to ask for a position teaching piano. The applicant wept when Sylvia's music teacher told her she had no opening. If she didn't find a way to earn a living soon, Sylvia heard Mrs. Weintraub say, she would have to sell herself on the streets.

"Yes, my child, your sorrows will soon be behind you." Mrs. Weintraub issued an ingratiating grin and opened her hands, allowing Frieda's to fall on the velvet.

Sympathy for the resourceful woman flooded Frieda. "Is it possible, Madame Angelica, that I, too, have a touch of clairvoyance?"

"Why do you ask?" The woman's expression was wary.

"I picked up some vibrations."

"You did?" Madame peered at Frieda through her near-sighted eyes.

"Yes. You recently experienced a painful jolt."

"True," Madame Angelica said, emitting a heavy, self-pitying sigh. She took a long swig from her tea cup.

"You've had a difficult time regaining your footing."

"What else did you see?"

"You are growing steadier."

Mrs. Weintraub nodded. "See anything about my future?"

"I think I do."

"Is it good?"

"Yes, good."

"How so?"

Frieda took Mrs. Weintraub's hands in hers, closed her eyes, tilted her head, and for several seconds was silent. "I see you entering an elegant house on Nob Hill." She paused, registering pleasure. "You're elegantly attired, and eagerly awaited."

"Are you sure?"

"Absolutely sure."

"And soon? I do hope soon."

"Very soon."

"Thank you for telling me, my dear."

Frieda resisted an impulse to throw her arms around the woman and pat her brightened cheek. "And thank *you*," she said, rising and heading for the front room.

"Miss," Mrs. Weintraub called after her.

Frieda turned back to Mrs. Weintraub.

"You forgot something."

"Have I?" Frieda asked, puzzled.

"One dollar, please."

Frieda laughed; she had forgotten. "My friend in the waiting room is going to pay for me."

When Frieda appeared from behind the screen, Minnie said peevishly, "What took you so long?"

"She's waiting for you, go on."

"How was it?"

"Nice, you'll like it." Frieda said, taking her friend by the shoulders and shoving her toward the back room.

A half hour later, Minnie emerged, bright faced and bubbling. On the street and in the carriage, she raved about

Madame Angelica's extraordinary powers. The clairvoyant had told her that she had been frail and nervous as a child, and had suffered ill health—that she'd been timid and afraid to reach out for the love that was due her.

"That's what she said, Frieda," Minnie said, sliding along the carriage seat until she was pressing against her companion. "'The love that is due you.'"

Minnie grabbed Frieda's hand and drew it to her hot cheek. "All that is going to change soon; that's what she told me. I wasn't supposed to say anything to anyone, but I want you to know. An able and handsome man is hurtling toward me. Isn't that wonderful?" Minnie studied Frieda's face. "Why do you look so strange? Madame Angelica said you're going to have a terrible future, didn't she?"

"Not really," Frieda said.

"She told you something awful is going to happen. I can tell from your face."

"No she didn't."

"Now I'm sorry I told you about me. Madame Angelica told me not to say anything to anybody. She said one jealous person could ruin everything. Now you're going to wish away my good fortune."

"I wouldn't do that, Minnie."

Reassured, Minnie gushed, "Aren't you glad we went?"

Frieda was glad. Whether from Madame Angelica or Annie Weintraub, the bright prognosis had lifted her spirits.

Minnie put her mouth to Frieda's ear. "Promise me," she whispered, "you won't tell my mother."

"Not even your mother, Minnie?"

"Especially not my mother. She'll be wild with joy if she knows there's a man hurtling toward me."

"Don't you want your mother to be happy?"

"Not that happy."

"Why not?"

"She might run off and leave me before he gets here."

CHAPTER SEVENTEEN

The Rainy Season

RAIN INUNDATED SAN FRANCISCO most of January and into February. What looked to be a permanent stream of dirty yellow water filled Tehama Street from curb to curb. Some days it rose to the front steps of the boardinghouse, making it difficult to get out. Water seeped through the windows and door jambs, and trickled through holes in the roof. Everything in the worn clapboard began to look water-logged, including the kitchen. The residents went about in shawls and overcoats, and hovered around the kitchen stove—particularly the downstairsers, who had no place to go but der blotes. Their presence irritated Frieda; she shooed them away, but they crept back.

Deprived of her spiritual outlets, Frieda became increasingly edgy. For the first time, she began to doubt that she would ever be called to a new assignment away from the boardinghouse. At night she lay in the drafty crow's nest, kept awake by the sound of water plinking in buckets. Loneliness enveloped her. She felt as alien as a single animal in Noah's Ark.

She was also beset with ailments. Her head ached, her stomach felt queasy, or she was doubled over with menstrual cramps. More than half the inhabitants were suffering with one kind of respiratory or pulmonary infection or another, and she caught several varieties.

Terrors she had overcome or suppressed re-emerged, slowing her down by day, weighing her down by night. She cringed when "Bloody Blatner" came in the kitchen, and cowered passing Baum's retarded son in the hallway. Sweeping der blotes one morning, she imagined herself surrounded and assailed by its inhabitants and fled. When she was not the victim, she became the aggressor. She wanted to seize the oven paddle and swat the downstairsers like flies, lock her aunt out of the kitchen, burn the account books. One night, her knees rattling with exhaustion, she thought of shaking rat poison in the apples she was stewing for still another batch of strudel. (The poison, fortunately, was in the wine shed, and she was afraid to go there at night; it had been burglarized twice in recent months.)

Her self-control worn thin, she threw herself into the boardinghouse disputes. The night before St. Valentine's Day, Frieda and her aunt came close to blows. She was in the kitchen with seven-year-old Ida making valentine cards out of red construction paper and doilies, when Chava came in and wanted to know what they were doing.

"A Jewish girl shouldn't give no St. Valentine's cards," Chava said. "Jewish girls ain't supposed to have nothing to do with no saints."

"The cards aren't for saints, Aunt Chava," Ida said, "they're for sweethearts."

"A Jewish girl ain't supposed to send no cards to no sweethearts," Chava said, reaching out to grab the red-and-white papers.

"Why not?" Frieda demanded, jumping up and blocking Chava.

"Because it ain't nice," Chava said, trying to shove her aside.

Her arms raised to defend herself, Frieda told her aunt, "It's a loving custom to send a card to a sweetheart."

"Look who's talking about loving and sweethearts," Chava growled, ramming herself against Frieda.

Frieda stood her ground, glaring.

"I'm going to tell your father Ida is playing with saint cards."

"Frieda too," she cried after her departing aunt. "Give me some of those, Ida."

"Are you going to send some valentines?" Ida asked.

"Yes I am," said Frieda, stiff with defiance.

"To Minnie?"

"Not Minnie."

"Boys?"

"Yes, boys."

Ida watched her sister scrawl card after card. "You're supposed to send valentine cards to the people you like."

"That's what I'm doing," Frieda snapped. She reached for the envelopes and addressed them. "Mail these with yours," she told Ida, leaving her sister sounding out the names and addresses on the envelopes.

The first response came two days after Valentine's Day. A messenger appeared at the boardinghouse door with a book and a note for Frieda from Mr. Smithley. The white-haired, bespectacled assistant librarian at the Free Library knew American and English novels the way Kahane knew the Torah. Recognizing in Frieda an avid and intelligent reader, he watched over her literary sensibilities the way a doctor watches over his patient's health. Frieda often came away from the library intoxicated with book talk.

Mr. Smithley addressed her as "My dearest Frieda" (he had previously called her Miss Levie), and thanked her for the card, adding that he had slept with it under his pillow. The note was signed, "With all my love, Aaron;" Frieda had signed hers, "With love, Frieda." The book he sent was *Daniel Deronda* by George Eliot. He'd told her about it the last time she was in the library, saying that he'd save her a copy as soon as one was returned. He thought a person of her faith would be fascinated with the characters of Gwendolyn Harlech, a self-absorbed beauty of the Christian faith, and Daniel Deronda, an idealistic Jew.

Frieda was delighted to receive the book, but was distressed by the note. Mr. Smithley had taken her sentiment more personally than she had intended. She valued him greatly as a literary advisor, not at all as a lover.

A second response came that evening as Frieda worked in

the kitchen. Earlier, she had allowed several downstairsers to huddle around the stove while she prepared the ingredients for *Purim hamantashen*. But when she discovered they were filching the fruits and nuts as fast as she could prepare them, she chased them back to the basement. She was sitting in the kitchen cracking walnuts when she heard boots on the rear stairs. She ran for the paddle and stood at the door waiting.

The door flew open and down came the paddle, grazing her father's shoulder.

"What's the matter with you, Frieda," he cried, jumping back in alarm. "Have you gone crazy?"

He stepped aside to allow someone else to enter. A customer, Frieda deduced, judging by the hospitable sweep of her father's arm.

Embarrassed, Frieda returned the paddle to the corner, and was about to leave the kitchen when her father called, "Frieda, this gentleman is freezing. Offer him a cup of tea, can't you?"

As she prepared the tea, she heard the man struggling out of his raincoat. When she turned, cup in hand, she saw it was Harry, the bartender, seated at the kitchen table. His blond hair hung in damp curls, and his ruddy, ax-sharp face was still wet with raindrops. He was looking at Frieda, his eyes brimming with intentions. Her hand shook so violently, she had to set the cup on the table and slide it to the guest.

"Thank you, ma'am," Harry said, as though she were a stranger.

Early in their acquaintanceship he had asked to call on her at the boardinghouse. Frieda had been forced to explain why she could not receive him.

"So as I was saying," Harry told her father, "Carmody wants to pay up all his old bills and start afresh."

"Good, good." Abram was pleased. "I got a stack of bills for Carmody. Give the man a piece of strudel, Frieda," he ordered, as he headed toward the cupboard in the corner where he kept bills and receipts.

As soon as her father's back was turned, Harry reached in

his breast pocket and pulled out Frieda's valentine. Grinning as Frieda turned scarlet, he slid it back in his pocket and placed his hand over his heart. The trembling that had started in her hand moved up her arm and coursed through her body. When Abram returned to the table, his hands full of dog-eared bills, Frieda fled to the stove.

Harry was all business again. "Carmody told me to pay cash for the soft drinks. I'll tell him about the wine tonight. If he thinks we can use it, I'll pick up two kegs when I come with his check tomorrow night."

"I won't be home tomorrow night. I got a meeting of the Benevolent Society. Can't you come in the afternoon?"

Harry could not.

"If not, not," Abram decided, "Then come tomorrow night. My daughter will be here to take the money. I'll set the kegs out. She'll unlock the wine shed for you."

"Fine," Harry said. He ducked his head in Frieda's direction. "Is this your daughter?"

"Yah," Abram admitted.

"You're sure she'll be here?" Harry persisted.

"Frieda? Where else would she be?"

Amused with Harry's charade and annoyed by her father's disregard, Frieda did something she had never done before in her life. She winked at the bartender, and he answered her in kind.

The following evening after supper, Frieda walked her mother and aunt to the front porch. They were going next door to sit *shivah* with Mrs. Leibowitz, who had buried her husband the day before. A few minutes later, she watched her father and the rest of the minyan stomp down the rear stairs and pile into the wagon. Frieda found Ida in the parlor with some boarders, and hurried her off to bed in the crow's nest. Then she changed into a North of Market dress and swept her newly washed hair into a bank of shiny curls.

"Are you going to Mrs. Leibowitz's too?" Ida asked.

"I have to bake challahs for Shabbes," Frieda said. "Maybe I'll go after I finish."

Ida shuddered. "I don't like to go to places where people are screaming and crying."

"Nobody does," Frieda said, leaning toward the mirror to smooth her thick eyebrows with wetted fingertips.

"Mama and Aunt Chava do."

"I don't think they do, Ida," Frieda said, pinching her already inflamed cheeks.

"Aunt Chava told me she likes sad places. I asked her why and she told me better a house of morning than a house of mert."

"Better a house of mourning than a house of mirth," Frieda said. "It's from Ecclesiastes."

"What's ee-clee-zee-ass-tease?"

"A book in the Holy Scriptures."

"What does it mean—better a house of mourning than a house of mirth?" Ida sang the words as though they were the lyrics of a children's song.

"Sometimes, when people start having fun, they go too far and get themselves in trouble."

"Do you believe that?"

"It's hard for me to say, baby. I don't know a lot about fun."

"I do," Ida returned.

"What do you know about fun?" Frieda asked.

"Fun is fun!"

Back in the kitchen, Frieda found several downstairsers huddled around the stove, inhaling the fragrance of the first batch of challahs baking in the oven. More eager than ever to keep them out of the kitchen, she negotiated a deal. She'd prepare a pot of tea and a platter of strudel for them to take to the basement if they promised to stay there. Eyeing the strudel like ravenous orphans, they agreed.

Alone in the kitchen, Frieda donned a voluminous apron and set to work preparing the remaining bread dough for the oven. She was glad to be occupied until Harry arrived. She wasn't accustomed to sitting, hands folded, waiting for a gentleman caller. Nor did she wish to give the impression she was receiving him as a guest. When the back door opened, she was dragging a heavy tub of dough from the corner next to the stove to the table, where her rolling pin and floured board waited.

"Let me do that," Harry cried, rushing toward her.

The tub deposited on the table, Harry stripped off his slicker, while Frieda erased his muddy tracks with a mop.

"Sorry about that," he muttered. "I ain't thought about tracking up a kitchen floor since I left home."

Assuring him he had done no real damage, Frieda invited him to sit down. Harry sprawled in the kitchen chair, his arms folded on his chest, his eyes trailing his hostess as she washed her hands and returned to the work table.

"If you'll excuse me, I'll just finish preparing these breads for the oven," Frieda said, eager to conceal her nervousness. She was trembling from head to toe.

"Smells good," Harry said, sniffing.

"I'll give you one if you like," Frieda said. She glanced at him, and looked away; he was eyeing her like a fox stalking a chicken.

"Give me one what?" Harry asked.

"One bread." Frieda pulled a wad of dough out of the tub and slapped it onto the board.

"Oh, I thought you meant one kiss."

Ignoring his remark, Frieda spread the dough over the board and divided it into three strands for braiding. As she did, she automatically recited the blessing.

"What's that you're saying?" Harry asked.

"A blessing."

"You're a real Jewish girl, aren't you?"

Frieda thought she detected a sneer. "This is a boarding-house for traditional Jews," she told him.

"The likes of me would be turned away."

"Nothing personal," she soothed. "It's just that you're not Jewish." She was braiding the second loaf, wondering how to get the conversation back to business.

"If I came to the front door, they'd send me packing."

Frieda lifted her eyes, hoping to calm him with a loving gaze. "I wouldn't send you packing. You're a man who wants to improve himself."

"Improve myself," he scoffed. "I'll probably die first in a saloon brawl. I almost got knifed last week."

Frieda thought of her brother Sammy. She hated having him work in a place like Carmody's. "I'll wager you're the only bartender in San Francisco with enough grit to go to night school."

"What's the use? I'm going to quit."

She had turned to take the shiny brown breads out of the oven and set them on the table to cool. Her back to him, she said, "You mustn't quit, Harry."

"I'll never read and write perfect English like you."

Frieda turned to face him. "I'm sure you know many things I haven't a notion about."

"You're right there," he chortled. "If you'd like to learn, I'll be glad to teach you."

His lascivious grin made Frieda blush. The visit was not going quite the way she had imagined. "Did Mr. Carmody want the kegs of wine?" she asked.

Harry's face lit up. "Yah, let's go to the shed now."

"I'm busy with these breads. I'll ask one of the boarders to open the door for you. I don't want to keep you waiting." She wiped her hands and turned to the hall door.

"How about helping with a poem? I have to recite one at night school for Washington's Birthday," Harry called after her.

Frieda turned. "Do you have a poem with you?"

"No," Harry said. "You know a lot of them."

"None by heart anymore."

Harry slumped back in his chair. "Never mind, I'm going to quit night school anyway. I'm better at bouncing drunks than reciting poems."

Frieda reconsidered. "I do have a copy of 'Lord Ullin's Daughter' upstairs."

"Good. Go get it."

After four years of dealing with men at the boarding-
house, Frieda knew he was simply wheedling to get his way.
Still, she did love that poem and would enjoy teaching it to
Harry.

"We can't do it here," Frieda said, in a hushed tone.
"Someone might come in."

"That's why I suggested the wine shed."

"The wine shed?"

"Go over the poem with me a couple of times, then I'll
load up the kegs, pay you, and be off."

Frieda hesitated.

"You want to help me, or not?"

"I have things to do in the kitchen."

"I never would have bothered with night school if it
weren't for you." He was eying the door.

"Wait," Frieda said, taking off her apron. "I'll get the
poem and a shawl."

CHAPTER EIGHTEEN

Lord Ullin's Daughter

FRIEDA COULD HEAR ROTH and his *klezmorim* in the parlor scratching out a lively Purim tune as she led the way down the shaky rear stairs, a kerosene lantern in her hand. The rain had stopped but the night air was cold, and a golden half moon dipped in and out of fast-moving clouds. As she stepped down into the rear yard, moonlit puddles stretched before her like ponds.

"Allow me," came Harry's voice from behind her. Without waiting for her reply, he hoisted her off the ground and into his arms.

"No, please, someone might—"

"Nobody's going to see," Harry said, striding through the puddles in his rubber boots.

Holding herself upright, as if seated in a chair, Frieda scoured the yard. When Harry set her down, she yanked her dress straight, and planted her feet on the wood-slat mud scraper. Then for the benefit of a possible eavesdropper, she gave her keys a proprietary jingle and announced in an all-business tone, "My father said the two kegs of wine Carmody ordered would be near the door."

Inside, she deposited the kerosene lantern on the work bench that ran the length of the ten-foot shed, and tiptoed back across the damp floor to bolt the door from the inside. The drafty room reeked of oak wood and wine.

Harry inhaled. "Smells good."

Not to Frieda. One glass of wine made her tipsy; two, sick. She shivered and pulled her shawl tighter.

"No wonder you're cold," Harry said, "standing on the

wet floor in those thin shoes." He grabbed her waist and swung her up on to the work bench. "Sit there and have a swig of this." He pulled a flask from under his yellow slicker and handed it to her.

"What is it?" Frieda asked, jiggling her chilled legs.

"Brandy. It'll warm you up."

"I don't like wine."

"It's not wine."

"Whiskey?" She wrinkled her nose with distaste.

"It's not whiskey, it's brandy. They put it in little barrels and tie them around the necks of St. Bernards—"

"St. Bernards?"

"Rescue dogs."

Frieda wiped the opening with her hand and sipped. Sweet, warming, it hit her like hot sunlight. She gulped another mouthful, shuddered, gave back the flask, and fished the poem out of her bodice. A mistake. Harry was ogling her like a jewel thief eying a diamond necklace. A moment later, he was having another drink, then passing the flask back to her.

Already light-headed, she shook her head, shoving the brandy aside. "Here, read it, first to yourself, then out loud," she suggested, handing him the poem.

Harry jammed his hands under his thighs. No reading. She knew what a rotten reader he was. He'd listen to her and learn the poem that way. He had a good Irish ear.

There were some tricky words, Frieda acknowledged, fearing she'd shamed him. She shook open the paper, raised it to eye level, but couldn't make out the words in the dim light. Harry grabbed the lantern, hung it on a nail in the rafter above their heads, then settled alongside her, his thigh touching hers.

The first stanza sounded as flat as a grocery list. She grimaced, read it again with more emotion, then continued:

Now, who be ye would cross Loch-Gyle
This dark and stormy water?

Oh! I'm the chief of Ulva's Isle
And this, Lord Ullin's daughter.

"'Chief of Ulva's Isle'?" Harry chuckled. "You and that poem give me the shivers." He slipped the flask into her hand, watched her drink, had another himself, then wiped his mouth. Pressing his face close to hers, he murmured, "All alone, at last."

His hot, brandy-scented breath and his suggestive tone, set off one alarm, then another. "I've left challahs baking in the oven." She lowered herself to the floor.

"And leave Lord Ullin's daughter out there on the dark and stormy water?" Harry reached down, slipped his arm around her waist, and hoisted her back on to the bench.

Reprimanding him with a cross look, Frieda tried to wriggle out of his hold. Harry pulled her to him.

"You are the prettiest, smartest, most loving woman in San Francisco. You know that?"

"Behave, Harry, or I'm going right back to the house."

"Sorry, ma'am." He released her, put on a contrite expression, then had another swallow of brandy. "Last drop?" he offered.

Knowing she shouldn't, she took it. As she drained the flask, she felt Harry's hand creep under her shawl and caress the bare skin at the base of her neck. She moved away from him and laid down the law. Keep his hands to himself and his mind on the poem, or she had to leave. Promising to behave, Harry begged her to get back to the "dark and stormy water."

With heightened flair, Frieda read:

And fast before her father's men,
Three days we've fled together,
For should he find us in the glen,
My blood would stain the heather.

She flung out an arm, grazing Harry's face. He caught

her hand and held it while Frieda sought the next stanza.

His horsemen hard behind us ride,
Should they our steps discover,
Then who will cheer my bonny bride,
When they have slain her lover?

Frieda turned to Harry. "You like it?"

"I'm crazy about it," he crooned.

"You want to try it now?"

"Read it once more, start to finish. This time, do it like you were on the stage—gestures, voices, everything."

"I'd be embarrassed."

"No need. Just you and me here."

Giggling, she drew her feet under her, rose, and stood on the bench, clutching Harry's shoulder to steady herself. Her head almost touching the rafters, she bowed and spread her arms. "'Lord Ullin's Daughter', recited by Miss Frieda Levie." Eyes flashing, arms flying, switching voices and accents, she recited the poem as if she were playing to a full house. From time to time she glanced at Harry, who was gazing up at her, transfixed.

At she recited the last line, her arms flung wide, her cheeks blazing, Harry reached up, grabbed her around her knees, lifted her off her feet and pulled her onto his lap.

"Whee," Frieda squealed as she flew through the air. When he drew her close and pressed his wet mouth against hers, she did not resist. The shed, the wine, the kitchen, the baking breads—everything had dissolved, and she was aware of nothing but the commotion inside her. "Oh, oh, oh," Frieda gasped as his lips traveled to her cheek, ear, throat. When his mouth found hers again, she wound her arms around his neck and, trembling with excitement, kissed him back.

"Sweetheart," Harry groaned. Swiftly moving Frieda from his lap to the bench, he stretched out alongside. Head whirling, she nestled against him. When he lifted her skirt and tugged at her drawers, she gasped and tried to push away his hands. With her resistance, he became demanding, forceful. Undoing his pants, he flung himself on her.

"No!" Frieda cried out, turning her head, "Harry, please, no." Arching her back, she struggled to roll out from under him.

"Be good, honey. You'll love it," Harry whispered, tightening his hold.

She kicked her legs and pounded his shoulders.

"Jewbitch, you've been begging for this," Harry growled, rising to his knees to pin her shoulders to the bench.

"Don't do this to me, Harry, please, please," she cried, twisting her hips from side to side.

"Shuddup. You want them to hear you?" he hissed.

God, no. She didn't want *them* to hear her. Frieda gritted her teeth and stiffened.

"Relax, sweetheart. You don't want to die a virgin, do you?" Harry jeered.

She suddenly pressed herself against him, caressing his face, turning his mouth to hers.

"Good girl," he whispered, "sweet girl."

As his grip eased, she tensed her body and with one powerful thrust, knocked Harry off her and onto the floor.

"Jewbitch," he growled. Rising, he flung himself back on her, pinning her to the bench. She bit at his jaws, cheeks, mouth, and then, screaming hysterically, tore at his hair. Swearing, he raised his fist to strike her. Just then, the door burst open and Frieda heard her father keen, *"Oyyy gevalt."*

Harry jumped off her and onto the floor. Yanking up her drawers and pulling down her skirt, Frieda saw her father, his face white as wax, glaring at her with raw disgust. Behind him, boarders poured into the shed, and surrounded the bartender. One by one, he shoved them aside. Shouting and cursing, Harry fought his way to the door. Then he was gone, several boarders in pursuit.

"Get the *momser,*" her father called after them, "and give him the licking of his life. But no police, no police."

Frieda eased herself to the floor and backed into a corner, struck dumb.

Her father rushed at her. "I warned you something terrible would happen. Now you've ruined me. Are you satisfied?" he demanded, his voice cold and hard.

Mute, dry-eyed, Frieda stood, head bowed.

He pointed at the door. "Go. I don't want to see you."

Covering her head and most of her face with her shawl, Frieda trudged like a broken old woman across the muddy yard and up the rear stairs. The smoke-filled kitchen was empty. Someone had been taken the charred challahs out of the oven and piled them on the work table. Who? What difference did it make now? Her chin on her chest, on trembling limbs, she shuffled toward her room. Foot on the bottom rung, she dared a backward glance. Shadowlike figures hovered in doorways, and a trail of muddy footsteps marked her path down the hall.

CHAPTER NINETEEN

Betrothed

THE CROW'S NEST was empty—someone had taken Ida. Frieda tore off her clothes, put on her nightgown, and crawled under the feather bed. Alone, in the dark, her body had its say. Spasms swept through her arms, back, and loins; her head spun, and the area from her chest to her mouth convulsed with nausea.

The first wave of vomiting caught her unprepared; she barely managed to get to the wash basin. Holding the basin under her chin, heaving as she went, she made her way to the water closet on the second floor. In the little cubicle, on her hands and knees in front of the toilet, she discharged the contents of her stomach and what felt like the lining as well. The next few hours she spent walking, then crawling, between the W.C. and the crow's nest. Toward dawn she fell asleep. When she opened her eyes she saw her little sister, a schooldress over her arm, looking down at her.

"You smell awful," Ida said, pinching her nostrils.

Frieda groaned and rolled over onto her sore stomach.

"Aunt Chava says you're sick, and I should stay away from you. Are you going to die?"

"I already did," Frieda muttered.

"She says you dasn't leave this room," Ida said.

Where could she go? "Tell her not to worry."

Frieda was dozing again when Aunt Chava stomped in with a breakfast tray. Grim-faced as a mourner, she set down the tray alongside Frieda, and raced around the room flinging open the windows, muttering magical phrases and spitting to chase the evil spirits. Then she picked up the clothes Frieda had taken off the night before, and holding them at arm's length, left. A few minutes later, she was back with a bucket of hot water, a broom, and a scrub brush.

The crow's nest scoured, Aunt Chava brought in fresh sheets, soap, and a basin of hot water, and went to work on the bed and its occupant. Yanking her limp patient this way and that, Chava recounted the repercussions of the scandal Frieda brought down on the house.

"Your mother lays like a stone. Your father sits alone with the soda pop, praying and crying. The boarders are honking like geese. Kahane called a hearing after Shabbes."

Frieda remained in the crow's nest Friday and Saturday, the meal tray her only contact with the rest of the house. Most of the first day, she languished in a dreamless sleep. On the second, she paced the room, making up her story (the truth was unspeakable).

She was still in bed on Sunday morning when her aunt came to summon her for the hearing. She rose, washed, put on her gray Mother Hubbard, and wound her hair into a tight knot. Eyes glazed as if in a trance, she went down to the parlor. The door was closed. She tapped and Kahane bid her enter. For several seconds, she stood in the doorway, girding herself.

Seated in front of a long table brought in from the dining room were Kahane, Finklestein, and her father. They wore their black Shabbes suits and hats, and the grim expressions of men undertaking a difficult and distasteful task. Her brother sat in the green love seat, Harry's yellow slicker at his feet. Kahane nodded his head at Frieda and waved at the chair that stood like a witness box in front of the curtained parlor windows. In a tone even more magisterial than usual, he explained the purpose of the hearing.

"We are investigating the wrongdoing in the wine shed last Thursday night. Our aim is to determine what transpired, who was at fault, what damage was done, what punishment should be imposed and upon whom. He has testified,"

Kahane tossed his head in Abram's direction, "and so have they," nodding first at Finklestein, then at Sammy. "Now we want to hear what you have to say."

Kahane questioned her for an hour, then dismissed her while he and the men deliberated. Twenty minutes later, Chava rushed to the crow's nest with the results.

"Kahane blamed your father, not you. He said Abram made a big mistake to tell you to take a man customer, a goy yet, to the wine shed at night. He bawled him out good.

"Kahane, God bless him, knew what to do to fix up everything. You got to get married right away."

Right away? A week? A month? A year? The next morning while preparing breakfast Frieda learned right away was right away.

"When God mends a tear, you can't see the stitches," Aunt Chava crowed.

Frieda dropped coffee grounds wrapped in cheesecloth into a pot and watched it color the boiling water as Chava unveiled the divine stitchery.

"Your father already found for you a man. You'll be a Mrs. in no time."

Get married, get married, get married. For years she'd held out against her elders' shouts, tears, pleas, and accusing silences. They'd warned she'd be sorry, and now she was.

She alone knew how close she'd come to giving herself to that crook, that deceiver, that anti-Semite. And she alone knew how lust revisited her like attacks of malaria as she cooked, did the dishes, hung the wash, swept the floors, and most insistently, as she lay in bed at night. Again and again she imagined herself falling into an enveloping tangle of limbs and lips. Each relived experience seared her anew with the humbling truth. She'd been as eager as Harry to touch and be touched.

"Guess who the man is?" Chava cried.

"Who?" Frieda responded, ready, at last, to accept the remedy for her ailment.

"Isaac Gimel. A boarder, a good Jew, a Hebrew teacher."

Frieda didn't recognize the name or the description. That struck her as odd. She registered the boarders when they arrived, collected their rent, served them their meals, cleaned their rooms, knew their names, faces, habits. Why not Gimel's?

On Tuesday night, four days after what she'd come to think of as *The Fall*, Frieda finished the supper dishes, took off her apron and went to the parlor for the betrothal. Gimel, his hatted head bowed, stood waiting with the Levie elders, Kahane, and Finkelstein. Kahane had spent long hours calculating a suitable wedding date and working out the terms of the marriage contract. As soon as Frieda joined the assembled, Kahane proudly displayed the fruits of his labor.

The marriage had to take place soon. But not before thirty days had passed—the time nature required to either corroborate Frieda's account of the wine shed assault or to render her account of no further consequence. Once the possibility of a *complication* had been eliminated, they would move fast. The wedding had to be performed before the forty-nine days of *Omer*, a period during which marriages were prohibited by Jewish law. The date Kahane selected was March 22, three weeks before Passover began. That way, the bride could have the seven days' rest due her before and after the chasseneh and still have a week to help her mother and aunt prepare for the spring festival.

Kahane had negotiated for Gimel as if he were a son or a nephew, and read the pre-nuptial conditions with sacerdotal solemnity. Gimel was to receive a wedding outfit, a silver *Kiddush* cup, new bed linens, and employment as his father-in-law's assistant in the winery. "And last but hardly least, a move from der blotes to the crow's nest."

The contract unchallenged, Kahane smashed a dish—as was the custom—and proposed a toast to the *chossen* and his *kalleh*. Throughout the ceremony, Gimel stood between Kahane and Chava, shifting from foot to foot, his gaze darting back and forth between Kahane and his shoes. Stealing peeks at her future husband, Frieda finally placed him.

Gimmel was one of the downstairsers who huddled around the kitchen stove on cold days, nibbling whatever they could pinch. He was so low in the boardinghouse hierarchy, she'd failed to notice him.

Small, quiet, inconspicuous, Gimel commanded as little attention as he did space. He was, she noted, her height: five feet, two inches, and her weight: about one hundred and five pounds. His head was round and his straight hair and thin beard were yellowish-brown, like the skin of an onion. His blue eyes were as pale as a twilight sky. His features, while not unattractive, were made to appear so by his perpetual wince.

Aunt Chava gazed at him fondly as she whispered to her niece, "A marriage made in heaven."

Frieda wanted to agree, and found reasons why she should. Unlike her, Gimel had no dreams of distinction, no yearning for Progress, no thirst for worldly knowledge, no longing to improve himself or his society. Was it possible he'd been sent to teach her what had heretofore eluded her— how to be content among her poor, humble, God-fearing brethren? Hope dawned on Frieda's lips. Chava noticed and nudged Frieda's mother.

"*Du zehst?*" she whispered, "The bride is happy."

Frieda abandoned the unflattering attire and demeanor she'd used to discourage unwanted suitors and began to take pains with her appearance. Each evening before she came to the parlor, she went upstairs to put on a North of Market dress, arrange her curly brown hair in a smooth pompadour, powder her round, flushed cheeks, and balm her work-scarred hands. Her family and the boarders cheered her on, noting how much prettier and happier she looked. Frieda had the impression Gimel saw the difference as well, but was too shy to comment. Respecting his reserve, she didn't force him into conversation, but she did look forward to learning more about him before they became man and wife. The few words he uttered, she hoarded, and pieced together into a biography.

He was twenty-six, four years her senior, but looked

older—and younger. An only child, he had been born in Luck, Frieda's mother's birthplace. After his mother died in 1867, he and his father came to America. Hungry for news from home, Bella questioned him about her family and friends. His head hunched between his shoulders, his eyes lowered, Gimel knew none of the people in question.

"Who did you know?" Bella asked, alarmed.

"Beggars. My father went to the *schnorrers' schul*," Gimel answered. "All we knew were beggars."

His humility, his candor, his lack of pretensions, deeply impressed Frieda. She habitually lied about her age, her foreign birth, her South of Market residence, and any other vital statistic she supposed would lower her standing outside the boardinghouse.

Chava inquired about Gimel's life in the Mother Lode country before he came to San Francisco. He and his father had gone directly to a landsman in Sonora, but he had moved before they arrived. From there they went to Grass Valley, and then to Placerville. How had they earned a living? Chava wanted to know.

His father had tutored bar mitzvah boys, recited prayers for the dead, and occasionally officiated at a wedding or a funeral. They'd slept in the back of stores owned by Jewish merchants, earning their bed and board sweeping, arranging stock and serving as night watchmen. "A living it wasn't," Gimel sighed, "but we got by for eight years, Baruch ha Shem, praised be He." Then one night, when Gimel was out making a delivery, a thief broke into the store. His father took a pistol from the cash drawer and ordered him out. Gimel found his father sprawled on the floor, his face splattered with blood and brains. His blue eyes trickling tears, Gimel blessed the memory of his beloved parent. "He always told me, if something happened to him, I should go to the Levies in San Francisco. So I did."

In the honesty with which he told his story, and in the austerity of his life, Frieda found much to admire. All he'd ever known was was poverty and ignominy, yet uncomplaining, he took what came his way. Abram rubbed and rubbed at Gimel, hoping to ignite an enthusiasm for the wine business in him, but no sparks flew. Gimel did as he was told. When Abram gave him more orders than he could handle, or when he got tired, he simply stopped and sat down.

Evenings in the parlor, when the family was not interrogating him, he hummed liturgical melodies or dozed, exhausted, Frieda supposed, by his new responsibilities. When she met him elsewhere in the boardinghouse, she greeted him warmly, inquired about his health, or commented on the weather. His customary response was "Yeh." Once he muttered something about a princess and a peasant. Eager to understand him better, Frieda asked him to repeat what he had said. "Yeh," was all the assistance he gave her.

When words and smiles failed, Frieda reached out to him with a second helping of stew, another piece of pie, and cookies to take with him. With his perennial "Yeh," he accepted each offering, but never directly from her hands. An envious boarder seated nearby once joked about why the cook might want to fatten him up. Gimel granted the joker no more than his customary response.

One afternoon, Frieda met him coming out of the wine shed, dragging his feet and wiping his brow.

"How do you like working for my father?" she asked, concerned.

"How do *you* like working for your father?" he questioned in return.

Need he say more, Frieda thought, admiring the acuity of his response.

His remoteness she attributed to piety. The few ultra-pious Jews at the boardinghouse rarely looked at or spoke to a woman, and under no circumstances would they touch one. But they were old and unattached. Once they are married, he'll be more demonstrative. "Be fruitful and multiply" was the first injunction of a Jewish marriage, and no one had yet invented a way to make babies at a distance.

Frieda tried to emulate her teacher's reserve. Yet, hard as she tried, she couldn't keep from scratching for some sign of attraction, admiration, respect. The more she did to capture his attention, the more distant he became. After a while, even the *yehs* stopped.

She began to fear Gimel was not all there mentally, then chided herself for discrediting him. The failing was in her. The poor man sensed she was beset with sexual desire and didn't want her to defile him. She wished she could consult someone, but she'd have to reveal her malady, and that, under threat of torture, she refused to do. Frieda resolved to use the three weeks before her marriage to cleanse herself of her shameful preoccupation with lovemaking and make herself worthy of her pious bridegroom.

For two days she monitored and corrected her thoughts, discovering to her dismay that the more she did, the more she had to do. On the third day, while sweeping the second floor hallway, she overheard a conversation that froze the broom in her hands. Shapiro and Weinstein were in their room discussing the wedding.

"Levie is a fool," Shapiro said.

"Why?" Weinstein wanted to know.

"To marry off Frieda to Gimel."

"You know why," Weinstein said.

"Because of what happened in the wine shed. But how come to a schlemiel like Gimel?"

"He had to make it fast."

"Fast, yes, but it also is got to be good. Frieda and Gimel ain't a match."

"Levie figures he'll get a farzesseneh off his hands and maybe squeeze out for himself a grandson."

"Some grandson. From a *vantz*, a bedbug, don't come a *mensh*. From a vantz comes a vantz."

"He and the Missis want for Frieda a husband from the boardinghouse so she'll stay right here. Where would they find another worker like her?"

"All right, a boarder. But Gimel?"

"Sure. If they tell him to sit, he sits, if they tell him to stand, he stands. He won't make trouble."

"That's all he'll make is trouble."

"How come?"

"He ain't happy."

"Kahane got for him a new suit, bed linens, a Kiddush cup, the best room in the house, a good seat by the proprietor. Why ain't he happy?"

"He's a schnorrer and used to a schnorrer's share. It's too much for him. Frieda's too much for him.

After several seconds of silence, Weinstein wondered aloud, "So what will be?"

"What will be, will be," Shapiro said.

CHAPTER TWENTY

Please Say Yes

FRIEDA FLEW OUT of the alcove. For the rest of the day she chirped around the boardinghouse airborne. But after midnight, in the kitchen, baking the next day's breads and pastries, second thoughts grounded her. Shapiro was right about her elders' motives; she had battled them for years. But it didn't seem right to dismiss Gimel without an explanation....

Twenty minutes later she was heading for der blotes with a note inviting her betrothed to a private meeting. A lamp in one hand, her other on the railing, she paused halfway down the stairs, halted by the cold, malodorous air wafting up at her. She rarely came down to the communal room inhabited by the impoverished boarders. For what they were paying, let them clean up their own quarters, ordered her aunt. The stench reminded Frieda of a municipal prison she had visited as a Sister of Service. In an impassioned report she once described the inmates as "unwanted, unwashed, unwomaned creatures, stranded between their dismal pasts and their obscure futures."

Continuing her descent step by step, Frieda peered into the room. It was illuminated by a dim light emanating from several memorial candles burning on a low table—the boarders were never without somebody's death to commemorate. Her eyes moved from cot to cot, until she found Gimel. He was staring at her. As she approached, he shrank back, pulling the ragged cover up to his chin. Standing at his side, looking down, she whispered:

"I'm sorry I woke you."

"Who sleeps?" Gimel said.

"I just wanted to leave this note for you," she said, slipping it under his hands, which were folded on his chest.

Gimel shuddered, drawing back from the paper as though it were contaminated.

"I've no intention of hurting you," Frieda assured him. "Read it, you'll see."

Gimel lowered his eyelids.

"Read it now," she urged.

He lifted his head and looked around for help from his roommates, who were either asleep or pretended to be.

"Would you like me to tell you what it says?" asked Frieda, surmising suddenly that he couldn't read English.

Gimel nodded, looking relieved, but not greatly.

She wished she didn't have to stand over the man. It made her seem so big and him so small. But if she sat down on his cot, she feared he might jump up and flee. So she lowered herself to her haunches in the narrow space between his cot and the next.

Gimel flung his thin body as far from her as he could, and turned his face away.

"We have to talk," Frieda whispered.

Gimel's features contracted into his familiar grimace.

"You don't want to talk to me?"

He shook his head.

"Just enough so we can understand each other."

"It's against the law," Gimel pleaded.

"I promise I'll do nothing to compromise you."

Gimel's lips quivered.

"Do you understand what I'm saying?"

"What means *compromise*?"

"Shame you or make you commit a sin."

"Oy," the man wailed.

"Do you really like me?"

Gimel shook his head; he didn't like her.

"You're doing it because they," she jerked her chin toward the ceiling, "told you to marry me."

"Yeh," he whined.

"You don't have to marry me, Mr. Gimel."

Gimel looked up dubiously.

"Your father will throw me out in the street."

"No he won't."

A glimmer of hope crossed his gloomy face. "Who will tell him no wedding?" He had clearly sought the courage and found it lacking.

"I will."

Gimel's worried frown told Frieda he knew more about her and her explosive father than she thought.

"At the right moment I'll talk to him. It's a sin for two people who don't care for each other to marry." The words had a convincing ring. Frieda mentally filed them to use with her father.

"I got no place else to go," Gimel whimpered, drawing his shoulders up to his ears.

"Don't worry, Mr. Gimel. I promise you'll be able to stay right here." She patted the cot.

Clouds moved from Gimel's pale moon face and a new expression, one she had never seen before, appeared. She guessed it was a smile.

The wedding preparations were sailing along so smoothly, no one noticed that the bride had slipped overboard. In the calm before the inevitable storm ahead, Frieda floated like an eggshell on the ocean, drifting where the breeze blew. Mama wanted her to stand for a fitting of her wedding gown. Papa wanted her to send wedding invitations to every traditional Jew in San Francisco. Sylvia wanted her wedding gown to wear at her spring concert. Blatner wanted to breathe down the back of her neck. Chava wanted her to go to the *mikva* for a pre-nuptial purification bath. Ida wanted to be her flower girl and wear a garland of daisies in her golden hair. Mr. Gimel wanted her to ignore him. Baum's son wanted *matzo brie*, and it wasn't even Passover yet. Yes, yes, yes, yes, yes, March second, March third, March fourth, March fifth.

Late in the afternoon of March tenth, Frieda was on the front porch washing the parlor windows when Sammy returned from the post office with a thick letter for her from the Arizona Territory. She seized the envelope and studied it. "Bennie Goldson, Dos Cacahuates, Arizona Territory," read the return address. Her fingers trembling, she was about to tear it open when an inner alarm sounded.

Weighing the heavy envelope in her palm, Frieda searched her memory for an image of the man. Almost four years had passed since their chance meeting. What she summoned up was a tan Stetson, a cigar, curly dark red hair, mahogany-colored eyes, a ready smile, the brawny torso and weathered skin of an outdoorsman. He didn't look like any Jew she'd ever known, but he said he was, or had been, the last time he thought about it. She'd finish the windows, calm down, then see what he had to say.

When the windows gleamed rose and gold in the slanting light of the setting sun, Frieda carried her pail and newspapers indoors. Intrigued by the bulk of the letter—after so long a silence—she ducked into the little pantry off the kitchen for a peek before starting the evening meal. The light was dim with the door closed, but Frieda had no trouble reading Mr. Goldson's bold hand.

> March 7, 1880
> Dear Miss Levie:
>
> Now that the Southern Pacific Railroad is up and running in the Arizona Territory, this letter should take no more than a week to get to you. I was very happy to get your Valentine card. It reminded me of my schooldays in San Bernardino.

He must have received it almost three weeks ago. Why, Frieda wondered, had he taken so long to respond?

> For a collector of exotic postmarks, this letter should have special value. You are among the first

twenty people to receive a letter from Dos Cacahuates, Arizona Territory.

After all these years, he still remembered she had an exotic postmark collection.

> I have not moved, I'm in the same place, but the
> name of the camp and just about everything else in
> my life has changed. Let me assure you, all for the
> good. I better explain why I haven't written for so
> long lest you think ill of me. I received your letters,
> and I read them to tatters. (Ask my brother Morrie, if
> you don't believe me.) I just didn't have the heart to
> write you back. I will tell you frankly, I was too de-
> pressed. My business down here on the Mexican bor-
> der was not going the way I hoped. As I told you
> when we met, I am here for life, but things were not
> moving fast enough to suit me. I knew I had to make
> some kind of change, but I didn't know what.

Mr. Goldson was as free-speaking on paper as he was in
person, but she wished he'd get to where he was going.

> The way things worked out, I didn't have to go
> out seeking Dame Fortune. She came to me. On
> January 21, Yancy Nunes, the vice-president of the
> International Improvement Company, got off the
> stagecoach in front of my store and nothing has been
> the same since. He had a roll of plans under his arm,
> a suitcase full of handbills, and a scheme to develop
> this area that knocked my eyes out. Colonel Leigh-
> ton, the president of the company, had worked out a
> deal with Alejandro Ramirez, a Mexican gentleman
> who owns a huge former Spanish land grant that ex-
> tends to the north and south of the international line.
> Ramirez gave Leighton permission to plan a
> townsite on his land, and agreed to receive payment

as the lots are sold. But that is only part of the project. Leighton is also planning a shortline railroad from Mohawk Station, the Southern Pacific stop, down to Dos Cacahuates, and from Dos Cacahuates to Guaymas, Mexico. We never dreamed, my brother Morrie and me, that our little outpost would some-day sit on the route of an international railroad. Heck, we thought we hit pay dirt when we got the stagecoach from Yuma to Guaymas to stop here. Not that we don't deserve a little good luck after fifteen hard years in the Territory.

Why was he telling her all this? Was he trying to arouse her sympathy as Harry had, only to take advantage of her, and in so doing, humiliate her and her family?

The next thing we know Nunes is asking me and my brother to join the International Improvement Company as partners. Morrie's keen on ranching and farming, and was not too excited about the idea, but he perked up when Nunes offered to make him Di-rector of Physical Resources and me Sales Manager.

Frieda scanned the next three pages. At the top of page seven, she found what she was looking for:

So, it appears our town is about to become an in-ternational community, a gateway between nations. As we say down here, all we need now is good water and good women. Morrie is looking after the former, so it's my job to see to the latter. When we first met at the conservatory, I knew right away you and I think along the same lines. I been trying to figure out ever since how I was going to sell a fine San Francisco woman like you on the Arizona Territory.
    The problem was I had nothing to offer. Now that I'm on the ground floor of a big operation, I'm

ready to have my say. I'll be in San Francisco in the middle of March. Nunes wants me to pick up the architect's plans for the hotel and have some new handbills printed. If you say yes, I can promise you one heck of a train ride back to the Territory. This time you will have to travel the last leg from Mohawk Station to Dos Cacahuates by stagecoach, but in another year or so, there will be a train almost to your front porch. Nunes says to tell you that if you say yes now, you can go down in history as the First Lady of Dos Cacahuates. He also says that if I can't sell you, I don't deserve to be Sales Manager. In case I haven't made myself clear, I am asking you to marry me when I am in San Francisco. Please say yes.

Respectfully yours,

Bennie Goldson, Sales Manager
International Improvement Company
Dos Cacahuates Division

CHAPTER TWENTY-ONE

Bennie Goldson, A.T.

LATE FRIDAY AFTERNOON Frieda ran up the steps of the boardinghouse, hair streaming, face flushed, armpits dark with perspiration. She was about to open the front door when a man's voice called to her from the far end of the porch, "Ain't you Miss Frieda Levie?"

"Yes," she said, starting inside without a glance at the questioner.

The creaking rocking chair stopped and boots hit the porch floor. "Hold your horses, ma'am, we've got a few things to discuss."

"Later, I can't stop now." Frieda started over the threshold.

A firm hand took hold of her arm and drew her back out on to the porch. Looking up annoyed, she saw a Stetson hat, a green suit, a lit cigar, red curly hair, puzzled brown eyes, and a tooled leather suitcase.

"Bennie Goldson, Dos Cacahuates, Arizona Territory," the man said. "Your letter said you were looking forward to my visit."

Frieda let the door slam closed and strode toward the furthermost corner of the porch, signalling for the man to follow. "I can't talk now," she apologized in a low voice. "My father's wagon broke down and is holding up traffic. I came home to get help."

His face brightened. "Let's go."

"I can't trouble you," Frieda said, her eyes shifting back to the door.

"Fixing a wagon ain't no trouble. What's the problem?"

"A broken axle. The rear wheels collapsed." She showed

him with her hands.

"You got a tool shed out back?" Mr. Goldson asked, jerking his thumb in the direction of the yard.

She nodded.

"I'll see if I can find a wagon jack and a C-clamp." He started for the steps, then turned. "My valise will be all right here, won't it?"

"Of course."

"Back in a minute."

Frieda picked up the bulging case and opened the front door. Standing just inside were her mother and Aunt Chava, their faces alarmed, questioning.

"Who-is-he-what-is-he?" Chava demanded.

"I'll explain later," Frieda said, setting the valise down in the hall.

"What does he want from you, Frieda?" her mother cried.

"Papa's wagon has a broken axle. He's going to fix it."

Chava sucked her false teeth into place. "He says he came to marry you."

Frieda turned.

"Did you send him a letter, Frieda? He says you did," her mother called.

"When I get back." Frieda said, trying to close the door. Chava held the inside knob.

"He can't stay in mine boardinghouse," she cried, her wrinkled face setting like cracked cement.

"We're going to help Papa."

"Frieda, don't go with no stranger," her mother begged.

"He's not a stranger."

"We don't know him," Chava responded. "He's a stranger."

"We'll be right back."

"Don't make more trouble, Frieda," Chava yelled.

She hurried toward the street. Mr. Goldson was waiting for her on the sidewalk, one arm full of tools. They were starting off when she heard a thud. Looking back over her shoulder she saw Mr. Goldson's valise back on the porch.

"Lead the way," Mr. Goldson said.

Neither spoke as they half-ran down Tehama to Third. As they approached Howard Street, Frieda stopped, out of breath, her hand clamped to her side.

"I've got a stitch," she told her visitor.

"You set the pace, ma'am," was his reply.

They started off again, moving somewhat slower.

"You didn't tell them about me, did you?" Mr. Goldson said.

"I couldn't until you got here."

"They said you're getting married a week from Sunday. I thought they meant to me."

Frieda stopped again. "What did you tell them?"

"That I was the fellow from the Arizona Territory who had come to marry their daughter. They looked at me as if I was Billy the Kid on a rampage."

Frieda glanced away, shaking her head.

"They said you're going to marry a fellow named Gimel."

"Not if Gimel can help it."

Goldson shot her a incredulous look. "He don't want to marry you?"

"No more than I want to marry him."

"So who wants the wedding?"

He didn't mind asking personal questions, did he? "My father arranged it," Frieda said, tears welling.

"Why'd he do that?" Goldson asked, as if arranged nuptials were unheard of.

"He wants me to get married," Frieda said, her gaze fixed on the Post Street hill.

"So do I," the man from the Arizona Territory replied. "To me." They'd arrived at Market Street and were waiting to cross. "Think I can sell him on a switch?"

He was moving too fast. A chance meeting and a memorable conversation, a half-dozen letters, and now, after a four-year silence, a marriage proposal. Did she really want to spend her life with this man?

"I don't know," Frieda responded.

"Why not?" Goldson took her arm, rushing her across the street.

She didn't answer until they got to the other side. "They want me to marry a Jew."

"I'm a Jew."

"Not the kind my father has in mind."

"Am I the kind you have in mind?"

Trudging up Post Street, short of breath, a pain in her side, Frieda wasn't sure. "Sooner or later, you'll have to speak to my father."

"I say sooner." He released her arm, lifted his Stetson, re-settled it on his red curls, and picked up his pace. Then, as if suddenly recalling they were together, he slowed down and took her elbow.

A half-block from the accident, Frieda could see the commotion had heightened. The broken-down wagon, streaming homemade wine and soda pop, and the sway-backed horse rested in the middle of street, a foot or so from the cable car tracks. Carriages, victorias, hacks, buggies and delivery wagons, each with a shouting driver, were squeezing single-file past the impediment. Frieda caught her breath as a cable car clanked down the hill, just missing the horse and her father, who was kneeling at its side.

Reining in his mount alongside Abram, a policeman leaned down and shouted, "Do something, man. If you don't get that damned wagon out of here, I'm going to fine you and shoot that horse, or shoot you and fine the horse."

Searching the crowd for help, Abram spotted Frieda. He lunged at her, shouting orders. "Calm Yerushalayem, empty the wagon, find a repairman, bring Swifty Balderback, the Republican fixer."

Goldson had his own agenda. He set down the tools he was carrying, whipped off his green jacket, undid his stiff collar and tie, took off his hat, and placed them all on the wagon seat. He then rolled up his sleeves to his substantial biceps and strode toward the tailgate. On his way, he stopped to seize and pump the right hand of Frieda's distraught father, saying, "Bennie Goldson, Dos Cacahuates, Arizona Territory."

Abram yanked back his hand and hurried around the other side of the wagon to chase a small boy reaching for a bottle of soda. Goldson shrugged and ducked under the rear end of the wagon. When he re-emerged, he was smiling.

"Not much of a problem there," he called to Frieda. "I'll have her rolling in no time."

Back on his feet, he made a second try at Frieda's father.

Abram waved away Goldson's extended hand. "I got to get this wagon out of here before the dray cart comes."

"Five minutes, that's all it's going to take."

Abram studied Goldson, his small blue eyes aglitter with mistrust.

"I can't promise you won't need a new axle, but I think I can get you home."

"Right away, it's almost Shabbes."

"Then I better get to work." Goldson said, disappearing beneath the wagon.

Squatting on her haunches, her father standing alongside her, Frieda watched her visitor struggling with the jack.

"Mr. Levie," Goldson called.

Abram bent over, his hand cupped to his ear.

"Mr. Levie, I came to ask you for your daughter's hand in marriage."

Frieda's father either failed to hear or deliberately ignored Goldson's words. "You can't do nothing with that jack. That jack's broken," Abram called in return.

"Matter of fact, you're right. I'm going to have to lift the wagon on my back. I'll need your help."

"I don't know nothing about fixing axles," Frieda's father admitted.

"Come down here, I'll tell you what to do."

Frieda watched her father bend and ease himself beneath the vehicle. Bennie crouched, legs astride, grunted, and straightened, raising one end of the wagon off the ground.

"What you want I should do?" Abram asked.

"I want you should give me your daughter's hand."

"He wants he should give him his daughter's hand," mimicked one of the spectators.

"Who gets the rest of her?" another wisecracked.

Frieda, cheeks blazing, pretended she was deaf.

"To fix the wagon," Abram growled.

"That clamp near my shoe, take it," Bennie instructed.

"I got it. Now what?"

"See where that axle is cracked? I'm going to ease myself right over there and hold the two ends together. When I do, fit that clamp over the joint and screw it on. Here I go."

Frieda watched Bennie inch toward the axle.

"Right here, Mr. Levie."

"I can't see. I'm dizzy in the head."

"Give it to me," Bennie said, edging close to Levie. As he screwed the clamp in place, he continued his plea. "I want to marry Frieda next week and take her back to the Arizona Territory with me."

"He ain't bashful, you can say that for him," called someone in the crowd.

"And he's got a strong back," another heckler added.

"Will it hold?" Frieda heard her father question.

"Sure as shooting. At least until you get her home."

"Are you sure?"

"Ready to roll," Goldson said, crawling out from under the wagon. "I told you it wouldn't take more than five minutes."

Abram followed, looking dubious.

A smattering of applause came from the amused spectators. Frieda watched as Goldson rolled down his sleeves, put on his jacket, and started toward her father again. She signaled him to say no more, but he wasn't looking at her.

"I came to talk to you about marrying your daughter," he told Abram, "And I don't intend to leave off until—"

"Not now, Romeo," the annoyed policeman bellowed. "I'm giving you one minute to get that wagon off my street."

"We're going, we're going," Abram assured the policeman. When the officer trotted off, Frieda's father, rushed at her. "Who-is-he-what-is-he?"

"A man I know," Frieda said, patting Yerushalayem's trembling head.

"I can't ride, it's Shabbes," Abram told her, pointing at the darkening sky. "Can I trust him to get the wagon back to the boardinghouse?"

"Yes."

"How do you know?"

"He left his suitcase on the porch."

Abram gave his daughter a long, searching look, then turned to study the man from the Arizona Territory. "Goldson. He's a Jew?"

"Yes."

"But not a real Jew." Of that Abram had no doubt. Keeping his distance, he called to Goldson, "Mister, can you drive the wagon back to the boardinghouse for me?"

"Sure thing," Goldson answered. "Miss Frieda too."

"She's walking with me."

As her father rushed her off, Frieda heard a bystander shout, "Hey, Arizona, you ride on Shabbes?"

Over her shoulder, she saw Goldson crouched in a fighting position and heard him bellow, "If the son of a bitch who wants to know steps up, I'll be glad to tell him."

Frieda was in the steamy kitchen working on the Shabbes supper when Shapiro rushed in with the latest news.

"Levie told Sammy to tell the stranger if he *daven* on Shabbes, he should come to shul. You know what the stranger said?"—Shapiro paused—"'You bet your boots I daven, but you'll have to grubstake me to a *tallis* and a *yarmulke*. Must be some kind of Jew if he knows about prayer shawls and skullcaps."

"Abram's crazy," Chava grumbled. "Anyone can see the man's a no-good, a *paskudnyak*."

"What do you mean crazy, he saved Levie's life," Shapiro said.

"Last month Gimel saved his life." Chava removed a pan of hot *kishke* from the oven and thumped it down on top of the stove alongside Frieda, who was counting *gefilte* fish balls on a platter. "A *betrothed* girl sends a letter to a strange man," Chava chided.

Granting her aunt neither a word nor a glance, Frieda started for the dining room.

Chava yanked at her niece's skirt and warned, "We don't want no more trouble from you."

Frieda tugged herself free and disappeared.

In the dining room, the long, T-shaped tables were covered with snowy white linen. Her mother stood at the head table, lined with tall, carved mahogany chairs for the boardinghouse patriarchs. Bella was setting their places with what remained of the family's fine china, crystal, and silver. The intricately embossed ceremonial objects required for the table ceremony—candlesticks, Kiddush cups, a foot-long challah platter and breadknife—were already in place.

Frieda circled the tables counting the settings. The farther from the head, the more simple they became. At the opposite end, where the downstairsers sat, the settings were pieced together of unmatched, bent utensils and cracked plates. The total taken, Frieda returned to a midpoint and began setting another place.

"That man," Bella said, "he ain't coming to Shabbes supper, is he?"

"Yes. I'm setting a place for him here between Weinstein and Shapiro."

"What does *she* say?" Bella asked, jerking her head in the direction of the kitchen.

"I didn't ask *her*."

"That man, he lives in the Arizona Territory?"

"Yes," Frieda said, folding an embroidered linen napkin for his place.

"Oy," Bella cried in alarm.

"What's wrong?"

"It's so far away."

"Not since the Southern Pacific Railroad was completed."

"Wing Lee says it's hot as hell in the Arizona Territory," Bella reported dolefully.

"Thousands of people live there; it can't be that bad."

"Maybe that man knows Wing Lee? Is he in Yuma?"

"No, Dos Cacahuates."

"Dos ca-ca-what?"

"Dos Cacahuates."

Bella stopped what she was doing to sound out the word. "Dos ca-ca-wah-tes."

"That's right."

"Dos ca-ca-wah-tes," Bella tried it again.

"Exactly."

Bella's face puckered with distaste. "Frieda, I know what ca-ca is, but what *is wates*?"

"'Cacahuates' is one word, Mama. It means peanuts in Spanish. *Dos Cacahuates*, two peanuts."

"Spanish? Why Spanish?"

"The town is on the Mexican border."

"So far away?"

"Not since the Southern Pacific—" Frieda stopped, aware that she was about to repeat herself. "He says if I marry him now, I can be the First Lady of Dos Cacahuates."

"The first lady?" Bella paled.

"I'll be in the history books and everything."

"Don't do it, Frieda, you'll be so lonely."

Back in the kitchen, counting again—this time it was matzo balls—Frieda watched Ida show Shapiro how the cowboy introduced himself. "Pleasedtomeetcha," the seven-year-old piped. "Benniegoldsondoscacawaaatesarizonaterritory."

Home for Shabbes supper, Sylvia was dispatched by Chava to reason with Frieda.

"I could hardly believe my ears. A man from the interior? Have you no self-respect?"

"I'm tired of San Francisco," Frieda muttered.

"You *love* San Francisco."

She did love San Francisco. Even though, as Sylvia often pointed out, she wasn't a native daughter.

"San Francisco has everything—theaters, concert halls, parks, museums, department stores, lecture halls, schools, cultivation...."

"For you, maybe, not for me," Frieda said. "Excuse me, I've got to change before supper."

"I thought she was crazy, now I know it," she heard her sister tell her aunt as she left.

As Frieda put on her good dress, brushed her curly brown hair into a smooth pompadour, and powdered her blazing cheeks, she set aside her family's derisive opinions and considered her own. Watching Mr. Goldson deal with her family made her uneasy. He was so impulsive, outspoken. On the other hand, those same traits could be viewed as straight-forward, genuine. Besides, he wanted her. Not to toy with, but to marry, or so he said.

The cheerful Sabbath greetings of the boarders returning from shul wafted up into the crow's nest. Frieda rushed to the window. They were climbing the front steps and filing into the boardinghouse. Sammy and Mr. Goldson brought up the rear.

She found Sammy alone at the kitchen table, chuckling like a half-wit. She asked what he was laughing about. He started to tell her, but each time he tried, he broke down laughing. Frieda yanked him out of the chair, dragged him into the pantry, slammed the door, and shook him until he composed himself.

"Mr. Goldson wanted to sit up front, probably to impress Papa, who was on the *bimah*. Papa kept looking down from the platform; you know how he does," Sammy said, emulating their father's stern expression.

"Did Mr. Goldson know how to daven?" Frieda asked.

"He could pray a little," Sammy said. "He said he was 'real excited bout being in *shool*.'" He started to giggle.

"Go on," Frieda ordered.

"He ran out of prayers in no time. When he saw Papa watching him, he lifted his prayer book—upside down—and moved his lips." Banging the counter, Sammy rocked with laughter.

"You played some kind of joke on him," Frieda surmised.

"Naw, all I did was mention that they sometimes honor a visitor by asking him to read from the Torah."

"They never read the Torah on Friday night."

"I know, you know, but Mr. Goldson didn't know. 'Hell, I can't read from no Torah,'" Sammy mimicked.

"What did he do?"

"When Papa and the others went to the ark, he got up and ran."

"Outside?"

"That's what I thought. But a few minutes later, I saw Papa tearing off the bimah yelling, 'Nar, idjot, get out from there.'"

Frieda already knew, but she asked anyway, "Where was he?"

"In the women's section. Papa grabbed him by his collar, marched him down the aisle, and dumped him next to me. Mr. Goldson sat there, his face red as his hair, his eyes blinking; he looked like he was going to bust out bawling any minute."

Frieda raised her hand and swung from the shoulder, her open palm landing with a smack on her brother's cheek.

"You little saloon snipe," she hissed. "Is that any way to treat a guest?"

CHAPTER TWENTY-TWO

Pioneering

FRIEDA SPOTTED MR. GOLDSON as soon as she entered the crowded dining room. Seated among the ragged, pale downstairsers, he stood out like a Goliath among ghosts. With one shrewd gesture her father had taken the stranger in and rejected him as a suitor. Frieda's gaze turned to thin, balding, round-shouldered Gimel, seated alongside her father. Her features crimped with distaste. Nothing her father did or said could make her marry that odious onion.

Her eyes returned to Mr. Goldson. He was nervous; his thick, calloused fingers pleated the tablecloth, and his Mexican leather boots tangled with the legs of the wobbly, undersized chair. Even his unruly red curls seemed to be quivering. The black yarmulke on his head looked as if it had been dropped there by a passerby—as indeed it had.

The man to his left spotted her and nudged Mr. Goldson. Had he been questioning the downstairsers about her? Blood rushed to her face. His heavy hands planted on the table, he turned in his chair, first to the left, where she was not, and then to the right, where she was. The chair skittered as he bolted out of it. With two strides he was standing in front of Frieda, his teeth gleaming in his suntanned face. Hand extended, as if they were meeting for the first time, he said, "Bennie Goldson, Dos Cacahuates, Arizona Territory."

Conscious of the curious, mostly hostile, spectators, Frieda murmured, "I'm glad you came, Mr. Goldson."

"I am too—now that you're here. Call me Bennie," he urged her, his brown eyes seeking a commitment she was not yet prepared to make.

"Sit," Abram called, rising at the head of the table. Bennie dropped Frieda's hand and, like a naughty schoolboy, hurried toward his chair.

Frieda called after him, "Don't sit down there, I set a place for you here." She pointed to an empty chair near the center of the table, between her favorite boarders, Shapiro and Weinstein.

Waving his thanks, he scurried to his new seat, his eyes glued to Abram, who had raised his Kiddush cup. Seeing the other boarders raise their wine glasses, he lifted his, too, and with them recited, or pretended to recite, the blessing over the wine. When Frieda passed the platter of bread, she noticed that Bennie's forehead glistened with perspiration. "How am I doing?" he whispered as he helped himself to the challah.

She smiled encouragingly over Weinstein's shoulder. He grinned back around Weinstein's head, then stuffed the bread into his mouth. Before leaving for the kitchen, she set the platter with two remaining pieces of bread in front of him. When she returned, the platter was empty and Roth was leaning across the table, speaking to Bennie.

"You got bread like that to eat in the Arizona Territory?"

"Not lately," Bennie said, his tone jaunty but his face tightening.

The day they met in Golden Gate Park, Bennie told her that he and his brother cooked their meals from provisions they kept in the store and edibles they gathered in the surrounding desert.

"Not lately," Weinstein mocked. "You think we don't know about the wilderness? I got snowed in one year at Ringel's Slope, and for one month I ate nothing but dried herring and beans."

"Dried herring, hah," Katz, a Hungarian Jew with an ocean of wavy hair, commented from the other side of Shapiro. "In Fiddletown, where I was, the only dried herring we had was in our dreams."

Frieda passed the gefilte fish, knowing where the conversation was headed. The woes of the wilderness—a favorite topic among the boarders when someone from the interior was present. All but a few of them had suffered hardships and disappointments in or around the gold fields and silver mines of California and Nevada. They were of one mind: pioneering didn't pay.

"Some more fish, Mr. Katz," Frieda asked, hoping to divert him.

He shook his head and continued.

"The wilderness, phooey," Katz waved his fork. "Take me and my brother." The men within earshot leaned back, their eyes fixed on Bennie. There was no need for them to listen; each lugubrious story had been told many times.

One finished and another began. Shapiro had taken his young wife's dowry and plunged it into a gold mine in partnership with his second cousin from Kovno. When their baby died of a burst appendix, Shapiro's wife refused to stay in the interior. He took her back to San Francisco and settled her in a Clay Street boardinghouse, planning to divide his time between San Francisco and the mine in Placerville. When he got back to the mine he found his partner had sold it and run off with the money.

"We had no more children, then my wife died. Who do I have now?" he wanted Bennie to tell him. "Weinstein," he answered.

Frieda picked up the fish plates and put down the soup bowls, noting how Bennie pounced on the offering. Glazer, a wizened one-hundred-pounder sitting next to Roth, leaned forward to inform the guest that their Frieda was the best cook South of Market. Bennie caught Frieda's eye. He raised his right thumb and forefinger in a sign of excellence and pointed to the soup, mouthing, "the best I ever tasted." Frieda flushed and fled to the kitchen.

Conversation lagged as the boarders attacked their full plates—chicken, lokshen, tsimmes. Then suddenly, over the clinking of silverware, the smacking of lips, the sucking of bones, rose a reedy whine. Frieda looked around the table to see who was speaking. It was Gimel.

"I wouldn't step out of San Francisco," squeaked the small Hebrew teacher. He slumped back into his chair.

"Go on," Chava urged him.

"I came a bar mitzvah boy to this country with mine father, a poor teacher. Who would he hurt?" Gimel closed his eyes. Kahane whispered in his ear.

Gimel shook his head tragically. "From morning to night, lying Jew, stealing Jew, miser Jew, Christ-killer." He recited the epithets with as much emotion as his passive nature could muster.

"Listen, Gimel," Greenblatt called, "the goyim taunt the Jew, but are they so nice to each other? Irisher, Bohunk, Guinie, Nigger, Limey."

"They shot my father like he was a dozing dog," cried Gimel. "It ain't so good in San Francisco neither, but at least I'm with mine people." He leaned back, finished.

"Listen to me, Gimel," called Greenblatt, a tailor whose neck extended like a turtle's. "I was born in Minsk. Rodnos was my village. Let me tell you, there were Jewish bullies, thieves, and madmen there, too."

"Rodnos wasn't paradise," agreed Glazer, Greenblatt's landsman, "but it wasn't Bodie, neither."

Quarrels broke out like little fires all around Bennie. The sound of wrangling grew louder. Frieda watched Bennie's eyes dart from flame to flame.

"Quiet!" Abram shouted, slapping the table with his hand, then rising to impose his authority.

"Levie," Roth called, "we been telling this gentleman that it don't pay for a Jew to stay in the wilderness."

Abram leveled a long, demeaning look at Bennie.

"What do you say?" Roth prompted.

"A Jew is supposed to chase God, not gold," her father asserted.

"And stay together with his people," Chava added, "not run away, each for himself, scrambling one on top of the other to get rich."

"What do you say to that, mister?" Greenblatt asked, pointing his finger at Bennie as though it were a gun.

Bennie turned to Greenblatt. "If you are an orphan boy," he started slowly, "or a lone immigrant with little education and no capital, and you don't want to stay that way, you got to make sacrifices, take risks. Isn't that why Jews leave the old country?"

"We ran away from a bad life," Abram cried angrily.

"And to a better one," Bennie said. "Take me for example. I was born in Marysville and lived there until my father was murdered by robbers, just like that gentleman's." He pointed at Gimel. "Not long after, my mother died. My brother and I went to relatives in San Bernardino. But they had children of their own, and not much else. Back in '61, a prospector turned up with a chunk of gold as big as a fist that he'd found in La Paz on the Colorado River. A party of men set out from San Bernardino the next day, my brother and me among them. We been in the Arizona Territory ever since. Sure it's a dangerous life and a hard one, but it's a new land and there's plenty to do. I found work in mining, merchandising, freighting, cattle-raising. Better yet, I found hope. I been up and I been down, but I never doubted that I would come out on top."

"Bah," Weinstein rudely discounted the stranger. "How many win? A handful. You'll lose too."

Bennie's words stirred Frieda deeply, but the boarders were unmoved. Thirty against one, and they wouldn't be satisfied until he was ranting or worn down. It had happened many times before. She wished she could warn him to give up now.

"I won't lose," Bennie pressed on, his voice loud and sure. "I been through bad times too, and seen terrible things—things I would just as soon forget, but I didn't give up. So when Lady Luck got to my doorstep, I was right there waiting for her." His gaze turned to Frieda. "Now my wildest dreams are coming true." His eyes proclaimed her as part of his good fortune.

"Your dreams," Kahane scoffed, rising on his sacerdotal authority. "What about our dreams, my good man?"

Bennie turned respectfully to Kahane, clearly a learned Jew. "Ain't had much learning in Torah," he told him, "but enough to know God wants us to be good to one another. When a person is down and out, it's every man for himself. Sure, I'm working to better myself in the Arizona Territory, but I'm also helping to Civilize the West," his gaze flitted back to Frieda, "and Make the World a Better Place." He looked around, openly satisfied with the words that had risen from his heart to his lips.

What remained of Frieda's doubts dissolved; her face bloomed with allegiance. He need say no more. She would steal away with him at midnight if necessary. Her father's head was bent over his prayerbook, but his eyes glanced up. He called abruptly in Bennie's direction, "What you got down there?"

"Mining, agriculture, cattle-raising, commerce, soon a resort hotel. And by the end of the year there will be a rail-road bringing people in and taking natural resources out. The International Improvement Company out of Washington, D.C., is the biggest thing in the Arizona Territory, maybe in the West. They have plans to open up all of northern Mexico and southern Arizona with two short-line railroads to the West Coast..." Bennie stopped. "But I'm getting ahead of myself. We're planning a big land sale after the hotel is finished. That is why I came to San Francisco—to pick up the building plans, place some ads for the sale of some pre-view lots and company stock, and..." he paused bashfully, "take care of some personal business."

"A hotel?" Glazer questioned.

"And what a hotel!"

"How many rooms?" Roth wanted to know.

"Fifty to start. We're also planning a dining room, ball-room, gymnasium, gardens, a bridle path, hot springs. Yancy Nunes, a Spanish Jew from Charleston, is vice-president of the Dos Cacahuates Division. He brought folders with him from the East, full of pictures of famous European hotels and gardens to copy." Bennie broke off with a laugh. "I guess I get carried away. They didn't make me sales manager for nothing."

"What you figure the hotel will cost?" Abram asked.

"We don't know yet. Once we have the plans on the site and the Mexican workers estimate the local costs, we'll have a better idea. Some of the materials will have to be freighted in from the coast and from Mexico."

Abram slapped his hand on the table. "No more business talk on Shabbes. It's time for the *Birkas ha Mazon*."

After the closing grace, Abram, Kahane, Finkelstein, Blatner, and a few others sat singing Sabbath songs, while Shapiro, Weinstein, Roth, and Glazer escorted Bennie to the parlor. Frieda trailed after them.

In the parlor, Bennie noticed a piano and asked if he could play it.

Roth, ever ready for a little music, responded. "Help yourself, Mr. Goldson. We're Jews, but we're not fanatics."

Bennie settled himself at the piano stool and exercised his fingers on the keys. Then he turned to ask for requests. "Tramp, Tramp, Tramp," "Maryland, My Maryland," "Listen to the Mockingbird." Bennie's fingers needed no prompting. From time to time, he looked up to smile or wink at Frieda standing at his side.

"In this Mexican love song," said Bennie, "a man is telling his sweetheart that he's going to tie a ribbon around the world and give it to her." Frieda swayed and tapped her foot.

When he finished the song in Spanish, Bennie began one in Hebrew.

"'*Adon Olam*,'" Roth identified. "Where did you learn that?"

Laughing, Bennie explained, "There was an ex-cantor from New Haven who played the piano and sang at a saloon up in Clifton, next to Abraham's Hotel. The cantor was a *shikker*, and whenever he got good and oiled, he always broke into 'Adon Olam.' Everyone in town could sing it that year—

even the girls."

"Which girls?" Sammy asked, who had just returned with his saxophone.

Bennie looked at the piano keys and started to sing again, as though he had not heard Sammy's question.

"Which girls?" Sammy questioned again.

Frieda rested her hip against him and placed her hand on his shoulder.

Bennie slid into "Buffalo Gals."

"I asked her if she'd be my wife. Then I'd be happy all my life, If she would marry me."

Entering the parlor with Chava and Kahane, Abram shouted, "Quiet. What do you think we got here, a music hall? Frieda, I want to talk to you out here."

In the kitchen, the Levie elders, Kahane, and Sylvia drummed out an angry dirge. Mr. Goldson had to leave the boardinghouse at once. He would not be received again. Frieda was not to meet him outside. She should remember she was marrying Gimel in a week. Sylvia added her own coda. "I want that man to stop playing my piano *now.* He hits the keys too hard."

Unperturbed, Frieda, still floating on her decision, went to deliver her own version of the message. In the front hall, her bodice grazing Bennie's vest, Frieda tenderly translated her family's edicts. Then rising on her tiptoes, she breathed her answer in Bennie's ear.

"I'd be honored to become Mrs. Bennie Goldson. To-morrow morning, I'll speak to my father in private and make my position clear. Meet me in the Grand Court of the Palace Hotel at two, and I'll tell you what he said."

Elated, Bennie wrapped his arms around her and pressed a long kiss on her upturned mouth.

At six in the morning, Frieda went to find her father before he started morning prayers. He was dressed in his black Shabbes suit, a worn black yarmulke on his gleaming bald pate. Under his arm were a prayer book and a velvet sack containing his phylacteries. His exhausted eyes hovered impatiently over Frieda's head when she asked to speak to him.

"I can't talk now."

"There's something I want you to know."

"It's time for the morning service."

"I told Mr. Gimel I am not going to marry him."

Anger jolted Abram into wakefulness. "You told him? You got no business to tell Gimel anything."

"He doesn't want to marry me, either, Papa."

"What does she want from mine life?" Abram beseeched the ceiling.

"Papa," Frieda pleaded. "It's Mr. Goldson I want to marry."

"Plagues, boils, pestilences—daughters."

"He's a good man, Papa, and a Jew."

"I saw what kind of Jew," Abram spat.

"He loves me."

"Let me *live*," he begged, as if she were his executioner.

"I want you to live, but I want to live too—with Mr. Goldson in the Arizona Territory."

"Hah," Abram snorted. "In two months you'll cry to come home."

"No I won't, Papa. I'm not Mama."

"Don't be an idjot, Frieda, you'll work like a horse."

"Harder than I work at the boardinghouse?" Frieda retorted. "Without a cent in salary or a word of acknowledgment?"

"I'm a poor man," Abram sputtered. "What do you want from me?" He was furious, struggling for control.

"I want you to talk to Mr. Goldson."

"I don't talk to strangers."

"Talk to him, then he won't be a stranger."

The boarders were passing on the way to the parlor, lending eye and ear to the dispute between father and daughter.

"You're going to marry Gimel and that's final," Abram said, turning abruptly.

Frieda followed in his footsteps. "If you won't talk to Mr. Goldson, speak to a rabbi."

"Yeh, I'll talk to a rabbi," Abram mocked.

Frieda strode ahead of him and blocked his path. "Promise me you'll speak to a rabbi?"

"I said I would," he hissed, pushing past her.

Frieda ground her heels into the thin carpet. "When?"

"Tomorrow," Abram answered, his face lighting up, "if you dress up nice and come to shul today to listen to your chossen read from the Torah."

CHAPTER TWENTY-THREE

The Redheaded Stranger

FRIEDA SEARCHED THE Saturday afternoon crowd in the Grand Court of the Palace Hotel for a tan Stetson and a green suit. Bennie stood under an arch to the side of the carriage entrance, talking to a group of well-dressed men. He was facing the street and saw her at once. He excused himself and pushed through the crowd to greet her.

"You came," he cried, taking her hands in his.

"I told you I would. My father's speaking to a rabbi about you tomorrow."

"A rabbi?" Bennie's face clouded.

"I'm hoping he'll advise him to give us his blessing."

"And if he doesn't?"

"I'm still yours," Frieda answered, her gaze locking with his.

Bennie emitted a love-stricken sigh. "Then I won't worry about a thing." He calculated for a moment. "We'd better get a marriage license on Monday morning before I go north. I'll be gone until Thursday, Friday, the latest. We'll get married on Sunday and leave on the Southern Pacific the same day."

Frieda nodded happily.

"Wear this dress," Bennie said, fingering the folds of green silk. "You look like a ripe pippin apple in it." He took her hand and pressed it to his mouth.

"I'd like a bite right now."

Mindless of the crowd, Frieda took his free hand and drew it to her lips. They gazed transfixed into each other's brimming eyes. When the Grand Court clock struck three, Frieda straightened as if apprehended.

"You don't have to go, do you?"

"The men will be coming home from shul soon."

"I'll walk with you."

"Oh, no, someone might see us."

"That reminds me," Bennie said. "I met your best friend's mother this morning."

"What's her name," Frieda asked, wary of his answer.

"Mrs. Cohn. I spoke to a group of Western investors this morning, her among them. Seems like a shrewd operator." Bennie's lips formed a lopsided grin. "She asked me if I was taken."

"And you told her?"

"Lock, stock, and barrel."

"Oh, Bennie, you shouldn't have."

"Couldn't help it, I'm bursting with pride. She said her daughter would be broken-hearted at losing her best friend."

"And you said?"

"Maybe she didn't have to lose her. Maybe she could come along. My brother Morrie's looking for a wife, too."

From Bennie's self-congratulatory look, Frieda deduced he thought he'd hit pay dirt.

"Minnie's not strong enough for the rigors of the frontier."

"What ails her?"

"She has a weak chest, and...."

"The Arizona Territory is just the place for lungers."

"And weak nerves."

"Nothing like the desert to calm a person down."

"Bennie, Minnie is a spoiled, rich girl with...."

"So her mother tells me. She invited me to come see her and Minerva on Monday afternoon. She wants to discuss an investment in Dos Cacahuates."

"Don't go," Frieda pleaded. "Once Rosamund Cohn gets her hooks into you, you're...."

"She's my best prospect in San Francisco. I've got to make at least one substantial sale to cover expenses."

Scowling, Frieda studied the carpet.

"Mrs. Cohn asked me to bring you on Monday." He studied her dubious countenance and coaxed, "I need your help, sweetheart. They'll be suspicious if you don't come with me."

"Then I will." And let Minnie convince him she wouldn't make a good wife for his brother.

On Sunday morning Frieda watched her grim-faced father set out in a downpour to consult the rabbi. He failed to return in time for the midday meal. In the afternoon the rain grew heavier, as did the faces of the older Levie women. A little after four, Abram stomped up the rear steps, his boots squishing and his hat brim supporting a small pond. Chava and Bella whisked him through the door, removed his sopping outer garments and wrapped him in a bathrobe. In minutes they had him in a chair next to the cookstove, his feet immersed in a tub of hot water. Then sitting down, one on each side of him, with *nu*'s and *so*'s they drew from Abram an account of his deliberations with the rabbi.

"Not one rabbi, three," he corrected them. "We got real tsoris." His eyes flashed balefully at Frieda, who stood opposite her elders, peeling carrots, a blank expression masking her emotions as her father described their *trouble*.

Rabbi Gosshanger, spiritual leader of the Beth Am Synagogue on Stockton Street, had concurred with his and Kahane's opinion.

"So why didn't you come right home?" Chava wanted to know. "What more did you need?"

"A good bawling out," Abram told them. "The rabbi said I got no business letting my daughter go out alone and talk to strange men on the streets. I told him I don't let her—she goes—so he said I should watch her better or she's going to get into big trouble. The newspapers are full of terrible stories about Jewish girls ruined by thieves, fakers, white slavers."

"White slavers, oy," Bella wailed.

"Sure," Chava said, "they take Jewish girls and sell them

to filthy Chinamen."

"Not only Chinamen," Bella corrected.

"Sha," Abram said. "That ain't all. Gosshanger told me to talk to Rabbi Kurtz and Rabbi Melzer. Both rabbis knew about a redheaded man chasing Jewish girls in San Francisco. One girl married this *rayter* without her family's permission. He stole everything she had and left her in Los Angeles, pregnant. Another girl who went off with a redhead vanished altogether."

Outraged glances flew across the table at Frieda. She stared back, spraying carrot skins over the floor.

"So," said Abram, "I went to see about it."

"See *what* about it?"

"Rabbi Kurtz said the girl's family belonged to his congregation, but he never saw the man in person. He said the people had to move out of San Francisco. With a red-haired baby—God knows who's his father—they couldn't hold up their heads."

"And what did Rabbi Melzer say?" Chava asked, ever eager for grim details.

"Rabbi Melzer said Kurtz made a big mistake. He didn't know nothing about no red-haired man. But he heard about a black-haired man, a *shvartzer* maybe, who deceived a San Francisco girl, he thinks was Jewish. All three rabbis warned me that in a time like this and a place like this, you can't trust nobody."

Abram rose, emitted a long-suffering sigh, and started for the door.

"How can you judge a man without listening to what he has to say," Frieda called after him.

"What would he tell me—lies," Abram countered.

"But, Papa...."

"No buts. If that man comes here, I'll call the police," Abram said, casting a final long-suffering look at Frieda before leaving.

The older women set about restoring order in the kitchen. They emptied the tub, wrung out the towels, gathered the wet clothing. As they worked, they eyed Frieda, clearly anticipating tears, shouts, threats.

Head bent, lips pressed shut, Frieda tore at the carrots with the small knife.

As she worked, her thoughts turned to Dorothy Helsman, who had lived on Sutter Street near the Levies. Dorothy had run off and married—at least, they said she married—the driver of a sleek black coupe drawn by a spirited white horse. No Helsman had spoken of, or to, Dorothy again.

Once, several months after she disappeared, Dorothy returned to Sutter Street with the man said to be her husband. The couple rode up and down the street in the black coupe. The neighbors had stared out the windows, and the children, Frieda among them, had stopped on the curb to watch. But the Helsmans had pulled their blinds and stayed out of sight until Dorothy and the man gave up and drove off. Dorothy's banishment sickened Frieda at the time, and each time she thought of her thereafter. What kind of man had been worth such a sacrifice? And how had Dorothy found the courage to stand with him against her entire family? Now Frieda knew.

CHAPTER TWENTY-FOUR

Best-Kept Secrets

"JEWISH FATHERS," Bennie snorted, his face turning dark and defensive. "They're all the same—in San Bernardino, Los Angeles, Tucson. What do they have against me?"

"They live for the past, you for the future," Frieda said, linking arms with Bennie as they climbed the steps to the San Francisco City Hall.

An hour later, a marriage license tucked in the inside pocket of Bennie's green jacket, the pair boarded the Clay Street cable car and sat thigh to thigh, gazing into each other's eyes, until the conductor called their stop.

A new maid answered the door at the Cohn house. (Mademoiselle had left the month before to return to Paris and her fiancé.) The sullen-faced servant led them to the parlor and went to summon her mistresses. As they waited, Frieda guided her impressed fiancé around the room, pointing out the wall-length fireplace ornamented with Italian ceramic tiles; the coffered ceiling; the heavy, carved beams; and the gleaming oak-panelled walls. The tour completed, she was inviting Bennie to sit down when Minnie flounced in and made straight for Frieda.

"I told you *you* were going to marry first and I'd be left alone," she lashed out.

Ignoring her bad manners, Frieda introduced Bennie.

Minnie shifted her gaze to the man from the Arizona Territory. "She said you were lost in the wilds of Mexico."

Taking a cue from Frieda, Bennie ignored his hostess's accusatory tone, and executed a gallant bow, "It is a great pleasure to meet Frieda's best friend."

Bennie was ogling Minnie—*Minnie*. Her pink silk dress rosied her sallow cheeks and the false bosom filled out her scrawny figure. Her unruly black hair was styled to conceal her low brow and the downy growth in front of her ears. She would have done Rosamund proud, were she not twitching like a rabbit. Standing awkwardly with her guests in the middle of the room, Minnie conversed in fits and starts until she heard the staccato of approaching heels on the hardwood floor. The moment her mother entered, Minnie, noticeably relieved, dropped with an exhausted sigh to the Nile green loveseat.

Rosamund was wearing a lilac-colored gown that accentuated her curves and softened her sharp-featured face. She greeted Frieda and Bennie effusively, then arranged herself alongside Minnie in a delicately harmonized composition of pink, lilac, and green.

Bennie took note and commented, "You and your daughter remind me of the Japanese garden at Golden Gate Park."

Rosamund rewarded him with a satisfied smile, then unsnapped her small, beaded bag and withdrew a yellow handbill. "Your project is extremely enticing," she told Bennie.

Unable to resist, Frieda asked, "May I see?"

Her eyes fixed on Bennie, Rosamund gave the handbill to Frieda, who, ignoring the others, devoured it as if it were an itinerary to her future.

ARIZONA'S BEST KEPT SECRET

Shrewd Western investor, we invite you into our confidence. A new international community is about to be established, one destined to become the leading trade and transportation center on the Arizona-Sonora border. It's name is—Dos Cacahuates.

Frieda's blood surged seeing in print the name of her future home.

This international community will soon serve as the gateway between the west coast of Mexico and the western United States. Two short-line railroads are planned. One will run from the Southern Pacific mainline stop at Mohawk Station to Dos Cacahuates, Arizona Territory. A second will travel from Dos Cacahuates, Sonora, to the Mexican port city of Guaymas. This vital life-line of transportation will provide the Arizona Territory with a much-needed seaport, low freight rates, and international passenger service. Rapid and inexpensive transportation is certain to speed the development of the region's fabulous natural resources—mining, ranching, farming—as well as international commerce and tourism.

The development was just as Bennie had described it at the boardinghouse: a grand hotel, a Latin-style townsite with a plaza at its heart, residential and business sites, public facilities, and the clear, clean air of a scenic desert wonderland.

Some hotel shares and building sites are now available in a preview sale for Western investors only. All at low, low, first-come, first-served prices. Advertisements for the lot auction in October will not be released to the general public until August. Serious investors—mine operators, ranchers, merchants, health-seekers, nature-lovers—and good citizens of every profession and persuasion, are invited to write at once for information: La Cíbola Hotel, Dos Cacahuates, Arizona Territory. Elevation: sea level. Rainfall: 9.5 inches. Population: 25,000 (on their way).

"Who is the president of the company?" Rosamund asked Bennie.

"Colonel Jack Leighton."

"Never heard of him."

"Leighton's well known in the East and in Texas," Bennie explained.

"Texas?" Rosamund repeated. "Was he associated with the Texas and Pacific line? I took a substantial loss when the Central Pacific blocked the Texas and Pacific in Yuma."

Leighton was not, Bennie assured her.

"I suspect this is a new drive," Rosamund said, "by the Atchison, Topeka, and Santa Fe to get a line through to the West Coast."

Bennie leaned toward Rosamund, with an admiring grin. "You're a clever woman."

"Thank you," Rosamund answered briskly. "But I wish you could be more specific."

"As soon as I am able."

"It strikes me as a good scheme, Mr. Goldson," Rosamund said, moving to the edge of her seat. "I consider it a privilege to bet against the Big Four-flushers. Particularly since I have a personal interest."

Did Rosamund mean her ex-husband and his holdings in the Central Pacific? Frieda wondered.

"Your future wife," Rosamund told Bennie, "is like a daughter to me." Folding her hands decisively in her lap, she asked, "How much would represent a genuine show of interest?"

"We're still waiting for the railroad stock to be issued. You'll be the first to know when it is. Right now I suggest you snap up hotel stock at an early-bird price."

"I have no experience with hotel stock," Rosamund said. "How much did you have in mind?"

Bennie spent several moments sizing up his customer. "Five thousand."

The figure was more than Rosamund had expected.

"I'm offering you an impressive return on your capital, Mrs. Cohn, and much more," Bennie said. "I'm inviting you to take part in the development of a rich, new region. I'll be frank, the International Improvement Company needs a woman like you. Someone with capital, style, and a sound reputation. Someone who can draw in equally qualified Western investors. For a five-thousand-dollar investment, I'm prepared to offer you a seat on the board of directors."

"You are a good salesman, Mr. Goldson," Rosamund said.

Frieda waited, poised to leap in at the first mention of Minnie.

"A crew will start digging foundations as soon as I return with the architect's plans," Bennie told Rosamund. "I'd like you to look over the layout. A woman of your taste," Bennie waved his arm around the parlor, "has much to contribute."

"I'd be delighted," Rosamund said. "But there is one other matter I must discuss first."

"Of course." Bennie attended.

Here it comes, Frieda thought, half-rising.

"Your brother," Rosamund said.

From her fiancé's surprised expression, Frieda supposed his brother was far from his thoughts.

"Is it possible that Morrie"—Rosamund uttered the name as though she knew the man personally—"is as intelligent and attractive as his brother?"

"Tell us about him," Minnie eagerly broke in.

Bennie closed his eyes and reflected, his features softening with affection. "Morrie is what you might call a gentle man."

Rosamund shot Minnie a pleased look. "A gentleman is precisely what I want most for my daughter." Adored, despised, constantly discussed, Leopold Cohn, who reigned in absentia, was, by his ex-wife's definition, not a gentleman. Rosamund measured all other men against him.

"Tell us more."

"Morrie's thirty-three," Bennie started. He was in excellent health, lived a moral life, and had a clean record. Together they owned Goldson Brothers, General Merchandise, a 360-acre ranch, which Morrie planned to put into cultivation, and now substantial shares in the International Improvement Company.

"Are you of German-Jewish descent?" Rosamund asked.

Frieda felt called upon to intercede, but Bennie was quicker on the draw.

"Morrie's American-born, like me," Bennie said, side-stepping the Goldson family's Eastern European ancestry.

"Do you have a picture of him?" Minnie piped up.

The Cohn women studied the photograph Bennie drew from his inside breast pocket. Frieda moved to where she could see too. Was the man pictured really Bennie's brother? They didn't look alike at all. Morrie's face was solemn and narrow, his hair fair. His eyes quietly questioned, and his mouth was unsmiling.

"He's sort of a spiritual type," Bennie told the women.

"Not a Spiritualist, I hope?" Rosamund inquired.

"A Spiritualist? Nah," said Bennie laughing. "Morrie peddled with an ex-rabbi one year and picked up some Jewish learning."

"But he is a down-to-earth businessman?"

"He's down-to-earth all right."

"And is interested in marriage *now*?" Rosamund asked.

"If not now, when?" Bennie answered without hesitation.

"I raised Minerva to live as a lady in civilized surroundings. But once she heard Frieda was planning to marry and move to the Arizona Territory, nothing would do but that she go too."

"No," Frieda protested audibly, but unheeded.

"She would not let up until I agreed to see you."

"I'll talk to Morrie about Minnie as soon as I get home," Bennie told Rosamund.

"That will be too late." Rosamund's expression turned firm, businesslike. "I need to invest my capital immediately. If we can't settle this matter now, I'll have to look elsewhere."

For an investment or a son-in-law? Frieda thought.

"Then I accept for my brother," Bennie responded. "I assure you, he'll be delighted with both the bride and the new member of the board."

"I'll write you a check for three thousand," Rosamund said, rising to her feet.

"Five thousand." Bennie stood to face her.

"Three thousand, a seat on the board, and my little girl."

"I can't do that, Mrs. Cohn. Three thousand doesn't qualify you for board membership."

"Take it or leave it," Rosamund said.

"I have partners to consider."

"Now or never."

"I'm not authorized to offer a seat on the board for under five thousand."

"My final word—three thousand."

"And a minimum of two thousand in lots at the auction in October."

"If all goes as planned."

"Agreed. But only to the mother of my future sister-in-law."

Rosamund settled the matter with a cordial handshake.

"I'd like to speak to you, Bennie—" Frieda blurted.

"Just a minute, sweetheart." Bennie stayed Frieda with a cautioning glance.

By then, Rosamund was ready for logistics. "I would have liked to take Minnie to Dos Cacahuates myself, meet my future son-in-law and see the development," she assured Frieda and Bennie. "But I have pressing business in Europe and am scheduled to leave on March twenty-fourth. Minnie will have to travel with you. I had a terrible time getting her a ticket on a Silver Palace car—the trains are booked solid; so many San Franciscans are going to Tucson to celebrate the completion of the Southern Pacific Railroad. I finally wangled not one, but three seats—two for the newlyweds as a wedding present." Rosamund beamed at Frieda. "Don't worry, I booked Minnie two cars away so she won't disturb you love-birds."

Frieda's mouth dropped open.

Interpreting the expression to be one of elation, Minnie rushed over and threw her arms around her. "Feel," she crooned, lifting Frieda's hand to her cheek, "Now it's me who's glowing like a gas lamp."

"We'll stay out of your way on Sunday," Rosamund said genially, "to avoid three-on-a-honeymoon jokes."

She rang for chilled champagne.

When they rose to leave, Frieda flinched when Minnie embraced her and whispered, "Thank you, dear friend. I would have died alone in San Francisco." She stepped back, radiant-faced, and gazed at Frieda. "Just think—you and me sharing an assignment again."

Back on the street, Bennie jumped in the air, kicking his heels and shouting, "*Ay-cac-caa-rrrray!*" He landed in front of Frieda, seized her in his arms, and hugged her until she struggled to escape. "I had to make a sale, but I never figured on landing one like this. I can't wait to see Nunes's face. With three thousand, we can start building the hotel right away. And Morrie's going to be crazy about Minerva."

"No one calls her Minerva."

"Morrie's going to be crazy about Minnie, and I'm happy for you too, Frieda," Bennie said, embracing her again. "You won't be so lonely with Minnie in Dos Cacahuates."

"Listen to me, Bennie, Minnie's not the pioneer type."

"Once she gets away from her bossy mother and out in the clear air and sunshine, she'll be a different person."

"Not Minnie."

"Trust me, sweetheart," Bennie begged, brown eyes aglow. He took her arm and entwined it with his. "Your friends are wonderful, the scheme's wonderful, you're wonderful. Oh, Frieda," he exclaimed, "finding you was the luckiest thing that ever happened to me." He lowered his face close to hers. "Promise me, while I'm gone, you'll remember how much I love you and how happy we're going to be together."

His hot cheek warmed hers. "I promise," Frieda said.

When she'd been alone and miserable, she'd consoled herself with Loving Everyone. Now that she had Bennie, she knew Loving a Special One was immeasurably more uplifting.

CHAPTER TWENTY-FIVE

Bay Windows

ON TUESDAY MORNING Bella and Chava were waiting for Frieda when she arrived in the kitchen.

"A kalleh is supposed to rest for a week before the wedding," Bella said, caressing her daughter's cheek.

"Besides," Chava added, "you're making a mishmash out of everything. Mrs. Pollock, who helps Reb Chaim in the yard, will work in your place."

Alone in the crow's nest, unaccustomed to leisure, Frieda moved from window to window, drinking in the view like a nerve tonic. A bank of fog mounted in the South Bay and rolled over the rooftops of the weather-beaten cottages and makeshift factories. In the east the sun pierced a striated stretch of iron-colored sky and cast beams of orange light onto the sea. The western window framed a geometric mosaic of downtown buildings, only partially visible in the gray morning mass. Great dark rainclouds rose menacingly in the northern sky.

For days, she'd dwelled on where she was going, without a thought to what she was leaving behind. San Francisco. When all else had failed her, she'd had her beloved city framed in the windows of the crow's nest. In that ever-changing panorama of sea and shore, valleys and peaks, erupting and collapsing buildings, there was always something new to distract and console her.

Her people. She was leaving them too. Hard as she tried, she could not imagine herself living with anyone but her family. She'd never spent a single night away from them. Could she eat, sleep, walk, work, think shorn of Levies?

She had no trouble at all imagining her family's distress when they discovered she'd eloped. She could imagine the sound of their outcries, the words they'd use to condemn her and Bennie, the search they would mount—at the Cohns', Miss O'Hara's, then in shame and desperation, the police station.

Gathering pen, ink, and paper, she searched for calming words to deliver her wounding message.

Beloved Family:

I know I am about to cause you pain and I deeply regret it, but there seems to be no other way. My deepest wish would be to marry with your blessing and add your happiness to my own. Since that is not to be, I am forced to marry Bennie Goldson in the presence of strangers.

When you find me gone, I pray you will forgive me and accept my decision. To be cast out by my family would distress me beyond measure. I love you all dearly, and will, evermore. Please know I am working to Make this World a Better Place for all of us. As far as Mr. Gimel is concerned, he wanted me as his wife no more than I wanted him as my husband. Even so, if I have caused him embarrassment, I am sorry. I hope he finds a mate with whom he can be as happy as I am with my beloved. I beg you not to think harshly of me. With fondest thoughts, I remain, now and forever,

Yours For a Better World,
Frieda

She read what she had written, addressed an envelope, "To My Dearest Family," inserted the letter, and put it under the mattress until she was ready to steal away.

The next day was Wednesday, March 17, her birthday. It was raining when she awoke. She lay in bed savoring again her last meeting with Bennie. It was in Maiden Lane, a quaint narrow alley off Union Square. She'd let it slip that her twenty-second birthday was two days off. He was sorry, so sorry, he couldn't be with her, and vowed on her next birthday to throw a *baile* for her in the plaza with *mariachis,* a *piñata, tamales.* He promised to find a present for her up north, something in silver or gold. In the meanwhile, she'd have to settle for his love and a birthday kiss.

After a moment's search for a secluded spot, Bennie pulled her into an empty storeroom. Cupping her shoulders in his large hands, he drew her close and gazed down at her, his features pulsing with passion. When their lips met, it was the wine shed all over again. Except this time she was with a man who loved her and wanted to marry her. She wrapped her arms around him, and let her ardor mount with his until a grinning warehouseman shooed them away, and they left laughing, arm in arm.

Miss O'Hara had taught her there can be no love where there is fear. Now she knew the reverse was also true. There can be no fear where there is love.

It was still raining on Thursday when Ida arrived with her breakfast tray and two bits of news.

"Aunt Chava told me to tell you that you have to go to the mikva tonight instead of tomorrow."

"Where is she?" asked Frieda.

"In the kitchen."

Chava had extracted from Frieda the date of the end of her last menstrual period and calculated when she was to begin counting seven clean days. At the completion of the seventh, she explained with the precision of a priestess, they would take her to the mikva for her bridal purification ceremony. There, her hair would be shampooed and brushed free of tangles, her fingernails and toenails would be clipped, and she would immerse herself in a pool of water.

"A bride is supposed to go to the *chuppah* clean and pure as a baby."

The idea of purifying herself before starting her new life appealed to Frieda, but what if Bennie came for her that night while she was out? Feigning a cold with coughs and sneezes, Frieda headed for the kitchen to argue for an afternoon trip to the mikva.

At seven-thirty that evening Frieda was back in the crow's nest, brushing her hair. When her long brown tresses were dry and rolled into curls, she sat rocking and dreaming of Bennie. At about one she put on her nightgown, looked down once more on the empty, rainswept street, and stretched out to rest, her ears straining for a sound.

In the morning when she awoke, Bennie's words echoed in her mind—"at latest, Friday." She rose, washed, and put on a housedress, wondering how to fill the day. She considered helping out in the kitchen to pass a few hours, but decided against it. She preferred to remain apart, cleansed of her old sorrows, quietly waiting for her shining new life to begin. So she remained alone in the crow's nest, arranging her curls in different styles, filing and buffing her newly-clipped nails until they shone, and creaming her work-chafed hands and round face with a French lotion Minnie had given her. After the midday meal, she lay down and fell into a deep sleep.

It was after three when she awoke. A new storm was tearing in from the north, and with it a new thought. *What if Bennie didn't come for her?* Frieda jumped up and ran downstairs to find something diverting to read.

Back in the crow's nest, she opened the *Alta California* to an article about the Southern Pacific festivities in Tucson that weekend. A large number of San Franciscans were going to the Arizona Territory to take part. Trains leaving on Thursday and for several days thereafter were completely booked. Thanks to Rosamund Cohn—and her eagerness to pawn Minnie off on them—she and Bennie would be on the Sunday train. Frieda reached for the *Pacific Traveler's Guide* and flipped to an effusive description of the Southern Pacific's luxurious Silver Palace cars.

•

On Shabbes Eve, Frieda pled a bad sore throat and settled in front of the north window to watch for Bennie. As she peered out at the slashing rain, the thought struck her for a second time: *What if Bennie didn't come for her?*

At that moment Chava arrived with a supper tray, her last meal before her pre-nuptial fast. When Frieda told her she wasn't hungry, Chava sat down to force a bowl of soup, spoon by spoon, down her niece's supposedly constricted throat. On her way out, Chava stopped to pick stray threads from the wedding dress hanging on the wardrobe door. Caressing the white silk, her wrinkled face curled in a self-congratulatory smile.

"Next year, God willing, your father will have a grandson, *a kaddish-zuger.*"

CHAPTER TWENTY-SIX
With or Without Him

FRIEDA SPENT THE NIGHT in the rockingchair in front of the window. Saturday at dawn she was sick with worry and fatigue, but resolute. Bennie loved her and she loved him. They belonged together, were promised to each other. He had had some kind of mishap or he would have come by now. She ached to go out and look for him, but if she left the boardinghouse he might come and be as disconcerted by her absence as she was by his.

On the other hand, she had to get out of the boarding-house before Sunday or she'd be caught in the wheels of the wedding and rolled to the chuppah to meet Gimel. Her face frantic, her heart throbbing with indecision, she stared out into the rain.

By three in the afternoon she had settled on a course of action. She resolved to wait for Bennie until a little before dawn. If he didn't appear, she'd leave alone. She had no choice; her mind and spirit had already departed, only her body remained. She'd go to Miss O'Hara, explain her pre-dicament and, with her help, search for Bennie. And if she didn't find him? Frieda's mind went blank. Not finding Bennie was unthinkable.

The rain stopped Saturday evening. A full moon rose in the royal blue sky, painting a white road across the South Bay. Visitors streamed through the crow's nest, cheerfully promis-ing the fasting bride clear skies for her wedding day. Frieda nodded, blank-faced. The last to arrive was Bella, who had come prepared to spend the night. Someone had to sleep with the bride to prevent the demons from stealing her away.

Frieda protested; she was nervous and restless and wanted to be alone. Bella persisted until Frieda hit on a compromise; Ida would stay with her.

Nestled in Frieda's lap, the little girl babbled about the wedding cake, the chuppah, the flowers, the guests. At ten o'clock, to settle down the excited child, Frieda put on her nightgown and joined her under the covers. When Ida finally fell asleep, Frieda pressed a farewell kiss on her damp forehead and got out of bed. She drew her shawl around her shoulders, placed a lantern in the window, and pulled up the rockingchair so she could see the street below.

As she waited, jumbled images of Bennie fluttered across her mind. She saw him up on Powell Street under her father's wagon, in the Grand Court of the Palace Hotel, in the Golden Gate Conservatory, at the boardinghouse Shabbes table, in the storeroom in Maiden Lane—his lips pledging love, his hand on her breast. Please, Bennie, please come for me, Frieda begged as though her wishes had the power to transport him to Tehama Street. The St. Patrick's Church bells chimed eleven, twelve, one, two.

Her fervor spent, her hope for his arrival that night all but gone, Frieda began to prepare her alternative course. At four she would dress, take her valise, steal downstairs, and walk to Market Street. The cable cars didn't start running until six, but she had to be out of the boardinghouse before the men arose for morning prayers.

Frieda was about to rise and start dressing when the first pebble hit the window.

She sprang to her feet and rushed to the door. As she started down the stairs, she heard a second pebble shatter the glass, and Ida's startled cry. Bursting through the front door, Frieda saw a fog-shrouded figure waiting at the bottom of the stairs, arms spread to receive her. She leaped over the last three steps and flung herself at Bennie with a force that would have knocked down a less sturdy man. He wrapped his arms around her and squeezed her.

"Bennie, Bennie, Bennie," she cried, her hot tears wetting his cold, stubbled face. "I was so worried something happened to you."

"Two bridges washed out and the trains couldn't get through. I was terrified I'd get back and find you married to that Gimel fellow."

"I would rather have died." Frieda's lips searched for Bennie's. Their kiss vibrated with the ecstasy of having faced disaster and eluded it. Pulling back with a sigh, Bennie told her, "I finally had to rent a horse in Santa Rosa and ride all the way to San Francisco." Taking her face in his hands, he whispered, "I've never been so glad to see anyone in my whole life."

"My love, my love, my love," Frieda croaked. "I was about to leave without you—to go to Miss O'Hara and beg her to help me find—"

His lips silenced her. She was pressed tightly against him, her arms wound around his neck, when she heard alarmed voices emanating from the boardinghouse. Looking up at the crow's nest, she saw faces in the lighted window.

"Friedaaa," she heard Chava call. "Are you down there?"

One after another, lights were going on all over the house.

"Come on," Frieda whispered, seizing Bennie's hand. "We've got to get away from here."

"Where can we go?"

"South Park," Frieda said, after a moment's thought. "No one will be there at this hour."

The sun was coming up when Frieda and Bennie, hand in hand, climbed the front steps of the boardinghouse. In the morning light, they looked like survivors of a catastrophe. Bennie's face was dirt-streaked and covered with a three-day beard. His green suit was mud-splattered and his Stetson pushed out of shape. Frieda had her black shawl pulled tightly around her nightgown; her hair hung damp and disheveled around her cheeks. Their faces glistened, triumphant. Bennie pulled open the front door and protectively entered before Frieda. Their appearance brought an outcry from a knot of boarders marshaled for action in the front hall.

"They're here, they're here!" Roth shouted. "*Levie, Levie,* Frieda's back, and she's got no clothes but her nightgown."

Abram rushed out of the kitchen, flanked by Kahane and Finkelstein, Bella and Chava in his wake. Glaring at his daughter, eyes narrowed with fury, teeth bared, Abram hissed, "*You,* get upstairs."

"After we talk," Frieda responded.

"No after—*now.*"

"You must listen, Papa."

"I'll kill her," Abram cried, lunging at her with his hand raised.

"You'd better calm down, Mr. Levie," Bennie said, stepping in front of Frieda.

Kahane and Finkelstein restrained Abram. Struggling to free himself, Frieda's father growled at Bennie, "You demon, you, get out from mine house or I'll have you arrested."

"If he goes, I go too," Frieda said, stepping out from behind Bennie.

"Somebody run call the police. And you, Frieda, *upstairs.* Chava, Bella, take her now. Out, mister."

Frieda watched her white-faced, dumbstruck mother and aunt creep toward her as if she were bewitched or insane. "Don't worry, Mama, Aunt Chava, he loves me."

A wild cry broke from Abram's throat. He tore himself from Finkelstein's clasp, grabbed Frieda's left arm and yanked her from Bennie's side as though he were snatching her from the devil. Bennie seized her right arm and pulled her back.

"Stop, both of you, you're tearing me in two." Facing her father, Frieda said, "It's too late, Papa. I'm Mrs. Bennie Goldson. You can't keep us apart."

Abram dropped Frieda's arm as though it were unclean, and stepped back between Kahane and Finkelstein. "What do you mean?" he stammered.

"We're married," Frieda said, slipping her freed arm through Bennie's.

"Where?" her father asked, dubiously.

"South Park."

"What do you mean, South Park? Without a marriage contract? A license? A rabbi? Your family?" demanded Frieda's equally incredulous aunt.

Frieda held out her left hand with the gold band on her third finger. "You told me, Aunt Chava, that if a man puts a ring on a woman's finger and says the words, *'Behold, thou art consecrated unto me with this ring, according to the laws of Moses and Israel,'* he and she were married."

"In the park? Like dogs?" Abram groaned with disgust. "You don't know what you're talking about." He turned to Kahane for corroboration.

"Who else was present?" Kahane questioned.

"No one, just Frieda and me," Bennie said.

"Then it's not legal. There has to be two witnesses."

"Say what you wish," Frieda cried wildly. "I'm pledged to this man, and can marry no other."

No one disagreed.

"You'll get no dowry from me, Mister." Abram flung the words at Bennie as if they were stones.

"Your daughter is all I want," Bennie said, his adoring eyes fixed on his disheveled bride.

"Hah," Abram barked.

Silence followed. No one seemed to know how to go forward. For weeks, the entire boardinghouse had thought of little but the approaching wedding. Eyes turned to peer into the parlor decorated with white ribbons and flowers, and then into the dining room, where the tables were set with holiday finery.

Frieda's bewildered mother expressed what the others must have been thinking.

"We been cooking and baking and sewing for weeks. The food is ready, the clothes are ready, the musicians are ready, the rabbi is coming, the guests are coming. And now we're not going to have a chasseneh?"

CHAPTER TWENTY-SEVEN

All Brides Are Beautiful

AT ONE-THIRTY Frieda stood in the front hall in her wedding gown, aquiver with anticipation. Beneath her veil, her cheeks, torched by compliments, blazed like twin fires. Female relatives, neighbors, and guests had gathered in the crow's nest to watch her dress. The women, weeping and laughing, assured her that hers was the most beautiful wedding dress they had ever seen; that she was the most beautiful bride; Ida, the most beautiful flower girl; Bella, the most beautiful mother of the bride; and Chava—once she had been wheedled out of her solitary sulk—the most beautiful aunt of the bride, anywhere. No one mentioned that the bridegroom's name was different from the one on the wedding invitation. Few people outside of the boardinghouse knew—or would know.

Every inch of space in the parlor was filled. Rising on tiptoes, Frieda could see the red velvet chuppah in front of the windows. Bennie was already under the canopy, Sammy at his side, and the minyan behind him. If Frieda had not known it was Bennie, she never would have recognized him. A wide-brimmed black hat had been set on his head and a huge prayer shawl draped over his green suit. He looked like Gimel. She had already met Rabbi Gosshanger—a small, thin man supporting a capacious black robe and tall, black crown—so she knew he was there somewhere. Probably at the side of Kahane, who with his usual priestly authority was directing the men supporting the chuppah, Bennie, Sammy, and everyone else in earshot.

At the first notes of Mendelssohn's wedding march, Ida

darted to the doorway, basket in hand, waiting as directed until the entire march had been played and started for the second time. On cue, Ida set out. The excited crowd parted like the waters of the Red Sea for the bride's pretty little sister. Chava followed, her mottled face tilted toward the ceiling, her candle held high, as though she were lighting the world. Before she reached the chuppah, the eager guests had turned to look for the bride. Eyes nervously averted, Frieda and her parents arranged themselves three abreast.

Cries of delight resounded as they entered the room.

Walking slowly, they moved down the makeshift aisle to the accompaniment of the music and the audible pleasure of the guests. Never in her life had Frieda been the object of so much approbation. The good will surging at her swept aside what remained of her defenses. Pierced to its depths, her heart opened to the two human beings on either side of her.

I am of their bone, their blood, their flesh, their union, and the unions of countless women and men who preceded them, marveled Frieda. *I was born of these two in a cruel and distant land and carried by them to a new and better world. Here, they sustained me while I grew, suffering and searching for my missing mate. Now they're leading me to be joined to him. So that he and I can create new beings whom we will care for while each of them grows, suffers, and searches.*

Frieda wanted to stop and embrace her mother and father, something she had not done since she was a tiny girl, and thank them for having given her life and for having sustained her until this happy moment. They had arrived at the chuppah. Her father then left them and joined his minyan, while her mother gazed about, wet-eyed and confused, until Chava yanked her to her side. Under the canopy, Frieda's nascent thanksgiving, still unvoiced, gave way to ancient ceremony.

The moment the bride arrived, Rabbi Gosshanger was off and running. Someone had mentioned that the couple had to catch a train in Oakland at six-thirty. Besides, he had another wedding to perform that afternoon—North of Market. He half-chanted, half-spoke the ceremonial words in Hebrew, with an occasional line or two in English. Both languages sounded the same to Frieda; she could understand neither. Miss O'Hara had once discussed at length the beauty of the Hebrew wedding ceremony and the high regard the Jewish faith held for women, marriage, and the fruits thereof. Frieda presumed what was transpiring would be uplifting, if only she understood it. Longing to be touched, she listened, drank the wine proffered her, extended her hand to receive Bennie's ring again, and repeated fervently the few words required of her. But it was not the ceremony that stirred her. It was the visible distress of those standing under the canopy with her.

Abram and his cohorts were as grim-faced as warriors. Her mother and her aunt were sobbing as if Frieda were dying instead of being reborn. Even the bright-faced little Ida was whimpering. Of them all, Bennie alone aroused her compassion. He was trembling like a surrounded captive. His eyes shifting between Rabbi Gosshanger and Kahane, who was assisting the rabbi, he listened as though his life depended on decoding their words. The undisguised scorn his religious ignorance aroused had clearly damaged his usual self-confidence. He faltered, stuttered, and had to be prompted repeatedly. His hand shook so, he could barely get the ring on Frieda's finger. And Sammy was supposed to be helping him, but it was all he could do to keep from laughing out loud.

When the rabbi finally got to a ritual familiar to Bennie—the breaking of the glass—he stamped so hard, he almost put his foot through the sagging floor. Encouraged by the ensuing shouts of *mazel tov*, he cast restraint aside. Seizing his bride, he threw back her veil and kissed her long and hard, as may have been customary in the Arizona Territory, but was evidently frowned upon by the *good Jews* of San Francisco.

In the dining room after the ceremony, Abram gave the speech he had prepared with only one change—the name of the bridegroom. Inundated with good wishes, he stood beaming as though the event were going exactly as he had planned. The wine flowed as toasts were offered to the new-lyweds and the family, and soon platters of festive foods were streaming out of the kitchen. Roth, the wedding jester, seized control of the festivities and lifted the celebrants to hi-larity with jokes and stories. Frieda's spirits rose along with everyone else's. Even Gimel managed a faint smile. Then Roth, Sammy, and several other musicians tuned up and the singing and dancing began. The women claimed the bride, and the men, the bridegroom.

Light-headed from the wine, Frieda whirled, glided, stamped, and clapped until her rosy face glistened with per-spiration and her heart pounded. Sylvia cornered her to slip napkins under her armpits so she didn't ruin her dress. When she could dance no more, Frieda retreated, her hand clutch-ing her side. For a while, she stood watching Bennie, half-delighted, half-appalled. With the help of wine, vodka, and the music, he had overcome his reserve. His arms draped on the shoulders of his fellow revelers, singing and shouting, he danced a *sherele*. Then, surrounded by a circle of hand-clappers, he squatted and executed an energetic *kozatskeh*. When the musicians swung into a freilach, he was off again, dancing as though Jewish festivities were an everyday occur-rence in the Arizona Territory.

At three o'clock, Frieda went upstairs to change into her traveling suit and prepare to depart to the train station with Bennie, her family and the boarders willing to leave the still-lively celebration to accompany them.

As Frieda closed the door behind her, her heart lurched. Moving down the front steps, she began to tremble. She marched down Tehama Street stony-faced, until compelled to turn for a final look at the boardinghouse. Fighting back tears, she reminded herself that she could always come back for a visit. Afraid to speak and reveal her distress, she rode the cable car to the Ferry Building in silence.

On the deck of the ferry boat, Frieda stood looking back at San Francisco, illuminated by the rosy light of the setting sun. She felt as though she were bodily connected to the city; the farther she went, the more painful became the tug in her midsection. Was she making a mistake?

Frieda looked around for reassurance. Her mother, exhausted and seasick, hovered close to the railing, green with nausea. Her aunt was going from boarder to boarder, still loudly protesting Frieda's marriage and defection. ("Like rats in winter they run away, American children.") Her father and Bennie were only inches away from her, still heatedly arguing the pros and cons of pioneering. Frieda wished Bennie would stop trying to convince him. Her family would never understand what they hoped to achieve on the Arizona-Sonora border.

Not as Miss O'Hara would. Frieda winced with remorse; she was leaving San Francisco without a word of farewell or a syllable of appreciation to her longtime teacher. She pledged to write to her as soon as she got to Dos Cacahuates, and tell her all about Bennie and her long-awaited new assignment.

She could see Miss O'Hara hush the Sisters of Service II, saying, "Girls, I have an inspiring letter to read to you. It's from Frieda Levie Goldson, one of our most dedicated Sisters of Service. After a long apprenticeship giving Service to Family, Frieda was called to a challenging new assignment in the Arizona Territory. She and her husband are helping to build a new international community, a gateway between two great nations, a place where people of different races and faiths...."